Revelle

a novel

Alison Wiley

Alison Wiley

Diamond-Cut Life Publishing
Portland, Oregon

Copyright © 2012 by Alison Wiley
All rights reserved. Published 2012.
Except for the purposes of reviews and brief quotes, no part of this document may be reproduced or transmitted in any form or by any means, electronic, mechanical, photocopying, recording, or otherwise, without prior written permission of Alison Wiley. For information regarding permission, write to alison.wiley@live.com

Diamond-Cut Life Publishing
Portland, Oregon
www.diamondcutlife.org

Printed in the United States of America

ISBN: 978-0-9856096-0-3
Library of Congress Control Number: 2012946506

The characters and events in this book are fictitious.

Cover art by Chris Cartwright
Book design by Jennifer Omner
Author photo by Louisa Moratti

Acknowledgments

I always thought authors were exaggerating when I read those (often gushy) preambles to their books called acknowledgements. But now I get it.

It turns out that books are shockingly big projects, vast as the Australian outback. I hope you'll never have to write one. But if you are compelled to as I was, get smart earlier than I did on all the help you'll need. Find people like the ones I acknowledge here—because it does take a village to turn out a book. All those authors are telling the truth.

Heartfelt thanks to:

Colleen Kaleda, for countless shared writing/critique sessions and introducing me to PDX Writers. Particular thanks for accepting my suggestion that our novels, i.e. the worlds of our heroines, could intersect, and for sharing the Shasta character with me. (Shasta rocks).

Erick Mertz, my editor, for embracing Revelle, climbing into her world and significantly improving the story.

Vicki Lind, for believing in Revelle from the beginning, providing lots of problem-solving and referrals, and for sharing the protagonist's freedom-loving spirit.

Cime Bruce, Erin Butler, Thea Constantine, Karen Frost, Gene Latimer, Jennifer Springsteen, and Sue Staehli of PDX Writers, for reading, contributing and cheerleading.

Thor Hinckley, my husband, for encouraging me to start my blog Diamond-Cut Life, and for our shared life-path in general.

The developers of WordPress, home to Diamond-Cut Life. WordPress is a tremendous, ongoing source of empowerment to this writer and countless writers worldwide.

Special remembrance and thanks to Jean Wiley, my late mother, for her artistic soul and nature-loving spirit. Love you, Mom.

Chapter 1
Fire

September 1993
Portland, Oregon

The day that my husband set my truck and possessions on fire I was stunned but dry-eyed. I had felt an explosion coming, but I hadn't known which of the three of us would ignite it.

I was dancing in my new home that Labor Day morning in 1993 when the doorbell rang. I was dancing barefoot on the hardwood floor to Tom Petty's "Listen to Her Heart." Sunlight was streaming into Marisol and Ruben's living room, its beams marked by little dust-motes because I was moving so much air around with my body, and I remember the small Celtic cross on the silver chain around my neck bouncing against my collarbones as I whirled, kicked and undulated. My skirt was flying. I decided to use the whirl-kick-body wave sequence in the class I would be leading on Wednesday in my studio on Hawthorne, which was named Dancing Fool. I was breathing hard, joyful in my skin. In that sundrenched moment, the pain about my imploding marriage had been chased away.

The song ended and the doorbell rang. I turned the volume down before walking to the door. The aroma of the morning's coffee was lingering in the air as I opened the door to find my husband, standing on the front porch of Ruben and Marisol's house. His lean, ropy-muscled body was familiar, but the expression on his face was strange, several degrees left of center, making my stomach re-clench into the old anxiety. I looked up at him, my five-three to his six-two. The height advantage was his, too.

I had left him five days ago, after a marriage of one year that had felt more like an affair. He had moved to Portland just three weeks earlier. Prior to then, he had lived in Anaheim as I lived in Portland, Oregon, he steadily promising to move up and live with me and, just as steadily, breaking his promises.

"I need some salve for my hand," he announced.

"What? Why?" I was confused and off-balance, something I had felt about half the time in the two years I'd known him. The other half of the time I'd felt enchanted by his vitality, admiring his competency as a carpenter and amused by his antics. I'd been hopelessly in love with him.

"I set your truck on fire with all your things in it. Now my hands are burned." His tone implied I was the one responsible.

I looked at him more closely. His light brown eyelashes and eyebrows seemed to be partially missing. Were they singed?

"I don't believe you," I said. Not believing my husband had often turned out to be the path of reality. But my heart was racing. He'd been furious last week when I'd told him I was ending the marriage.

"It's over in the Nature's parking lot," he said. He was referring to the local grocery store. "I'll show you."

I put on my sandals and we walked four blocks west in the warm, hazy sunshine. I trailed behind him, not because I was afraid, but because he was a jerk. I didn't want to be seen with someone crazy enough to ask me for help, for salve, because he'd set my own things on fire.

When we'd met two years ago we couldn't get enough of each other, he found me so beautiful, and I him. "You're a heart stopper," he'd breathed in my ear during more than one sweaty, love-soaked moment. I had come to believe beauty was overrated, that it carried more liabilities than benefits. Beauty made a person into prey, a target, the way that an antelope that is colored or built differently than the rest of its herd draws the eye of the cheetah, capturing its laser focus, and triggering the deadly chase.

At the Lloyd cinema parking lot, I found that at least this morning, he was telling the truth. There was my red Toyota pickup truck, the entire back of the truck and camper shell a charred, steaming ruin. The firemen were packing up their things. Their big, shiny red truck looked like an older, healthier, better-fed relative of my mutilated one. The white foam that came from the extinguishers was strewn about like semen, the fire having triggered their explosive release into the world.

"You can't just leave me for another man and get away with it," my husband said.

I repressed the scream rising in me. I had learned as a child to hide my pain. "It would have happened with or without the other man," I said.

"Cheaters always say that. It's bullshit. You don't get off scot-free."

I walked closer. The door of the camper shell was up. "I smell gasoline," I said.

"I poured gasoline over it before I lit the match."

The withered, caved-in shell of my guitar case lay beside the charred remains of my good down parka. My wedding dress that I'd designed was now as black as the old-timey Singer sewing machine I'd used to make it. The hiking boots that had taken me through hundreds of miles of wildish backcountry were melted into deformed piles. Fallen-over stacks of my favorite paperback novels, pages curled like arthritic hands. Notebooks of dance sequences and choreography, textbooks on teaching I had kept from graduate school.

My husband watched me closely, craving a reaction, some outrage, a screaming match. But I knew that coldness was what would hurt him, so that was what I gave him. I turned away from the sickly sweet smell of the smoldering mess that was my old life. I refused to make eye contact with the man who just a year ago had embodied my new life, but was now bonded by fire, like welded steel, to the old. I walked back to the house, leaving Sonny in the parking lot with his singed eyelashes and hands that needed salve.

"My name rhymes with gazelle, but starts with an R-e-v," I explained to the policeman an hour later back at the house. "Revelle Jones Champagne. Spelled like the drink. No hyphen."

"That's quite a name," he said, smiling. He was probably trying to put me at ease. He needn't have worried. All I would let him see was calm courtesy. I was dissociated, the part of me that was frightened and furious over the fire locked away into a box.

"I think my name will be changing," I said faintly. Marisol and Ruben, whose house we were in, smiled. Jones was my maiden name, Champagne my husband's name. Marisol, my best friend had taken Ruben's last name of Lopez when they had married ten years ago, after much discussion and debate. "I'm still an independent person," she had declared at the wedding reception, done in the style of the old Mexico of their grandparents. "Oh that is clear," Ruben had said in his dry, understated way.

"So let me see if I have this right," Officer Chilstrom said. He had arrived soon after Marisol called him, and looked to be about my age, 34. "Your husband still lives in Northwest, near Wallace Park. And you moved in here with your friends five days ago?"

I nodded. Ruben and Marisol sat on the couch in their living room where I had been dancing as the fire had been lit. They sat, sides pressed together, faces grave. I was sitting cross-legged on a pillow on the floor, wearing the off-white hip-yoke skirt I'd been dancing in that morning, the one I used for ecstatic dance. My dusty-blue camisole had 'Cowgirl' scripted on the front, and I felt self-conscious that the officer might read something unsavory into that. I felt unsavory.

"And this morning your husband drove himself all the way up here, parked, got into your truck, drove that vehicle back to, uh, your former shared home in Northwest, and . . . filled it up with your personal possessions?"

I nodded.

"And then he drove all the way back up to the parking lot at the Lloyd Cinema and set it on fire?"

"He poured gasoline over all of it first," Marisol said, helpful and angry.

"Gasoline," Officer Chilstrom nodded, writing busily.

"I blame myself," Ruben said. All eyes turned to him. "I told Revelle earlier this week that we needed to go down to her old house and bring her clothes and everything up here. We ... didn't make it our highest priority."

"I wouldn't blame myself if I were you," Officer Chilstrom said to Ruben. "If he couldn't have attacked her clothes and other things, he might have attacked her instead. That happens all the time. I hate to say it, but this could have been a lot worse."

Ruben visibly relaxed, and I realized that had been a brief man-to-man talk, one male protector to another. Ruben had felt that he had failed me. The policeman had assured him he hadn't. I agreed with the policeman. My husband was a wild card.

"How soon can you arrest him?" Marisol said. The officer and I started talking at the same time.

"Go ahead," he deferred to me.

"I'd like to think it over about pressing charges," I said. "I haven't had time to think yet."

"OK," the officer said. "I was going to ask if you think he's running at this point or sticking around in town."

I shrugged helplessly. After a moment, Ruben offered, "He's never been a real predictable guy."

"What about a restraining order?" Marisol said. She was clearly the person in the room most in touch with her anger.

"I would never advise someone not to get a restraining order," the policeman said, rubbing his chin. "But they don't work like an electric fence. People walk through them all the time. Restraining orders tend to be more valuable after the fact. Are there any children in the picture here?"

I shook my head no, thinking that was a blessing now, despite my passionate desire for a child.

"If there had been children, and he broke the restraining order, you'd then be in a better position to get full custody of them."

The three of us nodded. Marisol wouldn't want to hear it, but a restraining order sounded useless to me, another lame attempt to control the sideways-tilted force of nature that I'd married in a time of weakness.

"Here's my card," he said, extending it to me. I took it and then got up from the floor in the spiral motion I'd learned long ago, the one that starts with one foot crossing in front of the body. I could feel the policeman noticing it. We all walked him to the front porch.

"Thank you so much, Officer Chilstrom," I said, looking him full in the eye. "You've been really helpful."

"If I were you, I'd press charges," he offered. Marisol nodded energetically. "The pattern with these domestic violence guys is that they start with something small."

Ruben nodded sadly. He had grown up in the East Los Angeles barrios where domestic violence happened more publicly than in neighborhoods where higher incomes bought space and privacy.

"They get addicted to their own anger," Officer Chilstrom went on. "Spending some time in jail can calm them down. But not always. Some people are crazy and nothing puts a dent in their violence." I wrapped my arms around myself in spite of the heat of the day. All I could feel was the weight of gravity, physical and emotional. I missed Kyle, wanted him to hold me. We had made plans to go out of town together that afternoon, to my friends' house near the coast. "I'm ready to arrest this guy as soon as you give word. The worst thing you could do, though, is to press charges and then drop them. That tells the perpetrator straight-up that you can be his ongoing prey."

He looked at me in a direct, pointed way. I held his gaze a moment, seeing he was attracted to me, feeling him challenging me to not be a perpetrator's prey, almost asking me to let him protect me. I looked down at the pistol in its black holster. I had never fired a gun. How did guns work at preventing fires from being set? They didn't. Men tried so hard to be strong and right, often in the wrong direction.

"I don't see a lot of victims as calm as you are," the officer said. When I swung my eyes back to his, he raised an eyebrow, asking for an explanation.

"I've got good friends," I pointed out. I did not add that Marisol and Ruben and I were part of a small, tight-knit church, or that I thought friends and community afforded me more protection than any single man could, with or without a gun.

"I can see that," he nodded. "Well, try to have a good day. You've got my phone number if you want to press charges. I can put him in jail in a heartbeat if that's what you want."

I stood on Marisol's porch in the late summer heat, sweating through my blue camisole, wondering how one could possibly send to jail the person to whom you had sworn a holy covenant. Especially when you had already betrayed that covenant with someone else.

You might be thinking that I'm a certain kind of person, the kind of woman, for example, that these things happen to, or that you know what direction this story is heading. But my experience is that predators can be plagued by vulnerability, and their prey can be strangely strong, even aggressive. Victimization is not always what it seems. Neither is revenge or forgiveness.

Mary, who performed my marriage, told me once that people always remember how things end, and that those endings then color all their experiences and memories, sometimes unfairly. She is right: I have always remembered how things ended with my husband. I have to work harder to remember that they began quite differently.

Chapter 2
Freefall

May 1991

My friend and housemate Paul and I were talking at the kitchen table after dinner, remains of grilled cheese sandwiches and tomato soup scattered around us. Gaylin, Paul's six year old nephew and the son of my housemate Jenny, was watching a Sesame Street video in the next room. Paul and I were taking care of him for the weekend while Jenny was out of town.

"Why did you and Mike break up?" Paul asked me, his large, bearded, workmanlike face riveted to mine, his big belly pushed against the table as he leaned toward me. I smiled. Paul had been in A.A. for eight years and in a men's group for four. He was the best listener I knew.

"The short answer? I loved Mike more than he loved me, basically." My voice broke. This time though, I willed myself not to cry. I'd done that already with Marisol, my best friend since college.

"All that that tells me is that Revelle Jones' heart is bigger than Mike Delaney's heart. No surprise there," Paul said, unimpressed. That set me back on my heels. I had thought he would sympathize with me. I'd never thought of unreciprocated love that way before. It was true that I loved easily. But loving Gaylin and Paul and Marisol was much less problematic than romantic love.

"Well, there's more to it than that," I countered. "I'd wanted to get married and have a child. In the foreseeable future. And Mike didn't. He said he didn't find marriage or children . . . compelling." Tears formed in my eyes. At 32, I found those things quite compelling.

On the other hand, I hated self-pity.

"You know, in the bigger picture, this is nothing," I said, straightening my sagging spine and stacking our dinner plates. "Compared to people exposing their newborn girls in China. Or Sam at church watching his lover die of AIDS. I shouldn't be complaining."

"Pain is pain," Paul said, waving my comparisons away. "Other people's pain doesn't make yours feel any better."

"OK," I said, walking into his invitation like a guest to a downbeat party. "You're right, their pain doesn't help me. I feel like hell, except when I'm dancing. And the new principal disbanded the after-school dance troupe I was leading. He said our school has to focus on fundamentals. But he kept the *fucking fencing club!*" I whispered the last three words so Gaylin wouldn't hear. I slapped my palms on the table then threw my hands into the air, wishing I could slap the new principal across his arrogant, thin-lipped, East Coast face.

"What a jerk," Paul concurred mildly. He, Marisol and I were all teachers, and had all had our disagreements with principals. "I think that Mike and your new principal have something in common. They're both sky-god men. They don't resonate with you. They're way up in their heads. Passion is too messy for them. You need a guy who's more soulful. Someone who'd be willing to crawl through a muddy swamp to be with you."

I started clearing the table for good this time, always more comfortable in motion than sitting still. Anyone who knew Mike—which of course Paul did, because we'd all gone out together—would have laughed at the idea of Mike in a muddy swamp. Mike was an M.D. in general practice, a take-charge, Type A guy, notably not hirsute, but clean-shaven and given to Brooks Brothers shirts and tasseled loafers. My parents would have liked him. My parents were a thousand miles away in Anaheim, California, where I'd grown up.

"Once Mike told me I was too wild for him," I said, almost to myself. "It wasn't on account of anything in particular I'd done. The context was more that..." My voice trailed off. Mike had said that to me after one of the last times we had made love. My intensity had filled the room and had contrasted with Mike's energy something like the way a cougar contrasts with a housecat.

"Well, wildness is sometimes a being-thing, not a doing-thing," Paul said. "I think he was saying something similar to what I'm saying: you and he were serving two different gods."

"Whichever gods were involved, I loved him," I said softly.

Paul's face fell. He turned away from me toward the wall, tossing the red napkin from his lap back onto the table. I sighed. I knew I should be asking Paul about himself, his own life, but my grief used up my energy like Gaylin's drawings used up entire pads of paper. Paul was going through a divorce, a complicated situation involving a strong-willed Israeli woman, Lena, whom he loved. The problem was that her primary interest had always been permanent residency in the U.S. I respected the fact that he never denigrated his soon-to-be-ex. Paul had met Lena at the small, eclectic church community that he, Marisol and I were all part of.

The phone mounted on the wall across the room rang, making me jump. We both held still, reluctant to let a call break our mood. Finally I moved to answer it.

"Hello?"

"Revelle, it's Mom." I tensed at the gravity of her voice, different from the breeziness of her usual keeping-in-touch calls.

"Mom, are you OK?" I already knew something was not OK.

"I'm OK. It's your father." She paused, and I could hear her working to keep her voice steady. "He's been diagnosed with a cancerous growth in his right kidney."

Paul was watching me alertly. "Dad has cancer in one of his kidneys," I whispered, my stomach clenching with fear. "Oh my God," I breathed into the phone, holding it in the air between us so Paul could hear. We leaned toward each other over the table, making an A-frame with our bodies. I had only seen my father ill, as in unable to work, once in my life, when I was 16 years old. The energetic way that he strode into rooms, the vigor with which he mowed the lawn and moved garbage cans from the backyard to the curb, made it hard to picture him being attacked by a cancerous growth.

"The doctor on the case wants to operate Wednesday morning," Mom continued. "The idea is to remove the bad kidney and see if the cancer has spread to the other kidney or not."

"God," I said again. I struggled to stay grounded. "Paul is here with me, helping me take all this in. You met Paul at my graduation, remember?"

"Yes," she said quickly, her tone warm with recognition. "I've learned that most people survive having a kidney removed but Dr. Gundell said we should be prepared for the possibility that the cancer in the left kidney has already traveled to the right kidney."

"This is all so sudden," I said, rotating my shoulders in forward circles since my neck was hurting.

"It's very sudden," she agreed. "He just noticed blood in his urine a week ago. I didn't call you at that point, because there was no reason to worry you if it turned out to be nothing."

Paul broke our A-frame but kept a close eye on me. He started walking softly in his stocking feet around the kitchen, stacking dinner plates in the sink gingerly to minimize the noise, putting Tabasco sauce, cheddar cheese and butter back into the refrigerator.

"Dad and I both have A-negative blood," I said slowly. We all knew our types because donating blood to the Red Cross was a tradition in my family. "It's possible I could give a kidney to Dad if the cancer has already gotten to both of his," I said.

Paul's head swung around toward me, eyebrows raised in alarm. I lifted a hand, palm facing up. Paul, like my older brother Rick, tended to be a little protective of me. I privately liked it, their care and concern feeling like a counterbalance to my habit of boldness, my attraction to a degree of risk.

"I'm thinking I should come down," I said, already weighing the cost versus quickness between driving and flying. Driving was winning. Two days to get ready and two to drive.

"I think that's a good idea," Mom replied. She sounded relieved, and I realized my coming home had been the goal of her call. After we said good-bye, I went to Paul like a stunned sleepwalker and lifted my arms for a hug. He held me like a bear wrapping itself around a sapling, his hands coming all the way back around to meet his own body.

※

The next day, Saturday, I got organized for the road trip. After I'd checked the oil, water and tire pressure in my truck, I went upstairs to my bedroom and started packing my clothes, dance notebooks and some novels into duffel bags and boxes. Gaylin wandered in after awhile. His small, delicate-featured face was clouded with worry as he climbed onto my bed. I could see he wanted to talk, so I stopped packing and sat on the floor under the window. I reached my arms toward the sky, wrists crossed and palms together, since stretching always eased my tension, but he wouldn't make eye contact with me.

"What are you thinking about?" I asked him. I thought he'd say he was unhappy about my upcoming departure. I was. I wanted to stay right there in the Northwest Lovejoy house with him, Jenny and Paul.

"I think you and Paul should get married," Gaylin announced.

"Really?" I said, surprised. "Why do you think that?"

I loved Paul dearly, but didn't feel attracted to him at all. In his own words, he was an overweight mess, struggling with the end of his stormy marriage, going to extra meetings to keep from breaking down and taking that first drink. He had started smoking cigarettes again, going out onto the front porch late at night, when I assumed he missed Lena the most.

"You and Paul get along really well, and you both live here with me," Gaylin said.

"I get along pretty well with most people," I pointed out. Owen, the new principal, was the exception to this rule. "And people can be housemates without getting married. Paul and I just want to be friends with each other."

"I love you and I love Paul, so you should love each other and get married," Gaylin insisted. His tone indicated that I was really rather dense. Jenny had adopted Gaylin as a single mother. Paul was her older brother. They were from a Catholic family of six children, some of whom were married with children of their own, giving Gaylin lots of extended family and our house lots of sociability.

"I'm worried that my mom might marry Tony," Gaylin went on, twisting his hand anxiously into the hair above his forehead. "And make me move to Canada."

I nodded, unable to reassure him that this wouldn't happen. Jenny and Tony were in love, and she was visiting him right now in Vancouver, British Columbia.

"If you and Paul got married then I could maybe stay here with the two of you and not have to leave my friends and everything," Gaylin said. His voice was beseeching. "Then everything could come together for me." I was impressed by his initiative, his desire to chart the course of his life.

"Honey, it's pretty rare for things to come together the way we want them to," I offered in as warm a tone as possible. "To be honest, sometimes things come apart before they come back together again."

"I hate that," Gaylin scowled. I went to the bed and put my hand on his back, feeling his sharp shoulder blades and vertebrae like little sparrow bones through his brown T-shirt.

"Me, too," I said. You have no idea, I thought, wanting to scream, but knowing that wouldn't help either of us. Irrationally, from no place that made sense, I thought: I love my husband and I love my child. There was no husband and there was no child, objectively speaking. But they were already living in my heart, whoever they would turn out to be, and I yearned for them. I hugged Gaylin and he hugged me back, jumping into my lap and wrapping his bandy little legs around my waist like a monkey. It wouldn't help anything for me to wish aloud that he were mine, so I said nothing. After awhile he let go of me, fetched some Dr. Seuss books from his room and read aloud, sprawled on his stomach on my bed, while I slogged on with my packing.

When I said my prayers that night in front of the little altar in my bedroom, quieted my mind and listened for God's voice. Sometimes I could hear it like a whisper coming into my mind, things like 'have faith' or 'let go.' Occasionally a feeling would arrive, distinct as a human presence, like when I'd cried and prayed after my break-up with Mike, and I had gradually felt God's love burning in the room, distinct as a campfire on a chilly spring night.

Tonight when I waited on God, I got a visual image of myself. I was in profile, holding a small child, with a community of people around me. There was no man with me, though. I kept watching the image, eyes tight shut, until a man from the group, burly and strong-looking, stepped forward and held me and my child from behind, cradling us, protecting us.

I shook my head and got up from the altar. I wasn't going to have a child, and *then* find a man. The husband had to come first. I'd gotten that image from Jenny's current life, not from my future. That's what happened when you were close to people.

It was noon on Sunday before I reached for the phone to call my principal. I was nervous because I'd never had a conversation with him that had gone well. My church worshipped on Sunday evenings, with a group dinner beforehand. I was looking forward to it even more than usual today.

Owen's brusque voice answered on the first ring. I felt like he had pounced on my call and would now find a way to tear apart what I would tell him, in his Type A, New Yorky way.

"Owen, this is Revelle Jones. I'm sorry to call you at home," I said.

"Don't worry about it. What's happened?" he said. We both knew there was nothing normal about my call.

"It's my father. He has cancer in at least one kidney," I stated.

"I'm sorry," he replied, sounding as if he meant it. He probably did. Disliking me didn't mean he disliked my father.

"So I need to go be with him. In southern California," I added, since he'd never asked me where I was from or anything else about myself.

"I see."

"It's possible I'll be donating a kidney to him."

"Ah," he said, pausing before continuing. "So I need to find a substitute?"

"Yes. It's hard to know for how long. It might even be 'til the end of the school year. I'm sorry about this." It felt crappy to be leaving my students and fellow teachers, practically in the middle of the night, like an outlaw or a fugitive. I lived so much of my life at the school, in constant human contact and conversation.

"It's not your fault," he replied.

"No, it's not." I walked to my little altar restlessly, wanting to end the conversation.

"I need to tell you something," Owen said, in a different tone. "I'm sorry that the timing is what it is here." I waited. "I will not be able to renew your contract for next year."

I didn't respond right away. I sat down on the blue-painted wood floor in front of my altar and touched the items on it: the half-burned sage stick, the deep lavender geode, the textured cross with the reddish-brown glaze, the one that fit perfectly into my palm, that Luke Kavanaugh from church had made for me. He and his wife Cat were potters.

"I see," I said, holding the sage to my nose and inhaling its earthy scent. I wished that I were in the high desert of Central Oregon, near Bend, where it had come from. The concern at the top of my mind was that the smell of sage, which I loved, was going to become wedded in my memory to the moment I was fired from the job I loved.

"Enrollment is already down with the recession," Owen said, all business now, as if a private school with a couple hundred students was some Fortune 500 company and I was part of his sales force. I sensed he was relieved that I wasn't begging him to keep me on. But I would never have sacrificed my dignity like that. Silent self-control was my policy around people and situations I didn't trust.

"I have to lay off at least two teachers, and my high school English classes have the lowest student-teacher ratio. And I've gotten more complaints about you than anyone else."

"Two complaints," I clarified. They were from parents who were best friends. He acted as if two angry parents defined my whole teaching career.

"From the families that are the best fundraisers," he said flatly. Fundraising was central to a private school like Prentice.

"Good-bye," I said, choking back my pain. I hung up, humiliated, hating him in a way that made me understand how people could commit crimes of passion. Rather than plotting how to kill him I put on my running shoes, made sure Paul would stay home with Gaylin, and climbed into my pick-up truck for the short drive up to the Thurman Street entrance to Forest Park.

I ran through the spring sunlight, up Leif Ericson Drive until the Wildwood Trail offered itself to me on the left. I ran and ran on its hard-packed earth, climbing mostly, my feet dancing over the rocks and exposed tree roots. My legs were as steady beneath me as muscled metronomes. Even though my heart was imploding like a black hole, my body could remain stable and hold my world together. My root system could be as deep as those of the towering Douglas fir trees that comprised the forest.

I berated myself for having chosen to teach at a private school instead of in the public school system, as Marisol and Paul had done. They were in unions and could not have lost their jobs for the reason I just had. Beyond that, there was a pressure-cooker aspect to a place like Prentice that I should have realized had implications for job security. Annual tuition was almost $11,000, and the parents' agenda for their children was not just college, but the *best* college. I had once had a 16 year-old boy cry when I'd given him a B+ in my sophomore English class instead of an A-, sobbing between hiccups that his hopes of Harvard were now history. It took everything I had to refrain from suggesting that doing some service work at a soup kitchen might put his grades into a healthier perspective. I'd later told Paul and Marisol that some parents seemed to see their kids as extensions of themselves, their high performance child a status symbol as elegant and enviable as a Mercedes Benz.

When I'd sought and landed the job at Prentice, I'd felt that the higher academic standards, smaller classes and personal atmosphere made up for the lower pay. I felt less sure about that choice now, though. I was abruptly, jarringly, unemployed, and had large student loan payments. Despite years of buying my clothes at Goodwill, rarely eating out and vacationing only in campgrounds, I had less than $700 in my savings account.

The trail climbed, switched back and climbed some more. My breathing deepened. I imagined that the forest was absorbing my pain over Mike, my father's cancer and being fired. It was big enough to hold all my emotions, even if I wasn't.

When I got home almost two hours later my scalp, running bra and shorts were all sweat soaked. I climbed the stairs, still panting a little, needing to shower before Paul and I would head across the river to church. I found Jenny in her bedroom, back from visiting Tony in British Columbia. Her lean, tanned face was glowing with pleasure. We hugged. To her credit, Jenny never shied away from sweat. Then she told me, her eyes large and shining, that Tony had proposed to her and she had accepted.

"Congratulations," I said, producing a smile. Part of me was happy for her, while another felt insanely jealous that she got to have a great kid like Gaylin, plus a man who found the family proposition compelling.

"Gaylin and I will be moving to British Columbia," Jenny said. "I'll be selling the house, but don't worry. You'll have plenty of time to find a new place to live."

"I don't think that'll be an issue." I caught her up on my father's cancer, losing my job and the fact I was leaving for California tomorrow. I didn't know when I'd be returning to Portland. Jenny's facial features changed shape before my eyes.

"I'm so sorry, Revelle," she said. Her voice was subdued. She pulled me into another hug that was nothing like our welcome-home embrace of a minute ago. It made me think of two horses I had once observed in a pasture that had wrapped their heads around each other's necks, not tightly, but tenderly. They started by touching noses then moved side by side, and laid their chins across each other's necks. They had stayed intertwined like that awhile, before gently turning from the embrace, resuming their grazing and moving slowly away from each other across the pasture.

Chapter 3
Heading South

Lying on my back in my sleeping bag, I found Pleiades, the Seven Sisters, in the pantheon of stars arced high above me. It was Monday night, and I was camping alone in a small campground on the Klamath River, just over the border from Oregon in northern California.

I told myself the Seven Sisters were the friends I needed. The Seri tribe of northwestern Mexico, I had read, believed these stars to be seven women who were giving birth. I silently asked the star-women I was gazing at to share their fertility with me.

Camping alone was the type of thing I wouldn't tell my parents about. I'd camped by myself in the stunning San Juan Islands to the north, and on the rugged Oregon coast and I always enjoyed it, rarely feeling afraid. I had been so unlucky lately though, that tonight I pictured myself getting attacked by a bear, like in the stories I'd read about as a child in the *Reader's Digests* my parents kept lying around the house. My thoughts rolled on. I recalled that the Kiowa tribe legend of the Pleiades was that they had originally been seven maidens who had been discovered by huge bears, who chased the hapless girls up into the sky, where they remained and became stars.

Unlike those maidens, I couldn't escape from a marauding bear up into the heavens. And then who would be able to donate a kidney to my father, I thought darkly there in the dark, if my body was shredded, half-eaten by an ursine predator. My heartbeat accelerated with fear as the story I told myself unfolded. I sighed, turned onto my side in the flannel-lined sleeping bag, curled my knees up to my chest, and willed myself to think of something more positive.

Marisol had been supportive of the idea of kidney donation, while Paul had remained cautious. She was half Mexican on her mother's side, loyal as a lioness to family, sending gift checks to a complex network of relatives in East Los Angeles for everything from christenings to high school graduations. Last night she had told me that she considered me part of her family, and would give me one of her kidneys, in turn, if the need should later arise. The memory warmed and comforted me. She, Paul and I had been hanging out at her house after church. She said, "Funny how God gives everyone two kidneys at birth, when we only need one. It's a recipe for sharing."

"I'm good at sharing," Carmenita, Marisol's five-year-old daughter, announced from my lap.

"That's true," I affirmed. My skirt pocket was lumpy with the Lifesavers that the child had insisted on sharing with me: one for her, one for me, back and forth as I had cuddled her on the couch. I'd explained I needed to save my Lifesavers for my drive south, rather than telling her I disliked hard candy and risk her leaving. I loved the warm weight of her on my body and her silky black hair, which smelled of Johnson's baby shampoo, tickling my chin. I coveted people's children the way men coveted each other's beautiful wives. Marisol didn't mind. She had faith that I would marry and have children.

I sat up in my sleeping bag, worn out from worry and insomnia, and found I could read my watch in the moonlight. It was just 5:05 a.m., but there was no use in lying wide awake when I had a hard day's driving ahead of me. I got up, already clad in leggings and a big t-shirt, and did some stretching. Then I rolled up my sleeping bag and ground cloth, and drove the truck out of the dark, silent campground.

Dawn broke in rosy shades of pink over my left shoulder as I drove, like the blush of God. I climbed the part of the Cascade Range on which Mount Shasta was the showy, volcanic star. It was staggeringly tall as I drove past, snow-crowned even with summer approaching. I obsessed about failing in my job after initially succeeding in it. Should I even continue teaching? I loved to dance, but nobody made a living at that.

I bought gas in the little town of Red Bluff and used the dinky, rather dirty bathroom. In the mirror I saw a short, slim woman with large brown eyes, dark blonde hair that waved wildly down to her waist, and skin that appeared tanned but wasn't. I'd been light brown since birth. Only my close friends knew my mother was Palestinian, because the word created subtle hitches in any conversation, pauses fraught with people's thoughts of terrorists in the Mideast. I used the word Arabic, instead, when asked directly about my heritage. The woman in the mirror had an awfully sober expression. I shook my head at her, because she clearly needed to lighten up. Let Jesus back in, the one who wanted to carry her load.

I rinsed my sunglasses, brushed my teeth, rubbed myself down with a moist washcloth and changed into a tank top and shorts. It was already pushing 80, and I'd be sweating all day since my truck had no air conditioner. Yesterday the Klamath River had been deliciously cold when I'd walked into it at the campground. I had followed the example of a young woman already playing in the water. She had curly red hair, a fearless gaze and the unusual name of Shasta. I had welcomed the river's startling embrace after being melted all afternoon in my truck by the day's heat. It was as if the cold water had put me back together again, the Witch of the West's death in reverse.

I got back into the truck and resumed the drive, my sunglasses shielding my eyes from the bright sun. Shasta had approached my campfire later in the evening as I was softly playing my guitar, and I'd welcomed her company. "Sometimes I need a break from my college pals," she whispered with a smile. "Maybe I should camp alone next time, like you." Because she was interested, I'd told her about losing my relationship, job and home all at roughly the same time. But I held my tongue about my dad. I needed his cancer to not exist right then, as if it could break me if I let it into the gentle ring of fire we were sharing.

Shasta and I shared a love of wild places. I was intrigued that she knew some tree-sitters, people who actually lived for periods of time in old-growth trees to keep them from being destroyed by loggers. "Trees are just as alive as you and me," she murmured as she stared at the low flames.

"Maybe more," I said. Her smile was slow and sweet in the half-light. "Shasta's a beautiful name. Did your parents give it to you?"

"I gave it to myself. Just a few months ago. I've left Jennifer behind," she said with a small flourish of her flannel-shirted arm.

"Shasta suits you better." I gave her a little flurry of applause, and she parodied a bow. She was playful, which I liked.

"We both have unusual names," she pointed out. "How has yours worked for you?"

"It's been a good thing," I said without hesitation. "I've been Revelle all my life, and I've never felt attached to the status quo."

"Excellent!" She play-clapped for me, and I play-bowed for her. I decided to follow an impulse.

"I know we're new to each other," I said. "But it feels like we're old friends who just met. I've got a question for you, if you're up for it. What's your greatest hope and your deepest fear?"

She sat a little straighter on the ground, her red hair glowing redder in the firelight. She was clearly up for this.

"My hope is to make a real difference in the world. I want to do something that wouldn't get done if I didn't do it."

"Mmmm." The throaty sound came out of me unbidden, her words resonated so much in my body. After a minute she continued.

"And my fear is that I could fail in that." My spine relaxed a little in relief at the word. Yeah, a person can fail, I thought. "I mean, it would be terrible to not find the thing I came here to do. Or, I could find it, but then fail at doing it. Life doesn't have guarantees." I put another chunk of wood on the fire. Little sparks flew, then settled. "But I think I'm gonna find it. And I'm gonna do it."

"I think you are too," I said, convinced. She had that kind of force of character.

"Your turn. I feel like we're playing truth or dare." The radiant smile again. Her face wasn't beautiful, but it was striking.

"The hope is hard to say because it's not politically correct."

"Doesn't matter. Other people don't get to vote on it."

"I want to be a mother. I'm on fire to be a mother. It's hard to talk about because the world is full of mothers. It's the most mundane thing in the world."

"Not if you do it really well, it's not," Shasta declared. "Done well, motherhood can move heaven and earth."

"Thank you for that." I felt encouraged. "My other hope is to be a dance teacher. But it's a certain kind of dancing that does a certain thing for people."

"Tell me more." Shasta looked riveted. Her chin was on her knee, her curled legs encircled by her arms. She seemed ready to talk all night.

"This dancing gets people out of their heads, down into their bodies. I give my students structure, and steps we do together. But it's not about perfecting your technique. It's about being free inside yourself and connecting with other people from that place of freedom."

"Mmm." Shasta nodded, as if this readily made sense to her.

"That's the way I want to raise my child, too. With structure, for sure. We'd all flounder without that. But a deep freedom within that structure. Space to move, and be, and discover, and join into community." My breath was coming fast. "It's like I was put here as a conduit to help people to become themselves." I blinked. This was news even to me.

"I'd love to be your child. Or your dance student. Anybody would," Shasta said simply.

"Thank you," I said after a minute. It took me that time to quiet a sob that rose inside me. Crying wasn't bad, but this wasn't the time for it. This was a joyful time.

"And my fear is like yours. That I could fail," I added.

"But you won't. You're gonna do it." Shasta's voice brooked no doubt. It was certain. A gift of youth, I reflected. "Now, I need something from you, please," she said.

"Um . . . is it my phone number?"

We both laughed, breaking the tension in my chest and changing our shared mood from a good, deep one to a good, light one.

"Well, sure, that too," she said after we'd stopped giggling. "But your kind of dance is something I want. So, I'm thinking we need to dance. Here. In front of the fire."

She was already rising from the ground, and I followed. We shook our knees and shoulders out a little, loosening up. I was already smiling. I started gently pulsing my body, and she followed. Her movements began suggesting a river, so I let all my joints go fluid, and our bodies became flowing water that rushed, lapped, whirled and eddied around my campsite. Then we became warriors, leaping boldly about, brandishing fists and bows and arrows. Our eyes met often, with a warm knowingness. We gave ourselves to the night, our dancing as different from the kind everyone saw and did in public as a heartfelt conversation is different from a political debate full of posturing. Time in the usual sense fell away, though I knew the moon overhead to be our metronome, moving with us. We played and pranced, capered and cavorted. Eventually we slowed and faced each other across the dwindling fire. We came to a complete standstill, alert to each other to find the final movement.

I swayed subtly, and Shasta swayed with me. Then before my eyes she became a tree, tall and strong, highest branches moving in the wind. I became her fellow tree. Our feet had roots going down into the earth. Our arms and hands extended into the heavens. We were old-growth trees, ones who had seen it all, carried the secrets of the ages, and now felt no fear. Our bodies stitched earth and sky together.

But Shasta's fearlessness had not stayed with me. Driving toward Sacramento with its verdant fields on either side of me, I worried about when and where I would work again. Then I worried about my father whose life might depend on whether or not I donated a kidney to him. Further down the road, I devoted time to wishing, with the familiar dull pain, that Mike had loved me enough to still be with me at a time like this, when my life was falling apart. I wanted to be held. I wanted to make love.

"It's silly, what a person's mind fixates on," I had remarked to Paul a week ago.

"No, it's interesting what we fixate on," Paul had replied. "I obsess about Lena's ankles, the way they taper so sharply from her legs, like a racehorse's. My sponsor told me that when I've gotten over her, my fixation will fade away and she'll become a whole person in my memory instead of two beautiful legs that I obsess over. That's when I'll have forgiven her."

"Forgiveness." I perked up a little, since I probably needed to forgive Mike. "Well, here's what I've been obsessing over. A good-looking guy held the door for me at Prentice yesterday when we were both leaving the building. He looked Native American. I'd never seen him before, but we locked eyes as I passed through the door. I smiled and said thanks. He had these luminous hazel eyes that just held mine. It was the Look. I keep thinking about it."

"So, mythologically speaking, here's what your fixating on his eyes could symbolize" Paul ventured. He had read a lot of Robert Bly. "It could mean you need a man to see you for your true self, not just look at you physically, for your beauty."

Faster than conscious thought, my right finger went to the tip of my nose as my left finger pointed at Paul. He'd gotten it on the nose. I'd loved all of Mike. But his love for me had been largely physical.

I drove on now in the hot sun of the Central Valley. I'd wasted two precious years of fertility on Mike, a man who'd had no talent for loving in the first place. I pep-talked myself like a football coach would speak to a losing, hangdog team: I could choose better next time. I could choose a heartful man who definitely wanted children. Yes. This was doable; those men existed. I sat up straighter, like a revived quarterback, and played tapes to pass the long hours as the highway took me away from my home but toward my family. Jackson Brown, Judy Collins, Sinead O'Connor. Jackson's "Running On Empty" felt true for me as it never had before.

I tried not to think too far down the road about my dad's surgery tomorrow, which might find that both kidneys were already compromised by cancer. Unlike my mom, I hadn't done any research about the medical situation. I was simply willing to go under a surgeon's knife and give my dad a kidney. The risks were the doctors' concern, not mine, as I saw it, and so were the details. I had talked with Marisol about my irritation with science late one night in the dorm during our sophomore year of college.

"Here's what bothers me about this biology book," I'd said energetically, holding up the dense tome with the bug-eyed frog on the cover. "It's the disregard of spirit. They're obsessing about all these nitpicky details, all this frigging flotsam and jetsam minutiae. There's no sense of wholeness or spirit in motion, just of all these soulless material parts."

"Good point," Marisol had agreed. She was laying on her side on a worn-out sofa, wearing black leggings and a purple t-shirt, hugely oversized for her slight frame, that proclaimed "Take Back The Night" in bold, spiky black letters. Her major was women's studies. "It's just like the male power structure to break the world down into a series of mechanistic parts that they think they can control," she added, shaking her dainty, dark head dismissively. I nodded vigorously. It had felt so good at nineteen to find a best friend who shared my love of God, children, feminism and progressive politics, a combination that shouldn't be rare, in our view, but was.

The sun was high in the sky now, and I was hungry. At a rest stop with three skinny, sorry-looking trees shading its two picnic tables, I drank the iced tea, now warm, that Jenny had packed for me. I made two peanut butter and jelly sandwiches, eating one and wrapping the other for later. I peeled a navel orange, releasing nectar-like spray that I inhaled gratefully.

Suddenly I was six years old. I was sitting on my dad's lap in our backyard as he peeled an orange just-picked from the neighbor's tree that hung over onto our property. I was thrilled to be enclosed in his arms, intoxicated by the citrus spray in my nostrils. We broke apart the sections, his large hands around my small hands, and fed them to each other. The juice ran all over our hands, our forearms and chins and we were both laughing.

"We could never get away with this indoors," my dad said.

"Outdoors is better," I replied, grinning up at him.

On the hot picnic bench in the rest area, I still thought outdoors was better than indoors. But now I knew that my six-year-old innocence would have a short life span and meet a demise my dad could not protect me from. There was nothing I could do about that now. I rarely thought about it. The part I didn't know was whether I'd be able to protect my dad from the predatory growth in his kidney, or kidneys.

I threw away the orange peels, used the toilet, washed my hands in cold water and splashed more of it on my face and neck. The restroom had no soap or mirror, and the towel dispenser was empty. I dried my hands on my denim shorts and resumed driving.

I shifted miserably on the truck's spartan bench seat as I got into Los Angeles. I cursed myself for arriving there at the height of rush hour. I wished I could have stopped earlier to run or dance, get a reprieve from the solitary confinement of driving. It suddenly struck me that if I had still been leading the after-school dance troupe at Prentice when the two students had been rude to me, I wouldn't have found them so maddening, and reprimanded them in a way that invited their parents' complaints to the principal. Dancing had always kicked my frustrations down into the ground, creating joy and beauty along the way. In its absence, I'd verbally lashed out—at people who'd had the power to hurt me.

The gray skyscrapers and garish billboards of L.A. were ugly beyond belief, with my parent's home in Anaheim still an hour or more away. The Corvettes and Ferraris slithering around me with their phallic curves seemed obscene, like the male strippers of the automotive world. My eight-year-old pickup truck was distinctly low status in this environment, while I had never given a thought to my car status in Oregon. A gleaming black BMW zoomed out of nowhere on my right and swerved in front of me, no blinker, no hand wave from the driver seeking permission or forgiveness. It would have hit me if I hadn't quickly braked. The near miss frightened me and made me angry. I scowled at its black bumper and the white glare of the smog, concrete and tangled freeways and thought, *Toto, we're not in Oregon any more.*

Chapter 4
Descent

"Hi, Dad!" I smiled at my father as he lay in his bed at St. Jude Hospital in Fullerton. My smile was pure acting. I felt only alarm. The surgery that had removed his right kidney had ended five hours earlier. He looked ten years older than before the operation. His skin was gray, eyes sunken and his face deeply lined, haggard. The room smelled like antiseptic.

"Hi, honey," he said, hoarse, a little croaky. His right hand stirred slightly beneath the sheet in a body-memory of the little salute-wave he normally used for greeting people.

"It looks like I don't get to share body parts with you, after all," I said, pretending to be disappointed that his left kidney had been found free of cancer. The would-be hero in me actually was a little disappointed. With no job to return to, I needed a challenge, a way to contribute.

"We both got lucky," he smiled weakly. His weakness, in fact, was staggering to me. Mom, Rick and I were going to transform the family den on the ground floor into his new bedroom so he wouldn't have to climb the stairs when he came home.

"Is it hard for you to see Dad like this?" Rick had asked me in the hospital lounge yesterday, after my initial visit with them both. The green eyes in his thin, expressive face were concerned.

My face must have been registering culture shock around family and geography. The lack of trees and rivers, the labyrinth of freeways, the large sub-developments, parking lots and strip malls that had reproduced at rodent rates since my last visit were an assault on my senses. I hadn't been down in three years. Instead, I used phone calls and letters to stay connected to my family, mailing a big box of gifts down at Christmas.

"Yes, it's hard to see Dad like this," I replied. "He's never been in the hospital before." I've never been fired either, I thought. I had defined it to Rick and Mom as being laid off, which was technically accurate since three jobs, counting my own, had been dissolved at Prentice.

The last time my family and I had been in this hospital was when Grandpa Joe had died back when I was 14. He was my Mom's father. A car had hit him when he was out walking in his neighborhood before first light, dying just a few hours later. We had all wept inconsolably. He had been lively and vigorous, and we'd assumed he had many years left with us.

Grandpa Joe was Palestinian, with deep-bronze skin and bushy black eyebrows that made me think of caterpillars. I used to play Scrabble with him at his house, after he'd slowed down to where he could no longer play tag. The words we formed on the board sparked discussions. In fifth grade I had put "for" down in front of the word "give" and anxiously told him I'd learned in Sunday school that Jesus wanted me to forgive Leo.

Leo, I explained was the boy on the school playground, two grades ahead of me, who had tripped me at recess when I was running to home plate in a kickball game. He'd claimed it was an accident, which was an obvious lie. I was angry at Leo, and the big, ugly scabs on my knees that I showed Grandpa made him angry too.

"Elly," he said, since that was his nickname for me, He was looking into my eyes intently. "Forgiveness is for people too weak to take revenge." I blinked with surprise. I'd learned about revenge from the horse books I got from the library. One was about a stallion named Flame who lived in an island kingdom and fought other stallions for his herd of mares. Grandpa didn't want me to be weak, like the stallions who lost the fights. He wanted me to be like Flame, who won the fights.

"Should I kick and bite Leo tomorrow on the playground?" I asked, lost in the bright, hooded brown eyes under the bristling caterpillar eyebrows.

"You'll find a way," he'd said slowly. "You'll find an opening. Maybe tomorrow. Maybe much later. You've got to teach him to leave you alone without getting caught."

After a long, thoughtful moment, our Scrabble game resumed. At school, I had tensely watched at every recess for Leo. But he seemed to have disappeared. When I eventually asked his teacher where he was, she'd told me his dad, who was in the Marines, had been transferred to Okinawa. He was never coming back. So it was a standoff in my heart between forgiveness and revenge, with me taking action on neither the Christian path, nor my grandfather's path, which ironically came from the same part of the world.

Grandpa Joe had immigrated to California from Palestine right before the '48 war had ended. He had seen that the Israelis would win, and that fueled by the horrors of the Holocaust, the Palestinians would become, as he said, the next Jews, by which he meant the next oppressed people. He'd wanted no part of living under their rule, so he had taken his rug business, his wife, who we called Grandma Jean, and my mother, age 18 and their only child, to Anaheim, California. He had been keenly aware of the affluent Jewish population in Orange County and had promptly changed the family's name from Badareen to Beyer. My name was Revelle Beyer Jones, as if my parents had wanted to seal the deal with my middle name. My mom never wanted to discuss her Arabic heritage, particularly her shedding of it, or what I eventually learned from Grandpa Joe was the heartrending loss in '48 of the battle for the Holy Land.

ॐ

I visited Dad in the afternoons at the hospital as he recovered, reading the *Los Angeles Times* aloud to him since it tired him to hold the newspaper up, himself. When he had the energy, we discussed the recession, politics, and most of all the ups and downs of his beloved, mercurial Dodgers. His minister and church friends visited now and then with hokey get-well cards and the kind of cheerful banter my dad had always liked. He gained a bit of his former energy each day, but he still looked old and helpless compared to his former self. I wore my upbeat game face, concealing my worry since it wouldn't help him.

Living in my old bedroom in the Anaheim house was comforting in a nostalgic kind of way. I danced in the mornings after my mother left for work, moving across the well-worn, orange shag carpet my parents had installed in the living room in the 70's. I would have preferred leading a dance class in a studio setting or getting to perform, but this was better than not dancing at all. After coming home from the hospital I would cook dinner and eat with my mom when she returned from the rug warehouse and retail store. She had worked in Grandpa Joe's business in different ways for most of her life and then taken it over completely after he died.

"Are you going to look for a teaching job down here?" Mom asked me the evening before Dad was to come home from the hospital. We had eaten our fill of the enchilada casserole and the avocado-orange salad I'd made. We were leaning on our elbows, plates pushed aside, chins resting in our palms.

"I don't know. I might move back up to Oregon after Dad is back to normal," I said. My voice lacked conviction, because there was nothing solid to move back up to: no job, no relationship, no home. I placed my hands on the table, fingers spread out like the cards of a poker player. It was a losing set of cards, three of a kind at best, and my body wilted a little there onto the well-used, nicked-up dining room table at which we'd shared thousands of meals over the years. I felt like a loser, and the house of my girlhood seemed like a place that gave some permission for this state, at least temporarily.

"Mom," I said in a different tone, "what I really want is to have a child. A family."

"Well, Mike was just one man who wasn't ready for children.

There are probably thousands of men in this city alone that want exactly what you want," Mom said. She was petite and fair-haired like me. People thought Middle Easterners always had dark hair, which wasn't the case. The occasional photos sent to her by the extended Badareen clan in Palestine always featured a flashy minority of blonde heads, like Palominos popping up amongst brown and black horses.

"You *will* be a mother in time," she insisted. "It's not as if you're some special little person that God refuses to take care of."

I laughed.

"Good point." I liked her faith that God would not abandon me.

"Would you like to come to church with me tomorrow?" Mom asked hopefully.

"Um, no thanks." Her face fell, then rearranged itself into its usual composure. My parents' church left me cold. I saw it as a group of carefully coifed and dressed-up people performing a formal, rote style of worship as a prelude to coffee-chat about golf and keeping the Republicans in office. It was the opposite of my church, where people wore jeans, everyone was a Democrat, and we often had spirited discussions of Rachel's sermons, in the part of the service we called reflections.

"You could get a summer job down here while you get your teaching plans sorted out," Mom suggested, switching suddenly from church back to employment. I pushed my chair away from the table. She didn't want an adult daughter who was showing signs of depression living with her too long, or maybe becoming a dependent. I felt a little hurt because I'd always been the more independent of her two children, getting jobs as a teenager and moving out of the house before Rick had, for example.

"Teaching has me a little turned off at the moment," I admitted. "Dancing is what I really want."

"Disneyland employs some dancers every summer. They'd be hiring about now," she pointed out. Disneyland was five miles from our house, and every summer night of my girlhood its fireworks had boomed in the night sky, practically over our heads. Birthday parties in my hometown were held at Disneyland, making the Magic Kingdom mundane. Working there was what my friends had done when we'd been teenagers, selling ice cream and cotton candy to people who had traveled to the place like pilgrims to Mecca.

I cleared the leftover casserole and salad off the table.

"I'll look for a job," I agreed, without saying where. I did need to work, with Dad's cancer resolved. As I cleaned up the kitchen my skin felt cold even though the air was warm.

❦

"Thanks for meeting with me on the spur of the moment," I said to Mary Armour in the Claremont College chaplain's office. Her hand was firm and fleshy in mine as we shook, her left hand even joining in on the other side to embrace my thinner one. She was about twelve years older than me, a large-boned woman in a mud-colored dress. Despite her nice handshake, I dourly adjudged by her body-type that she had never danced a day in her life. She probably wouldn't relate to me.

I had been unhappily surprised to learn that Mary had replaced Ed Cunningham three years earlier as the chaplain of the Claremont colleges. Mary sat me down into a deep, comfy sofa in her office and got me a mug of coffee, which felt warmly comforting between my two hands. I recognized the lively art on her walls as coming from the Syracuse Cultural Workers calendar. She even had my favorite of theirs, women of color dancing gracefully in long dresses of bright colors. The scent of jasmine blossoms came in through the open window, something I seldom smelled in Oregon.

"It's a pleasure to meet you," Mary said. "It's not too often an alumnus comes to visit. When you were here, Ed must have been your chaplain." I nodded, smiling at the memory of the white-haired, pink-skinned man who had greeted me by name whenever I shook his hand or hugged him after a Sunday service. "Revelle, Revelle, my chapel belle," he would enthuse, making me feel like minor royalty in the little world he wove that was devout and exuberantly playful at the same time. Ed had been the first albino person I had ever known, and he had meant so much to me that when I had an albino student, Damien Waters, walk into my classroom the first day of my second year of teaching, I had immediately adored Damien, imputing all of Ed's good traits onto him.

"I'm looking for advice. A referral to a good church, actually. After I graduated from Pitzer in '83 I've been living in Portland, Oregon. But I'm back down in this area for I don't know exactly how long. My father developed cancer, and I came home to help take care of him. And there was a break-up" I trailed off, waving my hands to will away memories of Mike. "At any rate, I need to find a good church to attend down here."

"Wonderful!" Mary was into this. "Tell me a little more about yourself."

"Well, I'm a dancer, is the first thing I'd say," I told her, happy she was interested in me. "But my life has changed a lot all of a sudden. I'd been in a relationship, but we broke up a month ago. I wanted to get married and have children, and he didn't. So that hurts. I still think about him a lot." Mary was nodding. "And I'm an English teacher, but . . . well, my job went south pretty abruptly."

"Your job went south and you also went south," Mary observed.

"Without wanting to," I added. "I loved where I was living in Portland. I'd never been happier."

"You've sustained a lot of losses." Her plain-featured, open face was clearly feeling with me. Sitting there looking at her was like looking into a mirror, seeing what having things taken away from you looked like. She could have been a child told that Christmas had been cancelled.

"Nothing compared to the Kurds in Iraq," I contradicted her. "I just heard on the radio they think it was at least 40,000 people murdered in total. Chemical warfare on civilians, ordered by Iraq's own leader. Imagine the suffering. *Those* are losses."

"It seems like a different world when we think about a genocide like that, doesn't it?" Mary said. "It's hard to believe we're all living in the same world, being more alike to each other than different."

I nodded, feeling what she meant, and we regarded each other, sadness and warmth commingling in the room. I liked this woman. I softly put the now cool coffee mug onto the little table to my left, slipped off my sandals and crossed my legs Indian-style under my long skirt on the sofa.

"Should I assume you're looking for a church that would care about the Kurds?" Mary asked me.

I nodded again. "May I tell you about the church in Portland I'm still a member of?" I said.

"Please do!" she said, settling back into her armchair the way people do with a good story at hand.

"We worship on Sunday evenings," I began. "We meet in a big house, built about 80 years ago but restored and really beautiful. We take turns cooking dinner and once a month do potluck, and we all clean up together. You know that saying about many hands make for light work?"

"Yes. I'm a veteran of many fellowship dinners, too," she twinkled at me.

"Of course," I smiled back. "Our services are . . . really intimate and heartfelt. Technically we're non-denominational, which can sometimes mean you don't know who you are, but what we're really doing is borrowing from the richest parts of different traditions. A few times I've led everyone in some simple liturgical dance." I demonstrated, lifting one arm and then the other to join it in a circle above my head, wrists leading my fingers in the motion, head and eyes following the hand upward each time, *connoting reverence.*

"Ah," Mary said in pleased surprise, getting what my body had just said.

"When I had to leave Portland two weeks ago to come down here for my dad's surgery, everyone did a blessing circle at the end of the service to see me off. The children were closest to me in the center, since they're so short, naturally." Mary nodded, clearly picturing it. "They prayed for me and for my father. Our minister, Rachel, she happens to be gay; she can pray like nobody you've ever seen."

Mary pursed her lips, like, whew, and turned her head slightly to the side, eyes still trained on me, the way a gunslinger would silently marvel at the best draw in the west.

"Rachel had her hand on my shoulder, and my best friends Paul and Marisol had their hands on my neck and back, and Marisol's daughter Carmen, Carmenita Bonita I call her, had her little arms wrapped around my right thigh." I clasped my right thigh with both hands, reproducing the feeling of being held in the world, held closely with love. My parents had never been big on physical affection, either with each other or their children, at least not after we'd gotten big. But I loved to touch and be touched. I had trained my brother Rick to submit to my hugs, mostly a steady stream of side-hugs except for full-frontal hello and good-bye hugs, and I believed he secretly liked them despite never initiating them.

"Rachel was praying, 'Mother-Father God, we trust you to watch over Revelle as she journeys to stand with her father Ray, and please help her to feel our hearts journeying right along with our beloved sister' . . . only she really has the cadence going on, the rising and falling tones, like Martin Luther King Junior."

"Wow," Mary breathed. The room was getting warmer, the scent of jasmine stronger.

"And after that prayer my community said the Irish prayer of journeying, you know, 'May the road rise up to meet you, may the wind be always at your back'"—Mary was nodding vigorously—"and then we stood in a circle holding hands and sang 'God Be With You 'Til We Meet Again' and of course our eyes and faces were wet by the time we finished."

"I want to go to this church!" Mary blurted out. "It sounds wonderful."

"I miss them," I heard myself say in a broken voice. "And I miss my old job, the one I had before the new principal came." Mary nodded slowly, soberly, keeping eye contact. I could feel the feelings that had been lodged in my guts and womb for three weeks getting loosened up inside me. I gasped, sobbed once, and choked back another sob. "I know I've got it easy compared to most of the world."

"Don't fight it," Mary murmured, passing me a box of Kleenex, and I obeyed her, and let the crying rip. This little visit, this drop-in to collect a quick referral, had turned into something different than I'd planned. I collapsed in my middle, elbows on my knees. The delicious smell of jasmine was lost to me as my nose spewed snot into the Kleenex and mingled with my hot tears. I cried helplessly.

"You've lost a lot," Mary said simply, which triggered a new crescendo in my crying. My voice cracked under the strain, which set off a fit of coughing. I was a total mess. The coughing wouldn't stop so I groped for more Kleenex to reduce the risk of passing airborne germs to Mary. My hand grasped at air; the Kleenex was gone. Mary got up, I guessed to rummage for more. She returned after a minute with a roll of toilet paper. I smiled. "We used this all the time in college," I confessed as I helped myself to it.

"And I still do!" she smiled back, and we both laughed a little. I took a couple of deep breaths, traveling back from my wild grief to the peaceful, stable room.

"I'm worried that I'm taking up your day. I'm not even part of your official flock," I said.

"Bless your heart, Revelle," Mary said. "This is summer. I don't have any appointments scheduled today. And even if I did . . ." she waved her hand, giving me the impression that she would have cancelled other things to be with me right now.

"I wish I could refer you to a church just like your church in Portland. But I don't know of one," she said honestly. I nodded, having already sensed that. "I imagine it would only frustrate you to try to replicate down here what you're used to up there."

"But I have two thoughts for you," she went on. I nodded eagerly. A breeze came in through the window, the scent of jasmine coming back with it.

"One is that if I were you, I would do whatever it took to get back to where I belonged. I mean, after taking care of my family. Your tribe is in Portland. You need to return to your tribe at some point." Mary's tone was as plain and kind as her face. My left palm went to my chest, the word 'tribe' reverberating in me like the bass notes of rock music thrumming inside my body when I danced. Mary's matter of fact statements made me realize that I had lost my tribe. "My second thought is to ask, what brings you joy?"

"Dancing," I shrugged, as matter of fact now as Mary had been when telling me to return to my tribe. The tears were completely behind me now.

"Then that's what you have to do while you're here. It'll keep you grounded. I don't know the details of how you'll dance. But I do know that God wants you to dance. Maybe more than God wants you to go to church."

"Oh," I said. My body, which had been leaning forward, suddenly relaxed back against the sofa. I still wished for a good church, but I could see the rock-like solidity of Mary's reprioritizing.

"I sense you're in a kind of exile right now. It's subtler than the exile of Moses' people, because you're safe, and all that. I don't want to over-dramatize. But if the story of exile can help you to get through this period of your life, before you're able to return to Oregon, then you might want to use it. Just remember this is only one chapter of your life. It's not the last chapter of your life."

"Just one chapter. Return to my tribe. Dance," I murmured, working to absorb it all. Mary had given me my marching orders. I didn't yet know how I'd execute them, but I felt better just hearing them named by someone with compassion and common sense.

I rose to leave and Mary rose too, opening her arms to me. I stepped forward and stayed in her substantial embrace as long as I dared, not wanting to be too needy. In general, I felt like I'd stepped into an alternate universe where Revelle Jones was a neurotic wreck instead of the competent, confident Revelle Jones of the mainline universe. When I finally pulled away and walked to the door, my eye was caught by a framed photograph on the wall of a teenaged girl riding a Palomino at a gallop. The horse's golden hide gleamed in the sun, and its flaxen mane and tail flew behind in spiky shapes like white flags of surrender that had been artistically shredded.

"That's my daughter Isabel," Mary offered. I suppressed a shudder, thanked Mary and said my good-byes. I walked back across the campus toward my truck, not wanting to remember what I was about to remember.

Chapter 5
Palomino

My seven-year-old nose sniffed cotton candy and popcorn as I walked hand in hand with my mother at the school's spring carnival. It was a Friday early in May. The bushes that ringed the administration building had gone light pink with dense, countless small blossoms. We called them the bee bushes, named them for the bees they attracted that became intoxicated with the flowers' nectar and the riches they could bring their queen.

The carnival booths offered us their own riches: treats, games and prizes that kept my head swinging from side to side, not wanting to miss anything. When I saw a plastic model Palomino horse prancing on a back shelf at the basketball-toss booth I tugged on my mother's hand like a frisky puppy on a leash, but my mother was intent on delivering her homemade cherry cake to the Cake Walk.

I submitted, my head swiveling, eyes registering the location of the beautiful golden Palomino: right between the cotton candy booth and the dunk tank. A skinny, wet-haired sixth grader sat with his arms wrapped around himself, waiting for someone with a good arm to strike the bull's eye with a softball and dunk him again. A man with thick glasses, so tall that he stood and saw above everyone else, was standing near the basketball booth and was turning his head to watch me.

I assumed my new rose-colored dress had caught his eye, and I skipped a little, happy to have been noticed. This was the Easter dress that my mother had made for me on her black Singer sewing machine from a Simplicity pattern, and even though it was a church dress and not a school dress, I got to wear it to the carnival as a special treat. Mom had her cherry cake, a slightly darker pink than the bee-bush blossoms, in her other hand, in a clear plastic cake-carrier with a handle.

When we reached the Cake Walk at the far end of the booths, music was playing and people were walking around on the blacktop in a chalk-drawn track that featured large squares with numbers. I jumped up and down excitedly, wanting to be moving to the music, too. I recognized the song as "Elmer's Tune," because my dad played it at home on our phonograph stereo. People of all ages were in the Cake Walk—parents, teenagers, a white-haired grandmother with a cane, and kids from my school, including a redheaded kindergartener who took halting steps and kept looking anxiously at her mother, who nodded encouragement as if to say, yes, you can walk in a large circle without me. I was braver than the kindergartner. I would have been fine out there on the Cake Walk track. I liked doing things by myself and wasn't afraid of attention.

Suddenly the music stopped. The walkers stumbled slightly like dancers thrown off tempo.

"Stay right where you are!" a man with a barker's cone and hedgehog hair boomed authoritatively. The cake walkers' feet became glued to their chalk-drawn squares. Mr. Hedgehog made eye contact with me and I looked alertly back at him. "This pretty little blonde girl," he said. "She is going to draw a number now to see who will win this delicious-looking German chocolate cake." He stepped over to me and knelt down, holding out a fishbowl half full of little yellow squares of construction paper. I reached in, stirred the contents around like I'd seen a woman do on *Let's Make A Deal*, pulled a paper square from the bottom of the bowl, and pressed it into the man's large hand.

He shouted into his barker's cone: "Seven! Whoever is standing on square number seven, please come and collect your German chocolate cake at this time!"

The grandmother stared down at the chalk at her feet, grinned, waving her cane in the air jubilantly. She almost fell, swinging the rubber-tipped end of her cane back down on the ground just in time to catch herself. When she joined us at the table, the barker held the German chocolate cake out to her. It was wonderfully lumpy, with nuts and shreds of coconut poking out of the light brown frosting. She looked at her prize helplessly, cane in one hand, clearly unable to carry the cake and walk at the same time.

"Why don't I carry your cake over to your car for you?" my mother suggested.

"Thank you, dear," the grandmother smiled with relief, the well used creases around her mouth getting further use.

"I want to stay here," I told Mom. She nodded, obviously thinking I wanted to keep on jumping around to the music and pull winning tickets for the barker with the hedgehog hair.

"All right. I'll meet you back here," Mom said. She held the cake on its plate in both her hands and moved at the grandmother's slow, cane-assisted pace. The barker was busy taking tickets and had no idea my mom thought he was watching me. I slipped away in the crowd and ran so fast back to the basketball booth that I got out of breath like when we played dodgeball in P.E.

I stood at its counter, staring with yearning at the prancing Palomino on the back shelf amongst the brown teddy bears. I couldn't believe anyone would even look at a dumb teddy bear when a golden Palomino with flaxen mane and tail was standing there waiting to go home with you. I imagined playing with it at home, grooming it and making it a bridle and reins out of thin leather strips as I did with my other model horses.

"Hi there, Missy," a deep voice said from above me. "Looks like there's a prize you have your eye on."

I looked way up to see the tall man who had been watching me earlier. He was about my parents' age, with a big belly and glasses like the bottoms of Coke bottles.

"The Palomino," I confided to him.

"I like horses, too," he replied. He reminded me of Leslie Hoyt, an awkward boy with similar thick glasses. Leslie was in the special ed class and other kids were mean to him, calling him Four-Eyes and Fart-Face. I generally made a point of saying, "Hi Leslie," when I saw him in the cafeteria lunch line because I hated that people were mean to him and I knew he was lonely. The homely man trying to be my friend suffered similar things, and I wanted to be nice to him. I nodded at his comment.

"I'll bet I could win you that Palomino," the tall man said. I opened my mouth in surprise. He pulled a curly cascade of pink perforated tickets from his pants pocket. He counted some out, gave them to the woman at the counter, and started shooting baskets. Whoosh, whoosh, whoosh. I looked on amazed, my awkward new friend suddenly in command of the situation, not needing my pity, at all. Sweat darkened the armpits of his short-sleeved gray shirt as he kept raising his arms authoritatively above his head to aim and release the basketballs. In about ten minutes the tall man was out of pink tickets and had been handed the prancing Palomino.

"This is yours, Missy," the tall man smiled, holding it out to me. I didn't hesitate, but clutched the beautiful creature to my chest. It was as hard as bones or Rick's toy gun but I didn't care. I had great plans for it. "Thank you," I said.

"I've got some more model horses in my Volkswagen bus," the man said. "I could show them to you and we could play with them. You and me and your new Palomino." This time I hesitated. People his age didn't usually invite kids to play. He had been so nice to me though that it would be rude to say no.

"I can only play for a few minutes, because I'm supposed to be at the Cake Walk," I told him.

"OK, I'll have you back at the Cake Walk in a jiffy" he said cheerfully. He took my hand and led me through the crowd of people. He walked me to the long, narrow parking lot the teachers used and unlocked the sliding door of a blue VW bus. Someone had written, "Wash me" in the dirt on the door. The man put his hands on my waist and lifted me inside with a quick, sure movement. The bus was dirty on the inside too, littered with old rags and fast food trash. I smelled stale grease.

"Where are your model horses?" I asked him, already sensing there weren't any. A scared, tight feeling crept into my stomach as he slammed the door shut behind us.

"You know what? I must have left them at home," he said. The bus had dingy, dark-blue curtains on little rods all along its long windows that kept anyone from seeing in. "So we're going to play a different game," he announced in a singsong voice, as if he were reading *The Cat In The Hat*. He started rubbing his crotch in its khaki pants. His distorted, too-large eyes behind the thick glasses started to glaze over. I was terrified of his game, and since he was between me and the side door, I started to climb over the back of the front seat to get out the front door. His left hand shot out.

"You're staying right here," he informed me as he unzipped his pants, fumbled with both hands and produced a long, thick, purple-red object.

I had seen my brother Rick's penis many times when we were younger and took baths together. It had been small and innocuous moving in the water beside me like a diminutive fish, no bigger than my mother's thumb as she bathed us. This man's penis was so huge and inflated, like a hose, that I thought it was a deformity, like a tumor. A bit of clear liquid was seeping from the hole at the reddish-purple tip that I thought was pus. It reminded me of pictures I'd seen of infections. I feverishly linked his infected tumor in my mind with his bad eyes, distorted behind the Coke-bottle glasses. I had blundered into a terrible illness that was so rare and unlike the flu or measles of my experience that I had not yet learned the name for it. I could see though, that it made a person crazy.

The sick man grasped me behind the head. He pulled my face down and forced the big thing into my small, seven-year-old mouth, down my narrow throat. I gagged, squirmed, trying frantically to wriggle away, but his long, hard fingers were like fang-vices on my head and chin. It was a contest between lion and lamb. He moved his bloated organ in and out of my mouth and throat, and I breathed through my nose. The rest of my face no longer belonged to me. My bloodstream was flooded with terror and adrenaline, like before I had learned to swim and had found myself suddenly over my head in the community center swimming pool, floundering, legs churning, before my father, his feet solid on the bottom of the pool, had pulled me back to his chest, to safety.

"No teeth," the man grunted, bucking yet harder into my face for several beats then suddenly releasing me. I watched in horrified wonder as he spurted streams of white pus onto a crumpled old McDonald's bag he had grabbed from the bus's littered floor.

※

"Honey, you keep your Palomino horse," the man said as he placed the hard-hoofed thing back into my hands. "You earned it. Pretty girl like you, you're going to get everything you want in life. You walk on back and find your mommy. Tell her a friend gave this to you."

He was calm as a puddle, like when I'd first met him, his penis shrunken and put away back inside his pants. I acted calm, too, as if what he'd done was normal. I didn't want to cry since that would make him nervous and maybe try to keep me with him. I swallowed my fear and climbed down out of the bus's side door. He slid it shut behind me quickly, with a ker-chump. I held my horse by the head as if it were a handle and set off across the parking lot, immediately hearing the bus's engine start up behind me, coughing and hacking like the man who sat behind us in church and smelled of cigarette smoke. The bus's tires squealed as it went into reverse, then forward and out into the street, and I started running for the Cake Walk since that was where I'd last seen my mother. The bee-bushes came up on my right, the ones outside the principal's window. I stopped in my tracks as if a rider had jerked the reins to my mouth, and looked at them carefully. The bushes were pink and buzzing with bees. I looked down at the pink skirt of my dress and felt my head and body buzzing with what I would later in my life understand to be fear and rage. I thought: I am the bee bushes.

I knelt on the ground and shoved the Palomino under the bushes as far as I could, mashing my face into twigs, leaves and pink blossoms in the process. It hurt. Then suddenly my right cheek hurt badly, in one particular place. I pictured the tall man having jabbed a final needle into me even as I knew a bee had stung me. I sobbed with pain and shock as I rose and ran across the blacktop to the Cake Walk, bumping into people on the way. I found my mother standing near the barker, and I flung myself at her, crashing into her knees, crying frantically, reaching my arms up to her.

"Elly, where were you?" She bent, scooped me up and I wrapped my arms around her neck, desperately needing her comfort. "A bee stung my face!" I cried.

"You were supposed to stay right here!" she said, but I could tell she was more relieved than angry. We clung to each other as cake walkers shuffled around the chalk track on the blacktop to Kay Starr singing "Side By Side" and the barker continued with his happy shtick, bossing them around like a would-be TV game host.

Chapter 6
Magic Kingdom

I took a tepid spoonful of vegetable soup and gazed out the window of the Inn Between into Disneyland's so-called backstage area. Snow White, with her creamy skin, glossy, black-bobbed wig and fairy-tale dress, was smoking a cigarette, tapping the ashes irritably into a Diet Coke can. She appeared to be arguing with one of her seven dwarves, who held his oversized costume head in his hands. His real head sported dishwater-blonde dreadlocks. Characters who were completely hidden by their costumes when onstage were the only employees exempted from the Disney rules of short hair for men, minimal make-up and jewelry for women. I set my bad soup aside and checked my watch. There were 17 minutes left on my dinner break before going back onstage.

I'd asked to be a dancer in the job application I'd filled out two weeks ago, but ended up with a job in security. Casting, a pseudonym for human resources, had informed me that Disney dancers had many years of professional experience. Hollywood, after all, was just a few towns over, the woman had primly pointed out. However, teachers tended to make good security officers, she offered to me, like a secondhand Christmas gift. "They aren't too heavy-handed," she added. "Not like policemen tend to be."

"I won't throw anyone against a wall to frisk them," I had promised her, straight-faced.

Now, at the little restaurant where cast members took our breaks, a tall brown-haired guy, cute, sat down across from me.

"Hi, Revelle," he said, beaming brightly. His nametag said Sonny.

He had flirted with me in our security training class, attention I had ignored, because he seemed like a playboy. I'd chatted instead with my married colleagues, who in my optimistic moments, I'd thought might have single, stable friends they could introduce me to.

"Oh, you're on break now, too?" I said.

"No. But I saw that you were, so I came over to visit," he said. "I've been meaning to ask you, what kind of name is Revelle? It sounds like the offspring of a gazelle."

I let a chilly silence hang before answering. "It's a family name from Britain, my dad's side of the family. It dates back before the Norman Conquest in 1066."

"Really? Did you major in history?" His bright blue eyes were trained on mine like the tractor-beam in the Star Tours ride.

I shook my head. "My bachelor's is in English. I did my master's in education at Lewis and Clark."

"Isn't that in Portland, Oregon? I've always wanted to live in Oregon." He pronounced it Or-uh-GAWN, like most non-Oregonians. I managed not to roll my eyes.

I nodded. "I really miss Oregon, actually," I said, pronouncing it correctly, OR-uh-gun. "I've lived there since '84. I grew up down here, and I just came back last month when my dad got cancer."

"How awful! I'm so sorry," Sonny said, leaning in closer across the table.

"Thanks. It looks like he'll be OK though," I said, breaking the eye-lock tractor beam to look outdoors. Snow White had evidently concluded her spat with the dreadlocked dwarf and was sitting in a little gazebo with her feet propped on a chair. She was still smoking, exhaling moodily, chin thrust slightly skyward. She gave the impression of wishing herself elsewhere. I could relate.

"You're so tan. Have you been hitting the beach?" Sonny asked.

"No." This time I rolled my eyes. Would this dinner break never end? "This is my natural skin color. I have Arabic ancestry."

"That's cool. I like diversity," he said, his enthusiasm as boundless as his conversation topics. "Are those crosses you're wearing in your ears?" He reached across the table to touch one. I nodded. Disney dress code allowed only stud earrings. I usually wore dangling earrings.

"I'm a Christian, too," he offered.

"Oh really? What church do you go to?" I felt a twinge of interest.

"Um, I had been going to Calvary Chapel. But I think I'm ready for something different."

I nodded. Calvary Chapel was an enormous evangelical church that specialized in altar calls. Not my kind of church. We had something in common. Now I didn't resent his interruption so much.

"So, what do you do in the real world?" I asked him.

"I'm a self-employed carpenter," Sonny replied, confidently. "I specialize in remodels."

"Good," I said. "That's creative work. Is business slow right now, with the recession?" That would explain why he was working Disneyland security at slightly above minimum wage. A skilled carpenter would only do this as a last resort, I thought.

"Something like that," he said, shrugging slightly. "What do you usually do?"

"English teacher in a private school," I said. "But I'm also a dancer."

"Mmm, a dancer." Sonny's ruddy face became yet more avid. Again, I was irritated. He was coming on too strong.

"Not everyone is so keen on dancers," I said dryly. "Look, I'll be honest. I'm not having the time of my life right now, despite our, ah, upbeat environment here," I told him, extending my arm to indicate the Magic Kingdom. "You seem curious about me, so I'm just going to be blunt." Sonny nodded energetically. "I'd rather be in Oregon right now but I lost my job. And I'm getting over a break-up. The break-up was because I wanted to get married and have children." I checked my watch: three minutes, and I needed two of them to walk back to Tomorrowland. It should take just ten seconds for Sonny's jets to cool, for this obvious playboy to find a way to wiggle on out of this little flirtation he'd started in the Inn Between when he was supposed to be working.

"That's funny," he said slowly. "My last break-up was for the same reason as yours. But I was the one who wanted to get married and have children."

※

The hot July air smelled of popcorn and cotton candy at King Arthur's Carousel. Sonny was standing hardly two inches from me, too close for coworkers even in the crowded context of summer at Disneyland. I didn't move though. We'd gone on our first date the evening before, a walk in Craig Park. I'd declined on dinner afterward. But thoughts of him had kept me awake until late.

We watched a court jester in orange and purple costume juggle orange and purple bowling pins on the asphalt near the Sword in the Stone. People gathered around. He missed a beat, pin knocking him on his right wrist. He winced dramatically, bent in two and held the mock-injured wrist out to a pretty Latina girl in the audience. She hesitated, then kissed it. Her boyfriend at her side scowled.

The jester beamed at the girl, face aglow with delight. He recommenced juggling, pins flying higher and faster in the air, until he missed again, a pin grazing his mouth this time before it hit the asphalt. More agonized grimacing, this time over the lip injury, and then a second approach to the young beauty, pointing to his mouth hopefully. She grinned and shook her head—absolutely not—and the audience laughed, the girl's boyfriend loudest of all.

"What a hustler," Sonny grinned. He turned to me, and I felt butterflies in my stomach. We were close enough to kiss. "What's your favorite land?" he asked. I realized he meant in the park.

"Frontierland. I love the West. Horses." I told my stomach to calm down. He was just a guy. Just a human being.

"Calamity Revelle," he grinned. "OK Calamity, we've got a call. Lost child." He had actually been listening to the walkie-talkie on his hip. Or he knew how to adjust it. Mine never yielded much beyond static and squawks. I followed Sonny through Sleeping

Beauty's castle, out of Fantasyland into the hub at the bottom of Main Street, over to the Pavilion.

We found a solemn girl of about four with strawberry blonde pigtails sitting outdoors. An older African American man, dignified in his white food service costume, sat quietly next to her. The girl wore tiny blue overalls, a teensy red T-shirt and Lilliputian-sized red sneakers, which dangled two feet above the ground at the table under an umbrella. Her pale face was ominous. The man's nametag said Patrick.

"This young lady's family seems to have lost her a few minutes ago," Patrick said. His deeply lined face had the patience of Job and the kindness of Jesus. "We've been settin' together for a spell here. Haven't quite managed to exchange names." I assessed the situation. The tot seemed on the verge of crying, and she wouldn't look at Patrick, or Sonny, standing beside me. But she was looking straight at me. I got down on my knees, eye level with the child.

"Hi honey," I said softly. "Are you a little bit scared?" She nodded, eyes large and solemn and vulnerable. "We're going to find your parents," I assured her. "They'll be really happy to get you back." She nodded, looking slightly more hopeful. "What's your name, honey?"

Her tiny thumb went into her kewpie-doll mouth as her blue eyes regarded mine. The men looked on quietly. I sweated into the crotch of my nylons, ridiculous things to be wearing on a ninety-degree day. Her parents had probably told her to never talk to strangers. Good advice, except for now.

"Cammie Ferrante," she finally said. I impulsively kissed her little hand and sat down in a chair, relieved. Sonny radioed her name and description into the security office. Patrick and I chatted about his numerous grandchildren, some of whom he and his wife were raising.

As we spoke, a blond woman about my age arrived and swooped Cammie up with hugs and kisses. I smiled. We all smiled. The best day of this job so far.

"She's probably never been around black men before," Patrick said in his slow, kind way. I nodded, knowing that he would have liked to be Cammie's rescuer, himself.

"I look a little like her mother," I said. "That helped her trust me." He nodded.

"Only black men she's seen have probably been criminals on TV," Patrick said. He sounded sad, but not particularly bitter.

"Good point. Unless she's seen the Bill Cosby show," I mused out loud.

"Wish I could be a high-paid doctor like him," Patrick smiled.

"Amen," I said.

"You were born for that," Sonny remarked.

"Born for what?" I asked.

"Born to be a mother," Sonny replied. Patrick nodded in agreement.

A sob rose in me. I turned away from them to get hold of myself. It moved me that much to be seen.

✻

When I pulled my timecard from its slot one morning the following week, a handwritten note was paper-clipped to it. "Jones: working undercover tonight," it said. "No costume." When I found Jim, my boss, he explained that I would be roaming the park in my street clothes as if I were a guest. I would sniff for marijuana in the restrooms and watch for tram riders spitting on the guests on the ground below. Most importantly, he stressed, I would carry a walkie-talkie tucked into a Disney shopping bag, and call in if I discovered anything.

"Because we never know when they're going to turn on us," I said, nodding gravely. The whole pseudo-police nature of this Mickey Mouse security department brought out the devil in me. "Should I bust people who jump over the ropes in the line to Pirates of the Caribbean?"

Jim considered this carefully, rubbing his chin. "Only if it's really flagrant," he decided. "If you think it's likely to generate complaints."

I nodded slightly, tersely, like Peggy Lipton in a 90's version of Mod Squad. I was even wearing a short skirt, though my long blonde hair was wavy instead of stick-straight. You get what you pay for, I thought. I'm not a spy and I doubt I'll make any drug busts.

Hours later, I was in Frontierland, talking with Sonny on the plank-wood sidewalk outside the so-called saloon that served nothing stronger than Coca-Cola. He looked like a movie star from a Western, with his height, strong jaw, fake Stetson hat and red bandana at his throat. He looked at my legs and asked about my day as an undercover detective.

"Sniffing for pot in the women's restrooms is the most aimless waste of time I've ever been paid for," I replied. The steadily trained blue eyes were a little disconcerting. He had taken me out to dinner at a Mexican restaurant earlier in the week and tried to kiss me, but I'd turned away. I belonged in Oregon anyway, not down here, especially now that my father was out of danger. The problem was that here was where I was.

Sonny laughed at my disgust with my work. "Just think, the rest of the world is paying to be here, but we're *getting* paid to be here." He looked off into the distance, then back at me, and his tone changed. "Do you have plans after you clock out?"

"Not at the moment," I said, looking away at Big Thunder Mountain Railroad, where the mule ride had been when I was a girl.

"OK, Calamity Revelle. Let's go to Tom Sawyer Island when we get off."

The so-called River of the Americas had to be crossed to reach Tom Sawyer Island. The raft that took us there after we finished work was packed with guests, meaning Sonny and I had to stand with our bodies pressed together. He took my hand in his strong, warm, calloused-carpenter's hand as we walked off the raft onto the landing and led me onto a trail that went past the whistling caves that children were running in and out of, screaming with delight. He found a shady little spot under some trees and we sat down. I tried to keep breathing. Small talk was beyond me, and I couldn't quite meet the blue gaze trained on my face.

"I've got to kiss you," he murmured urgently. Without waiting for a reply, he did. His mouth came into my world as a shock. It felt as I had anticipated it would: strong, slightly chapped, impossibly warm. I was excited, completely alive. My nerve endings jangled with sensation. He kissed me and kissed me, the kisses an end in themselves, not needing to go anywhere else.

The other people milling around the island, many of them children, acted as our chaperones, transforming us back into teenagers who could only kiss. Everything in this place was about youth. We paused to breathe, panting a little like golden retrievers in the heat. We were retrieving each other from kisslessness, from lovelessness.

"I'm Tom Sawyer," he said. "You're Becky Thatcher."

"Tom and Becky didn't do this," I said.

"No they didn't." Another flurry of kisses on my mouth and neck. The scents of star jasmine and our saliva blended in my nose: earthy, sweet and delicious. I felt intoxicated.

"I love you," he said. The molecules in the hot air changed shape.

"I love you too," I said. The world changed shape again. I hadn't been walking around thinking I loved him, but his love for me conjured my own. Sonny had let the genie out of a bottle after she had suffered a hundred years of solitude trapped inside it. The desire and love for husband and child that had been steaming up inside me had finally found a shape. Sonny was the shape.

We stayed on the island until the last possible minute, running down the trail to catch the raft only when the speakers concealed in the trees announced everyone had to leave.

"Come home with me," Sonny said quietly into my ear, as we stood crushed together on the raft amongst the overexcited children and their footsore, sunburned parents. His arms were wrapped around me from behind, my long, thick hair crushed against his chest. He smelled like fresh wood and sweat. I canted my head back, up and far to the right to get my mouth close to his ear. It was a sharp angle only dancers and gymnasts were flexible enough to create, and I could feel curious eyes watching me. Stretching my neck that far to address him intimately in the crowd pleased my body and soul like hitting the high notes at the end of the Gloria Patri, which we sang in church. He bent his head down so that my mouth brushed his ear.

"No," I said. "We need to be outdoors for our first time." He absorbed that for a few seconds.

"Then I'll take you camping. Soon."

I nodded and relaxed, looking straight ahead. A thirty-something mom in a pink sun visor who was holding her infant to her chest met my eyes, and I smiled radiantly at her, winning a smile in return.

Chapter 7
Doheny

Campground Is Full, the sign said. Just like I'd thought would be the case at almost 10:00 at night at Doheny State Beach. I struggled to not blow up at Sonny, who was calmly sitting next to me in my truck. As if he hadn't been six hours late today. *Six hours.* When for once we actually had the same two days off in a row, Wednesday and Thursday.

I turned the engine off on the dark, quiet campground road without bothering to pull over. I bowed my head, draping my arms over the steering wheel, exhausted from an afternoon and evening of disappointment. The plan had been to take our first camping trip in the San Bernadino Mountains, at the Angel's Rest campground. Sonny was going to meet me at two, after doing some manly type helpful thing at his mother's house, I hadn't known exactly what.

When he finally rang the doorbell a little after 8 p.m., he looked impossibly handsome and innocent. I eyed him furiously through the screen door, waiting for him to speak first. At least he'd clearly been working. His white V necked t-shirt was soaked with sweat, blue jeans bagged at the knees.

"My mother had told me this morning she just needed me to trim her bougainvillea and tie it up in a few places because it was flopping all around," Sonny began, flopping his arms spastically, evidently like a misguided bougainvillea. I was unmoved.

"Then, once I did that she needed me to replace her downstairs toilet! I'm her only son in a hundred miles. I couldn't turn her down," he pleaded with me.

"Why didn't you CALL?" I shouted, setting the neighbor's dog barking. I didn't want to hear about his mother's rotted floor.

"I didn't know what to tell you. The whole thing just kept getting deeper, and I couldn't leave her with no working toilet downstairs."

"But you could leave me waiting for six hours?" I cried.

"I lost all track of time. I would have done the same thing for you if you'd been without a toilet," he said. "Look, let's go to Doheny. It's a lot closer than the mountains."

"I hate the beach!" I yelled. This was not exactly true but my anger dictated absolutes. Everyone in Southern California, and outside of it, seemed to think the beaches here were some kind of heaven restored to earth. I saw it differently. They were hemmed in by parking lots and streets, choked with people who craved them like people who had lost their god.

But now here we were at Doheny, sometimes termed a parking lot with picnic tables (I was the one who termed it that.) And the campground was full, anyway. We had eaten a quick, late dinner at a Carl's Junior on the way out. That was another sign of my newly pathetic life: eating too much at fast food restaurants. My friends and I rarely did it in Portland; there were enough *good* affordable places to eat, owned by real human beings instead of by soulless corporations who treated their employees like crap, most likely. My head swam there at the campground entrance with all the things I hated and wanted to get away from.

"Maybe we could just pitch our tent on the beach," I said, raising my head from the wheel.

"I've tried that before," Sonny said. "It didn't work." I waited. He'd created this situation and it wasn't my job to rescue us from it.

"Let's drive slowly through the campground," he said.

I started the engine and entered. We glided past hulking Winnebagos with satellite dishes and the inane laughter of sit-coms polluting the night. I glared balefully. That wasn't camping.

"What are we looking for?" I asked.

"Someone who'll share their campsite with us," he said.

I snorted with frustration, now feeling like a prowler, or even a stalker looking for victims.

"Stop here," Sonny said quietly. A small campfire softly lit a slight, young-looking couple in a tidy site. He got out of the truck and approached them. They were sitting cross-legged on the ground and he squatted on his haunches to be at their eye level. I shut the engine off, embarrassed but fascinated. I'd been in campgrounds all my life and had never seen anything like this. They're going to refuse, I thought. We'll have to either stay in a motel or drive home.

They listened to him though, earnest concern written on their baby-cheeked faces. Sonny gestured toward the truck and their eyes swung to me, brows furrowed. I saw two bicycles locked to a skinny tree and no car, and realized they must be bike touring.

Soon the couple were standing, nodding their heads vigorously as if trying to convince Sonny of something, pointing to the part of their campsite not occupied by their tiny tent and bicycles. My jaw dropped. We'd been given a place to sleep.

My tent went up quickly. Our hosts were from Germany and murmured charmingly accented concerns about my health. They looked to be 19 years old. I thanked them repeatedly for sharing their site as I pounded stakes into the hard-packed dirt, and hoped they didn't feel too snookered that I wasn't acting at all sick.

The air at the beach was cool, in the low 70's instead of the mid 80's we'd been sweating in when we'd left Anaheim. Climbing into the tent, I could feel my anger ebb a few degrees with the air temperature. The firstness of lying down with Sonny on my opened-out flannel sleeping bag was delicious. I was wearing a camisole and shorts, and Sonny had shucked his t-shirt and jeans, and was wearing just his underwear. The sight of his bare, muscled arms and shoulders, even in the semi-dark, made me feel dizzy. We nuzzled and stretched out, finding how our flat-bellied bodies, his rangy and my petite, fit together in the tent, in the world. His short-clipped, Disney regulation hair was soft against my face.

I breathed deeply, smelling salt air and wood smoke. Good smells.

I buried my face at the base of his neck. He did the same, wrapping his chin around my neck and cradling my long, wavy hair against his face. This was a different world than I had occupied all day and all night. This was the reason I hadn't sent Sonny away when he'd shown up six hours late.

Then he started kissing me. Then the kisses landed in unpredictable places—my eyebrow, my cheekbone, under my ear, the tip of my nose—and I found myself giggling. My noise made me worry that the childlike German couple would be way too nice to say anything if we were keeping them awake. Then Sonny started slowly undressing me and kissing me in other places and I wasn't thinking about the German couple. At. All.

༻ༀ༺

"I want you to marry me," he said afterward. The air in the tent changed shape. "I know it's really early. But that's what I'm feeling in my heart."

"Mmmm," I purred, snuggling further into him. I felt like an animal that could mate for life. Another part of me could hear Marisol and my parents saying, a thousand miles apart yet in unison, "You've only known him a month!" My mating animal said a month was plenty, not a problem. My common sense didn't have half the raw energy of that animal.

"Let's be engaged, but keep it private for awhile," I whispered after a moment. "It's too early to talk about it to anyone. I do love that you're asking me."

"So we're privately engaged?" he asked. "After a few months we'll tell everyone?" His face was so avid and open he seemed more like a child with a promise on the horizon than a 35-year-old man.

I nodded, cradling the side of his face in my hand. It was rough with new beard. Sonny didn't shave on the days he didn't work at Disneyland.

"We need to swim in the ocean!" I announced, sitting up in the tent, seizing his hand with excitement. I was positive of this. Sonny made a surprised snort of laughter.

"We do? To celebrate? Well, OK!"

The moonlight was bright enough to cast the shadow of our bodies onto the sand as we trotted hand in hand, barefoot, on the campground road down to the deserted beach. The sand was cool, yielding under our feet. I kept my blue bikini on, but Sonny shed his shorts in a swift motion before we ran into the white, foamy surf, the water too cold and then in a few seconds not at all cold. I loved the wildness of the wave that we dove under together. It washed me clean of my anger at waiting for six hours.

We made love all over again when we got back to the tent, my small limbs and his long limbs snaking and entwining around each other, the salt water that had dried on our bodies creating a delicious friction. I felt the most alive I had felt since dancing with little Gaylin in my Portland home right before everything had fallen apart. I felt that God had sent Sonny to me.

"Our children are going to be beautiful," he said afterward, dreamily. I smiled in the darkness, my head on his shoulder. Hearing that was even better than hearing that he wanted to marry me.

Chapter 8
Baroque Hoedown

Loopy, exuberant music came from the speakers so numerous and discreetly placed it felt as if the night air itself was creating the sound. I was in Disneyland's central hub, working the Main Street Electrical Parade as it made its way out of Fantasyland. The tune was called "Baroque Hoedown," and that was what it sounded like: fast-paced and rhythmic like a Virginia Reel, but also ornate, elaborate with detail in the way baroque music was.

It was late summer now, so I'd heard and seen this spectacle many times, and I had issues with it. For one thing, the dancers' movements were terribly constrained, with nothing of joy or freedom in their bodies. Yes, here was a prime example right in front of me: the dancers who accompanied Cinderella's pumpkin-shaped coach. In their glowing, lit-up hoop skirts and frock coats, they cavorted as carefully down the street as British courtiers in Victorian England. *Please.* Where was their spontaneity, their personal fire? It was all tamed out of them. A travesty of true dance.

The Electrical Parade also had too strict a barrier between performers and audience. I had expressed my beliefs on this matter to Sonny late last night in his bed. "The audience is too passive!" I cried. "They're as glazed-over as if they were watching a Disney movie. At some point they should be dancing themselves. And the performers should be encouraging them to do it. Everyone has an inner dancer, but for most people these days it's locked up. It wasn't like that back in the tribal days. The best kind of dancer acts as a turnkey for other people's dancing. That way everyone has a chance to be free."

Sonny grinned: "You're ranting. You're passionate. I like it."

I had never said any of those things before, but being around Sonny, feeling completely loved and emotionally supported by him, was helping certain things to crystallize in me. Tonight Sonny was working in Bear Country, on the other side of the park. I would be going home with him. My body was warm and fluid with excitement at the thought.

Snow White was moving down the street now in her glossy, bobbed wig, she of the backstage smoking and bickering with dreadlocked dwarves. You'd never know any of that by watching her stilted, straight-laced steps. I could dance so much better than that, I thought. It was hard not to grind my teeth with resentment. This was the biggest problem I had with the Electrical Parade: I wanted to be a dancer in it, not a silly security officer who sniffed uselessly for pot in restrooms.

The park guests strained over one another to see the floats and dancers. Children rode on their fathers' shoulders like miniature monarchs, their mouths hanging open in wonder, sneakered heels bouncing on the dads' chests in excitement until the men clasped the feet to still them. Of course you want to move to the music, I thought. Teenagers and even adults stood on the park benches to see the hoopla and razzle-dazzle, the exact thing I was being paid to get them not to do. Many couldn't even hear my request over the deafening strains of "Baroque Hoedown." So I started simply making eye contact, and once I had a bench-percher's attention, using elaborate arm gestures, starting high and sweeping down to the ground, my eyes and head following my hands, one big arc after another. Like a dancer.

A dark-skinned fellow watched my please-get-down gestures with pleasure from up on his bench. He started imitating my motions, arms up, then down, in rhythm to the music. He was dancing, smiling an invitation down at me.

I smiled back and went with it, my feet joining the rhythm, my neck and torso going loose and limber. Had I ever in my life rejected an invitation to dance? I would reflect afterward that I could not have played out what followed any differently.

The man jumped down from his bench, and I held my head up high. My arms folded out in front of me, Virginia Reel style. He immediately did the same, and we pranced merrily around each other in one do-si-do after another, which then evolved into doing the bump. People watched us with delight, so when they made eye contact with me I naturally started including them in the bump, jumping and turning in the air with every other beat, arms raised above my head. They loved this and joined right in. One great thing about being a small woman was that nobody ever felt threatened by my presence.

Dancing started to break out all around the hub: shimmying here, pseudo square dancing there, an older couple in Bermuda shorts doing a butter-smooth East Coast swing. Beautiful. Three Japanese tourists with cameras hanging around their necks were crowding around me now, confusion written on their mute faces: a security officer, dancing? "I was lost, but now I'm found!" I cried joyously to them. They may or may not have understood my words, but light bulbs went on in their faces, like: Oh! Another Disney act—Dancing Security Officer! They raised their cameras and started snapping pictures of me. I winked showily for them, like Madonna.

Now all we needed was to take our act on the road and join the parade. I skipped and sashayed down into Main Street, waving everyone to follow. Most did, and we were now the new tail end of the Electrical Parade, as distinct from its paid dancers as mustangs were different from draft horses. We were several dozen, with more joining every minute from the crowd that was lining Main Street six deep on either side. My Main Street 'costume,' the short-sleeved blue shirt and above-the-knee navy skirt, were not too bad for dancing; I was moving freely, without constraint. I wanted to rip off the navy blue tie at my throat and toss it into the crowd, but refrained—that would be going too far.

A group of teenaged black guys in turned-around baseball caps and huge, complicated athletic shoes were looking at me in amused disbelief, some of them pointing me out to others. I strutted over and pointed right back at them, then held up my hands as if to say, well, don't YOU dance? A couple of them grinned and started hopping and popping, shoulder-joints loose and fluid, faces beaming proudly. I beamed back and applauded them. As I moved down the street to stay with the new tail end of the parade, one of them was down on the ground break-dancing, starting to draw his own crowd.

The atmosphere on Main Street was by now truly electric, with spontaneity and joy buzzing in the air. Adrenaline was coursing through my body as I wove in and out of the teeming throng like a ribbon pulled by a muse. I smelled the vanilla of fresh waffle cones from the ice cream parlor as we danced past it. Seconds later it was buttery popcorn in my nostrils, then roasted coffee. The synthesized music looped up and down like the Space Mountain rollercoaster and I looped my arms up and down with it, others imitating me so that we became a flock of graceful geese.

Over at the street curb, a woman of about 70 in a wheelchair was making soft, gentle arm movements in rhythm to the music, her face blissful. I broke away from my bird flock and approached her, quieting my body language to match and mirror hers. She smiled at me, and I got down on my knees to be at her eye level. We arm-danced together in a lovely, dreamy world of our own, like geisha girls from different generations, our spread-out-hands our fans that we opened and closed, our heads tipping on our necks at slight, subtle angles as we regarded each other, bright blue eyes holding my brown eyes. I breathed deeply, happy beyond words, feeling I could do this with her all night. She finally broke the trance by taking my face between her hands. "You need to keep on leading the dance," she told me, nodding toward the throng.

"Do you want to come along?" I asked her, motioning that I could push her wheelchair.

"I'll dance here in place," she said serenely. I nodded and kissed her on the cheek, her skin soft under my lips. She smelled sweet, like baby powder. I stood and backed slowly away, my hands pressed together in a little prayer of respect before I turned and rejoined the parade in a series of flying deer leaps.

A little girl with Downs syndrome and black pigtails beamed at me from the right side of the street, her blunt face open and rapturous with wonder, her body bouncing to the music as if on a trampoline. I blew a kiss to her and she blew a sweetly disjointed kiss in return, her fingers going to her ear instead of her mouth before she flung her hand back out toward me.

A youngish, bald Asian man in a long orange robe belted at the waist was now dancing with us, arms spread wide, face lifted to the night sky. When he spun, his robe flew out in a billowing circle, spectacular as a Sufi whirling dervish. My heart swelled with love for the monk; we both knew our bodies to be instruments for loving God.

Near the Lincoln Theater I spotted Jim, my boss, among the crowd. He was staring at me drop-jawed, in a state of near shock, as if his world had fallen apart. I felt strongly that this man, of all people, needed to join the dance, the joyful throng. I knew it wasn't his time and place, though. So I smiled radiantly at him and pointed to the backstage area that the parade exited into, where the security offices were. "We'll talk!" I called to him, and danced on.

We were hundreds dancing in the street, the barrier between performers and audience fully dissolved, as I'd wanted it to be. Something else was dissolved, too. Every jot of the fear and dread that had occupied my body since losing Mike and my job and my home all at once back in May had been chased away by the influenza of joy that had broken out on Main Street. The face of Owen, the Prentice principal, popped into my mind. If I still lived in Oregon I'd be happier overall, but my fellows wouldn't have found their dance tonight, wouldn't have broken the bondage of their passivity to claim the fierce vitality of movement. Nothing could have been clearer than the fact that God intended me to be right here, right now, and I kept dancing all the way into the backstage area, near delirious and grounded at the same time, surrounded by the revelry I'd ignited.

"I guess you know that I have to let you go," Jim said from across his desk. He looked pained, his forehead furrowed. I was trying for a serious expression, but having trouble pulling it off. The little office in which he'd hired me was quiet, but the exuberant music was still ringing in my head, and my body was vibrating with energy. Wasn't there someplace we could have the after-party?

"Yes. I know you do," I said with compassion, wanting this to be easy for Jim. He was a good enough guy, just hopelessly locked into the rules.

"Revelle, you won't be eligible for re-hire," he announced, his shoulders going tense, as if thinking I'd fall apart at not getting to work Disney security again.

"I understand," I said. "Please don't worry about me."

Jim rubbed his chin regretfully. "Can I say something that can't leave this office?"

"By all means."

"The whole thing could probably have flown if you had just been working undercover tonight in plainclothes. You know, you could maybe have smelled pot on someone and followed him. And I could picture that he might have started dancing since he was stoned, and other people joined in, and you didn't want to lose him. And things . . . just got out of hand from there. As you were trying to stay with him, you know."

I nodded thoughtfully. "I can see your point, Jim. That would have been a different scenario. But . . . it played out the way it did." I shrugged and held out my hand. "No hard feelings."

He shook it, his hand gentle. "You're one hell of a dancer, Revelle."

"Thank you." I looked him in the eye and did not demure from the praise. For all of its silliness, Disneyland had helped me move toward who I was.

"I won," Dad declared. The Scrabble board on our dining room table looked like a confounding maze that only the cleverest creature could escape from.

"That's only because you got to do 'quiz' on the triple-word score," Mom retorted, sipping her wine, but her expression was warm. Sonny and I had our ankles wrapped around each other under the table. I was glad Dad had won. It reminded me of when I was a little girl and thought him invincible. At age five I had confused him for a while with Jesus, having taken literally a dinner guest's joke that he had turned water into wine. Now, Dad held the bottle of wine across the table with his eyebrows raised. I shook my head since I'd already had two glasses, but Sonny nodded and Dad poured for him, his arm and hand more-or-less steady. He was back to working part-time, doing the books for the rug business. As if thinking about work himself, he asked me, "What's new on the job search?"

"I researched private schools at the Anaheim library today," I said. "In order to stay down here." Sonny beamed brightly. My return smile was a little forced. With all respect to my parents, living in Southern California was a form of misery for me. But Sonny and I were in love, and the relationship needed more time to develop. Moreover, he'd enthused about Oregon the first time we'd talked, saying he'd always wanted to move there. I was sitting on a hopeful egg of a plan that wasn't yet ready to hatch.

"So I made a list of schools and started calling them. First I asked if they were interested in an experienced English teacher. The front office people just said flat out they weren't hiring. Even when I figured out how to get through to the principals, they just said they'd been laying teachers off, and they were sorry." My parents were listening quietly, their faces well-lined and kind. They had never had their own personal agendas for Rick's or my careers. "We just want you to be educated, employed and happy," they had said more than once in my youth. But I wasn't so young now. Now, I was just educated.

"I think you should stop teaching English and teach dance instead," Sonny announced with conviction. He set his wine glass down hard, and the red wine jumped and splashed as if it were cheering. "You have a unique gift. Millions of people can teach English," he went on, waving the arm not attached to his wine, evidently at a world overloaded with English teachers. "But very few can inspire people to dance like you can."

"There's no money in teaching dance," I said. Maybe I was warning myself as much as him. But I sat up straighter, my body already feeling lighter at even the idea of leaving surly English students behind.

"I can support both of us," Sonny replied, chewing his pretzels confidently. My parents exchanged a glance, amused and curious. "I've asked her to marry me, but she's keeping me dangling," he informed them. "I want to have children with her, but she's thinking about it." He threw his hands up in fond frustration, as if to say I was hopelessly fickle. "I am but a humble carpenter, but I—"

"OK," I interrupted him, laughing, pleased and embarrassed at the same time. "You've had too much wine. We're cutting you off." My parents were laughing now, too. I kissed Sonny on the side of his chiseled jaw and rose to put the Scrabble game away.

※

"Talk to me more," Sonny murmured. "I love the sound of your voice." He was holding me in his bed later that night after making love. It was past 1 a.m. but I was wide-awake, still leaning into his long-boned leanness, unable to get as close as I wanted to get. His taut biceps and corded forearms triggered my desire. He never smelled like medical antiseptic or cologne like Mike had, but rather, like freshly cut wood and sawdust.

Earlier, he had told me about his father's death. Sonny was eleven when a drunk-driving accident took his life. "It was his fault. He drank and drove a lot." Sonny had said, his usual gaiety gone. His voice was barely audible even in the still room. "I never talk about any of this. It hurts too much." I'd nodded, barely able to imagine the pain of losing one of my parents as a child.

"I'm glad you're telling me about it."

"What's been the most painful thing in your life?" Sonny asked me. My heart stopped for a minute. I wasn't able to recount the afternoon at the carnival. It would have been like dumping a severed horse's head into our bed. It was too ugly to be thinkable. Instead, I said, "Did I ever tell you the principal at Prentice fired me two minutes after I told him my father had kidney cancer?"

Sonny shook his head in dismay. "How could he? What an asshole."

"He also cancelled my after-school dance troupe for a stupid karate class. I want you to know, though, I forgave Owen the night of the Hoedown." Sonny loved the story of the Hoedown I'd led at Disneyland, and said the biggest regret of his year was not having been part of it.

"The conflict between a principal and a teacher makes me think of that movie from the late 60's. It was about a high-spirited teacher in Scotland," Sonny said. "Maggie Smith played her. She was blond like you, creative like you. She broke the rules and pissed off the Man. I related to her."

"The Prime of Miss Jean Frigging Brodie," I said after a minute, sardonically, and we both burst out laughing. Sonny sat up and started to sing the theme song from the movie, ad-libbing his own lyrics as he went. "Revelle, Revelle, I'm under your spell," his baritone voice soared, impressively on key. I clapped, tickled. "How I yearn for thee . . . you should be with me . . . Give me a chance"—he clasped his hands to his heart—"I'll help you dance." I gasped with laughter and delight at his spontaneity, felt tears rise in my eyes. He *got* me.

We made love again, then talked more. We didn't sleep until after 3. Sonny didn't leave for his job site until 9:30 a.m. He'd promised the client the night before he'd be there at 7.

"It's cool that you like to cook," I said. Sonny was setting the table with sky-blue plates on top of tangerine-colored placemats. "I like to cook, but not every night."

I was housesitting at Vicki and Frank's condo for three weeks as they worked on building their earth ship in Taos, New Mexico. Sonny would be with me most of the time, I'd told them, which they had said was fine, since they both liked him, especially Vicki, who laughed her head off when he did things like turn cartwheels in the park. Their place was in Diamond Bar, a narrow, tall and lovely space with huge glass doors opening from their living room to landscaped pine trees.

"You know, I called your mom's house this morning to make plans for tonight," I began, my tone casual. "You hadn't gotten there yet." Jane had been having more plumbing problems that needed his help. "At first she thought I was someone named Paula. She was saying she hadn't seen me in awhile and she asked me where I'd been."

"Oh really?" A hitch in Sonny's chopping of onions followed. Then silence and resumed chopping. I wished he would volunteer who Paula was to him. I hated playing investigator.

"Your mom said you asked Paula to marry you not long ago," I finally said. "And that she thought you were still engaged to each other."

"It's true I asked her to marry me," he finally said, washing a green bell pepper at the sink and then slicing it open and removing the white membrane and seeds.

"And she said yes?" The story was moving way too slowly for me.

"She said yes. And then, you know, I lost interest. We didn't have much in common, and I didn't respect her very much."

"Wait a minute." My hand went to my head, which was starting to hurt. "You told me the first day we met that your last relationship had ended because you wanted to get married and have children and she didn't." It was hard to keep the confusion and pain out of my voice.

"It *had* ended because of that," he said. "That had been Katie. OK, so Katie was actually my next to last relationship. *Then* there was Paula. I was kind of on the rebound. I built a fence for her because her dog was always running away. One thing led to another."

"Are you still engaged to Paula?" I kept my voice calm, but my neck and shoulders were aching and my stomach was churning, the way it had in the final conversation Mike had had with me.

Sonny went back to dicing the green pepper strips. "I stopped calling her three weeks ago. I'm sure she's gotten the message by now. I was trying to give her the pleasure of breaking up with me."

Some pleasure, I thought. "So you're actually still engaged to her."

"Not really. I asked her on an impulse. She might not have taken it very seriously, either. I hadn't really thought it all through." He'd put the knife and peppers down and was giving me his full attention. "I would never have asked her if I'd known that you'd be coming along. Believe me, Revelle, I never saw myself being with Paula the rest of my life, like I see myself being with you."

"You know, I have to say I have a problem with this, Sonny," I said. "It's not that I feel jealous. It's more like, do you ask everyone to marry you? Did you mean it at Doheny when you asked me? What do you think it means when you say you're engaged to a woman?"

"You're questioning my integrity?" he asked, haughtily, fixing me with a dramatic blue gaze. *I thought, you've just shown me you lack integrity.*

"What's your plan?" I asked.

"Plan for what?" he responded blankly.

"Telling her you're with someone else now. Breaking the engagement."

He shrugged. "I could call her at some point, I guess."

The phone sat on the counter that separated Vicki and Frank's kitchen from their living room. I pushed it over to him, sliding the cutting board away from him in the process.

"Now?" He was confused, at the same time that my confusion had vanished.

I nodded. "It's better both for me and for Paula this way."

He hesitated while I prayed silently: God, please help me be willing to spend the night alone if he doesn't break off this thing with Paula. Then he pulled a small, well-worn black book from the hip pocket of his jeans. He opened it out on the counter and dialed the number penciled next to Paula. I heard a series of rings, then a voicemail greeting and a beep.

"This is Sonny. I just wanted to let you know that I've met someone else. I, uh, think I was being premature when I suggested awhile back that we get married. I won't be calling again, but I hope you have a good life. Take care."

Dinner was strained, the angel-hair spaghetti with its homemade sauce tasteless in my mouth. Most of it we stored as leftovers. We flipped a coin for which movie to watch. Sonny called tails and won, but then nicely chose *Flashdance* instead of *Terminator II* since he knew it was what I wanted. Afterwards we padded out to sit in the hot tub, and the steamy heat soothed me a little. When we went to bed our bodies stayed on opposite sides of the bed, as if we didn't know each other. On some level, maybe we didn't.

I lay awake reflecting that if this had happened in Oregon, I wouldn't have been desperate to not be alone. I would have gone to Fideles House the following Sunday evening, eating dinner with the community, worshipping, then hanging out, debriefing from worship and socializing. At some point I'd have told people what had happened. Paul and Marisol would have hugged me, jokes would have flown about narrow brushes with polygamy, laughter would have flowed and my perspective would have improved. But down here, I was like a woman in exile, as Mary had pointed out. I felt strongly that if Sonny and I could be in Oregon, close to the Fideles community, our relationship would have different dynamics altogether. In Oregon, I'd always lived from my strengths, not my weaknesses.

Chapter 9
Aerobics

"I'm a dance instructor," I said, trying to be confident and inquisitive at the same time. "I'm interested in leading aerobics classes here in your gym."

"Aerobics," Red replied thoughtfully. "I've never thought about that." He was listening with interest and didn't seem opposed to the idea, so I felt the most optimistic I'd felt all day. The gym owner had a reddish-gray crew cut, a big, blunt face and the bulky arms and shoulders of a former bodybuilder. We sat across from one another in his tiny, cluttered office that smelled of exhaust fumes from the auto body shop that occupied the ground floor below.

"But you're willing to think about it now?"

"Well, it's an interesting idea."

I had spent the day driving from gym to gym in Orange County. Six gyms had said they already had all the dance instructors they needed, while two added that they had recently cut some of their aerobics classes due to low attendance. Three gyms had asked if I had a following, as in students I'd be bringing with me who'd become new members of the gym. When I answered no, they told me that was required of new teachers, and politely showed me the door. This was a small, independent place in Santa Ana, my last stop of the day before I fought traffic to get back home.

"You know, I have a buddy who works at Nautilus. He tells me that this step aerobics thing is what everybody's doing now," Red told me. "Can you teach step aerobics? I gotta keep up with the times."

"I know what it is," I said. A more plodding and pathetic form of dance I could not imagine. Normal aerobics was dorky enough, like a caffeinated drill team marching in front of mirrors. My plan was to amend aerobics into dancing that was more flowing and expressive.

"Do you currently have any exercise classes?" I asked Red. All I could see from his windowed office was a single large room of weight machines with a smattering of stationary cycles and rowing machines. One middle-aged man was lying on a bench, lifting free weights shakily over his head, face strained and contorted. I felt worried the weights would crash down on him. A younger man kicked a rowing machine in evident anger, then sat down in the rowing machine next to it.

"Not yet," Red said, leaning toward me, "but a business has to be open to new things." I nodded. "Here's my problem," Red continued. "My memberships have been going down with the recession. A woman being here could bring in more men. It's real nice to watch women dancing. Even just normal dancing, with your clothes on and everything," he added hastily. "I'm open to this aerobics thing. I could move the rowing machines over, some of 'em are broken anyway, and rope off a little space for, you know, some dance activity that you could lead. It would even be OK if you didn't have any students at first. You'd still make the place more appealing."

I didn't answer immediately. I was trying not to laugh. Over Red's shoulder I could see the would-be rower kicking the second rowing machine and giving it the finger. "We could try two classes a week. I could pay you twelve bucks an hour, under the table, none of that tax stuff; it drives me apeshit, pardon my French. And I'm not hooked on the step aerobics thing. But I'd want you to wear those spandex dance clothes that look real cute. How about it?" I looked at him. I didn't have any other prospects, I wanted badly to teach dance, and I had to start somewhere. And Red's blunt face struck me as decent and honest, a few tax irregularities notwithstanding.

"Let's give it a try," I said.

Ten days later, "La Bamba" blasted from my little tape deck as I led three gym-goers in a grapevine step. The thin, beat-up carpet under my bare feet was gritty, but I always danced barefoot, unlike most aerobics instructors. I was wearing a black and pink spandex outfit I'd bought at the Goodwill on Harbor Boulevard.

A barrel-chested Mexican fellow danced proudly, head up, hips swiveling to beat the band. He was clearly an experienced salsa dancer. I started to swivel my hips too, adding castanet-type arm motions, and he smiled, letting loose a loud trill. This was my third class at Red's gym, with the most participants yet, and their faces told me they were having fun.

"La Bamba" ended and "Walk Like An Egyptian" began. I led them in jazz squares, feet crossing in front of the body with great big arm-swings like dancers in a musical. I danced facing the others since we had no mirrors, and saw right away that this step was too hard, or at least too new. I switched to jumping jacks to get them back in their comfort zone. They performed these with zeal, looking like a dedicated little military unit in a Third World country that couldn't afford matching uniforms. I beamed at them.

Four guys, Red among them, watched from the very nearby rowing machines, but they weren't dancing. "Join us!" I urged. They grinned and shook their heads. "I ain't no dancer!" Red called back.

"Old Time Rock 'n' Roll" was playing when the tall guy in the goofy goblin mask arrived. The mask covered his whole head, and at first I didn't think much about it, since Halloween was around the corner. I was leading my group in boogey and shimmy steps, watching them to see if this was working for them, or if one dancer might break into a move that the rest of us would then enjoy following.

Goblin Mask got onto our little dance floor and we all made room for him. His movements looked wrong though, even by this class's relaxed standards. He was lurching, barely staying on his feet.

He was drunk. I looked over at Red, anxious. He was already on my page, addressing the man.

"How about you watch with me from the sidelines over here," Red called to him.

"I'm dancing! I like where I am," a familiar voice replied. I did a double take. The goblin was wearing Sonny's sturdy yellowish work shoes and his green work-shirt with a collar, the one made of heavy, good-quality cloth. I tried to keep dancing, but my stomach was clenching, my mind reeling. This was Sonny, drunk, at my dance class. I had no idea of what to do.

His movements were erratic, spastic flashes between dancing and staggering like a drunken sailor moving through a brickyard. People scowled at him as he careened around and they dodged, trying to stay on their feet in the cramped space. I didn't want to address him by name and ask him to leave, because that would show I knew him, which was embarrassing. Then Sonny grabbed me, one hand at my waist and the other taking my right hand at shoulder height, in a sloppy parody of the ballroom dance position.

"Sonny, stop it!" I cried, and he actually obeyed and let go of me. But a minute later he was exchanging angry words with the tattooed fellow next to Red, and then suddenly fists were flying. I had the sick feeling of something ending as Red and the Mexican closed in on him. They were unclouded by alcohol and efficient, and the fight was over almost before it began, ending with the thud of the goblin's body onto the thin, dirty carpet. Bob Seger sang on about the joys of old time rock and roll, but nobody was dancing any more.

⚜

I slumped in the metal folding chair of Red's office. The gym was empty except for a couple of grim-faced rowers sliding forward and back noisily in their machines. I watched them to the side of Red's grayish-red crew-cut and reflected that no matter how hard they worked, they were going exactly nowhere. *I am the rowers*, I thought as Red propped his feet up on his cluttered desk.

"I used to get into fights, myself, when I was a young buck. But after a few broken bones I learned not to," Red told me. He looked mildly amused by the memories. "I did some damage before I quit, though, I'll tell ya," he added. I couldn't muster a smile.

"I'm so sorry this happened," I said. Red waved my words off, male shorthand for forgiveness. "Aw, the goblin guy was the problem, not you. I still love your dancing."

That did make me smile. I looked at him. "I really appreciate that, Red. You know what I love?" I asked slowly.

"That ain't hard. You love to dance."

"Even besides that. What I really love is Oregon. I used to live there. No offense, Red, but it's such a better place than down here."

"Hey, I grew up on a ranch in Texas. I miss that place every day of my life. I'd go back in a heartbeat, if I could. If Oregon's the place you love, I think that's where you oughtta be."

Energy shot through my sagging body as I thought about getting into my truck tomorrow and heading for Portland. Sonny had been the only thing keeping me here. That was over. I felt embarrassed that I had seen him as someone I'd marry, that I hadn't seen before tonight that he had a drinking problem. The weird double engagement thing by itself should have been enough to send me packing.

"I hate to bail on you after you've been nice enough to rearrange your rowing machines and make a space for dancing. It was great of you to give my dance classes a try. But I need to go back to Oregon. I need to say good-bye."

Red sighed. He got up, opened his arms to give me a hug. He was gentle, but I felt the power of his chest and shoulders, even two decades past his prime.

"You take care of yourself, honey," he said. "You've got what it takes to go places."

When I turned to look at him one last time before going down the stairs toward the auto body shop, Red was over by the rowing machines, listening as an unhappy rower gesticulated and complained.

ॐ

"I'm going to stop drinking," Sonny announced. He smelled like day-old beer and two day old sweat sitting in my truck the next morning. Showers didn't seem to be one of the amenities at the Anaheim police station, where I was parked.

"Good for you," I said indifferently. When he'd called an hour earlier, his voice had been as humble and contrite as that of a five year old who'd set the garage ablaze while playing with matches. He had spent the night in jail for driving under the influence. I'd initially refused to come pick him up. I had been packing my clothes at lickety-split pace to move back up to Oregon. I was confident that Marisol and Ruben would let me stay with them for a few weeks until I found a job. Any job would do—temp work, waitressing, hell, I was willing to clean toilets—until I found a real job. My parents were still sleeping, and I'd decided to leave them a note rather than wake them up and wade through a long discussion of my plans. I'd leave a note and then call them from Santa Barbara.

"I know you're going to break up with me," Sonny had said on the phone in his low, rich voice. "I'm just asking that you do that in person. I've never loved anyone like I've loved you. I'll never ask anything else of you again."

I thought that over, willing to let him sweat a few minutes on the other end of the line. I finally decided that since we had been in love, saying good-bye in person was probably the right thing to do.

"I'm going to an A.A. meeting tonight," he informed me now, looking straight ahead out the windshield. I ignored that and started the engine. "Just let me take you out to breakfast for our last talk," Sonny said hurriedly. "I owe you that much. There's a Denny's five blocks from here."

"No thanks." I shook my head and exited the parking lot.

"I'll take you anywhere you want," he pleaded. "Just name the place."

I sighed. I was hungry. If I ate breakfast now and also ordered a sandwich to go that I could eat as I drove, I could make a campground north of the Bay Area by nightfall. Ten minutes later we were sipping bland, weak coffee in a bright orange booth.

"I'll keep some good memories of our relationship," I said stiffly after we'd ordered. His beard-stubbled, handsome face regarded me gravely. "But you were right that I'm breaking up."

"I'd do the same thing if I were you. I was a jerk last night. I was out of control."

"What in Hades were you thinking?" I asked. "You know how much my dancing means to me, even if it is just in an old gym."

"When I've had too many beers I don't think. That's the problem. Two years ago I had six months clean and sober. I even went to AA some."

He added more fake creamer to his coffee. What was it with key men in my life who were alcoholics, I wondered. But Paul was so different from Sonny there was no comparison. Paul was steady and Sonny was sexy. It didn't matter anyway. I'd eat and be out of here.

"Then I made the mistake of thinking I was cured. I thought I could drink like other people," he said. "Big mistake. Here I am, losing the person in the world who means the most to me." His face was bereft, his eye contact with me unwavering. I was a little intrigued he'd once managed to go six months without drinking.

The overweight young waitress set our food in front of us. I forked my scrambled eggs and strings of hash browns into my mouth. Tasteless. I dumped Tabasco on and tried again. Marginally better. Sonny morosely cut up and ate his rubbery pancakes.

"Well, good luck with not drinking," I said politely into the silence.

"Thanks. I know I can do it. Just to let you know," he went on, leaning toward me, "that guy watching you last night, the one next to Red? He said something crude, I mean really crude, about your body and what he wanted to do to it. I asked him to have some respect and he ignored me. He just kept talking trash about you, and that was when I lost it and slugged him. That's not an excuse. It's just how it happened." I half believed him. Assuming it was true, it was depressing, though not surprising. Why did men have to sexualize dance so much? Why couldn't they enjoy dance for its own sake, without making it about sex?

"Revelle, if you'd give me another chance," Sonny went on, "I could get you set up in your own dance studio with a good clientele, not a bunch of bozos with tattoos lifting weights above an auto body shop. You deserve way better than that."

I looked at him. I wanted to stay detached, get the hell out of Orange County and drive straight up to Oregon as planned. But I also wanted what Sonny was describing. It was true that as a carpenter he knew how to create great spaces. I was crazy about him, even against my better judgment. He really loved me too, which was something your normal, standardized, reliable guy like Mike didn't seem to do.

"Being a self-employed dance instructor would go perfectly with being a mother," Sonny said energetically, forearms on the table. "You could set your own hours and put your children first. You wouldn't have to bow and scrape to some boss because you'd be your own boss." He shrugged and sat back up straight. "But you know what's best for you. I don't."

I pushed my plate of half-eaten eggs and hash browns away. "Excuse me for a minute." I found the payphone right next to the restroom. An unfamiliar voice with a heavy accent answered Marisol's number. I managed to gather that Marisol wasn't home. I thanked him and said good-bye, confused. Then I remembered her mentioning in a recent conversation that one or more cousins from East L.A. would be staying with them for a while. Showing up at her door wouldn't be a good idea at all. Marisol would just feel bad that she and Ruben couldn't take me in for a while.

Back at the table, Sonny had already paid for our breakfast. Two crisp one-dollar bills on the table awaited the overweight waitress.

With all his flaws, Sonny did have a wonderfully generous spirit. I loved that about him.

Thirty-five minutes later, I was in Sonny's bed, his long limbs warmly, deliciously wrapped around my smaller ones. As our mouths stayed joined for minutes at a time, alternately kissing and breathing each others' breath, I thought: *I am a tree, and he is my mistletoe.* Or, it might have been the other way around. Being with Sonny tended to scramble my brains. I wished we were both in Oregon.

Chapter 10
Revenge

"I wish my husband treated me like that!" I turned from Sonny's kiss to return the gaze of the woman addressing me in the strip-mall parking lot. She was fiftyish, with big bones and big hair like a Texan on TV, smiling broadly at the two of us as we held each other.

"Her brother says we're Siamese twins joined at the mouth!" Sonny grinned back at her.

"Keep it up, kids," she said as she climbed into her white minivan. It was a Friday night, and we had just bought a bottle of red wine for Liz's party the following night. We wouldn't be drinking it, but it was what Liz had suggested when I'd asked what we should bring. We'd also bought coffee and condoms—for an impulsive person, Sonny was surprisingly religious about using condoms every time we made love.

We strolled to his truck in the chilly January air, my frustration over my lack of a job forgotten for the moment. Instead, I was recalling my phone chat earlier in the day with Marisol. She had pressed me a little on when I'd return to Oregon. "We miss you," she'd said. Carmenita, who had been cooing in the background to the hamster she had received for Christmas, had then leaned into the receiver to yell, "I miss you, Revelle!"

"I miss you all too!" I'd replied, then had tried to explain to Marisol that Sonny made southern California almost bearable to me. "He loves me more than anyone I've ever known. When he's listening to me talk, it's like nothing else exists in the world for him right then. If a nuclear bomb exploded, he'd dust himself off and ask me to keep talking to him."

"That sounds, like, too seductive," Marisol had replied. "I think you should slow things down. Or bring him up here so we can check him out." Then, to Carmenita, "Honey, you've mauled Izzie enough. Put her back in her cage." Carmenita had asked me on the phone on Christmas morning to name her hamster and I had suggested Isadora after Isadora Duncan, the founder of expressive dance. That had quickly morphed to Izzie. I sighed now, wishing Sonny and I were in Portland, instead of a strip-mall parking lot. I spied a Hollywood video store three doors down.

"Let's rent a movie," I suggested. "I know, let's watch *Parenthood*. I love that movie, I've seen it three times."

"Isn't it time for something different?" Sonny was laughing at me.

"No, no, it'll be fun to see your reactions," I said eagerly as we walked into the store, arms around each other.

"And we want to be parents together," Sonny nodded, falling into agreement. We found the videotape, rented it and added it to the plastic bag holding the red wine.

Back at his apartment, the mood between us was so good that I decided to clear something up that had been bothering me.

"Sonny, about yesterday," I began. "Remember when we were driving back from Home Depot and my cramps were so bad?" I had been curled in a fetal position against the truck's passenger door, wondering if one's reproductive organs didn't sustain permanent damage from pain that severe.

"Uh-huh?" he said, blue eyes and blank expression trained on me.

"I was in terrible pain. I needed to lie down and rest in a quiet, dark room. I asked you to help me with that." My heart hurt just talking about this. But swallowing my feelings and not talking about it was even worse.

"And I did help you. Let's make some popcorn to eat during the movie," he said, rummaging noisily in the cupboard for his hot-air popper.

"Please listen to me. You stopped to shop at a yard sale. I was sitting in the truck doubled over for more than an hour." I didn't add that a small mountain of tools and dirty tarps in the section behind the seats had prevented me from reclining the seat.

"It was a yard sale that had *tools*. Almost none of them have tools. My circular saw broke last month and—"

"Sonny," I interrupted. My heart was pounding hard. I couldn't believe this talk with the man who loved me so visibly it swung people's heads around was going so badly.

"What, Revelle?" he said patiently, reasonably, as you'd do with a misguided three year old or a mentally ill person needing to be guided into the white wagon. "You'd taken Tylenol. We'd done what we could."

"It hadn't helped! Cramps don't always respond to painkillers! You don't understand; the pain was horrendous!" I kept feeling that if he only understood what I had been experiencing, he would apologize, and promise to be more considerate next time. There was always a next time with cramps. I was dreading my future, my very life as I watched his carefully blank face that registered no acknowledgment of me. It was as if I was an inanimate object. Or as if I didn't exist.

"I understand that millions of women all around the world deal with menstruation every month without expecting the world to close up shop on account of it," he replied with infinite calm. "You're overreacting."

"You actually don't care if I'm doubled up in pain," I whispered, feeling something cross over inside myself. I started backing up across the room toward the table, seeking a certain object and a certain distance from him.

"A relationship is about both people's needs, not just one person's needs, Revelle," he said, pious and patient as a Puritan minister, body still and rigid. He had no idea what was going to happen.

My right hand found what it was looking for behind me on the dining room table: the open-loop handle of the plastic grocery bag containing the wine and videotape. My pain had transmuted into rage as quickly as Jesus had turned water into wine. Maybe a little less fortuitously. My first two fingers in the handle, I hurled the heavy plastic bag like a slingshot. The bottle cracked on impact like David's stone hitting Goliath's forehead. Red stuff burst, gushed, streamed. In that moment I attacked, in the quick crouch, gathering of muscles and explosive release, the primal part of me felt fierce pleasure, and I understood how my ancestors must have felt in their battles and ambushes all those millennia ago, the bodily thrill of making a solid strike, violence-lust flooding the brain.

Across the room, Sonny slowly stood back up. He had ducked when I had hurled. The red wine dripping down the white wall behind him was at the same height as his head. He looked at me, face pale and shocked as a witness to a murder.

My body was trembling so hard my legs buckled at the knees, and I sank to the floor. I carried the guilt of having possibly killed a man seventeen years earlier.

✣

The smells of sweat and popcorn filled the air. I was sitting in the bleachers at a high school basketball game in 1977 with my friend Liz. It was a Friday night in February, and we were juniors, co-captains of the drill team and best friends. Our team and their rivals from Fountain Valley had already done their showy running entrance like gladiators, and were now doing their warm-up drills in their sweat suits as Queen's "We Will Rock You" blared through the sound system. Our feet and hands all moved with the music as we sat on the hard wooden benches: stomp, stomp, CLAP! Stomp, stomp, CLAP! The bleachers were a huge drum being pounded by a few thousand feet, and the vibrations going into my thighs and crotch gave me a primal thrill.

"I feel like we're a prehistoric tribe dancing around a bonfire," I murmured into Liz's ear. She smiled and nodded. We were sitting about two-thirds of the way up the steep, narrow-stepped bleachers, and I was next to one of the yellow-marked aisles that had to be kept clear, which was no small feat since our team had won three games in a row and the place was packed. Liz and I were pressed shoulder to shoulder, like much of the crowd. I wasn't a big fan of sitting still, and was attracted to aisle seats because they made it easier for me to get up and move around when I wanted to.

The game hadn't started yet and I twisted around to see whom I might recognize in the upper seats. I had flirted with Sam Hinckley that afternoon in U.S. History and it would be fun to banter with him some more if he was here. Standing in my aisle, at the top of our section with a wall behind him, stood a tall middle-aged man with a big belly, baseball cap and shaggy hair, taller than most of the players down on the court. My eyes passed over him to a bunch of senior girls chattering busily with each other, then moved of their own will back to the tall man. His eyes loomed bizarrely large through glasses thick as the bottoms of Coke bottles. I stared. It was him. My stomach lurched, sick with fear.

I turned back toward the court, where the referee and players were gathering for the toss. My eyes were turned toward the plays and baskets that followed, but all I was seeing was a pink Easter dress, a curly cascade of pink tickets, and a prancing Palomino horse.

I turned around again casually, like a girl who just happened to find the crowd more interesting than the game, and looked up at the tall man some more. He was hulking, slack-jawed, ugly as sin. He felt my gaze and our eyes met. But his gaze was blank and slid away to scan more of the people in the bleachers. Of course he wouldn't recognize me; any 16 year old looked far different than she had at seven. I sensed he was looking now for a new little girl, an unattended one that he could lure away to a Volkswagen bus so dirty that someone had fingerpainted "Wash me" into the filth on the long sliding door.

My body was gripped with fear and adrenaline, but I knew I was not a child alone with a predator now. I had a tribe all around me creating camouflage, and its energy had buzzed in my body earlier. Next to my fear, palpable as Liz's shoulder pressed against mine, was hatred and rage. I had had nightmares for years about the rape, and it was laughable to think his crime would ever face any kind of justice. Nobody would believe a memory from an event of nine years that had no proof, no physical evidence.

As if my emotions were contagious, the crowd suddenly rose to its feet, shouting. Later Liz would tell me that one of our players had stolen the ball near the rivals' basket, sprinted to mid-court with it, lost it to a rival, and then re-stole the ball to break away all over again, drive down the court and score a basket. In the moment, I simply rose with the crowd, in a trance, blind to the action down on the court, but sensing some kind of an opening in what was happening. Grandpa Joe had said I should wait for an opening, a time when I wouldn't be caught. I looked behind and up to the right. The big man was moving down the aisle, awkward as a hobbled horse, bag of popcorn in one hand, trying to watch the game and go down the steep narrow steps at the same time.

I was in a wordless zone, my normal mind dismissed, the one that conformed to rules and had a conscience. My primitive brain stem had taken over. I bent down pretending to tie my right shoe, looking down to the yellow-marked aisle on my right and back and up, waiting for him to reach me. There were his long, wide, dirty white sneakers two steps above me, then his right foot one step above me, then here came his left foot, landing just five inches to the side of my right foot. Perfect. The crowd was buzzing excitedly, completely focused on the basketball players darting around, gaining and losing control of the ball in turnover after turnover. The man's right foot landed on the step below me, and as his left foot came fully up into the air, my right heel hooked the front of his ankle, holding it in place. His ankle jerked automatically against it, hard, and I jerked right back, prepared, not surprised. *This time.*

His tall, ungainly body pitched forward, arms flying up and pitching his popcorn into the air like a reverse celebration. Then he crashed, first onto his right knee two yellow steps down, then onto his right shoulder two steps below that, then careening and rolling out of control, landing finally on the gym floor at the feet of a blonde cheerleader, whose face registered shock. She rushed to her advisor, Mrs. Howard, who took one look at the large man sprawled face-down on the floor and then ran to the lobby where the pay phones were located.

Our team's basketball coach crouched by the man and started shouting orders. The referee waved his arms and blew his whistle, halting the game. A coach and trainer from the other team came across the floor to kneel by the man, talk with our coach, and talk with the man, who wasn't moving and didn't look conscious. I knew from Girl Scout first aid training that they had to assess for broken bones and spinal injuries before they could move him.

The blue-shirted paramedics arrived, ringing authoritatively around the man to work on him. The coaches, outranked in this situation, went back to their usual sides of the gym. People went to the refreshment stand, and the players milled around their bench area, some talking animatedly with the cheerleaders, others resting on the bench, a few shooting baskets.

A part of me wanted to go down to the floor and learn the exact injuries I had inflicted. But the wiser part of me knew to keep my distance. I felt a warm, excited glow in my body. The prey had become the predator, and my body hummed with pleasure, a subtle tingling centering in my face around my lips.

The bustling, blue-shirted paramedics finally loaded the man onto a stretcher, his huge, dirty white sneakers sticking off the end of it, the crew straining a little under his weight. His long, big-bellied body looked more awkward than ever, like a killer whale that had been beached, and was still alive and breathing, but was out of its life-giving element. I watched, connected by thick, fibrous, psychic chords to the man now unable to walk. I knew him and his life more intimately than anyone else in the teeming gymnasium, because even if other victims of his were present, only I knew he had suffered not an accident, but an ambush.

"Who is he? Is he someone's father?" I heard a woman behind

me ask. I turned around. "I heard that he was, but Child Services took them away from him," I said "But that might have just been a rumor," I shrugged, as if I didn't want to spread idle gossip.

The following week the school newspaper mentioned the incident in its coverage of the basketball game, stating that an unidentified man had accidentally fallen down the bleachers stairs, received paramedic care while the game was suspended, and gone to the hospital. I toyed with the idea of calling the hospital to learn more. What condition was he in? Was he paralyzed? Dead? Alive? But I never called. I never even knew his name.

Chapter 11
Proposal

After shattering the bottle against the wall that night at Sonny's apartment, I felt shattered by how dangerous my anger was. I apologized to Sonny, and after an hour or so he forgave me and we went to bed. I lay frozen with shame for hours before I slept. It was the first time Sonny occupied the high ground between us.

I called Paul the next day at six. I knew he would be home from work, before heading out to his 7 p.m. meeting. I spilled all of it to him, supported by his little bass-note vocalizations, like punctuation marks to my story. "Mmm. Ah. Yeah. Whoa. Jesus."

"Sounds pretty rough down there in California," he offered when I finished. "Are you wanting advice, or for me to just be your sounding board?"

"Advice," I said, my voice tiny. Seven months ago I was a normal person, I thought disgustedly. What happened?

"To be honest, it sounds a lot like some of the scenes from my drinking days."

"Ah," I said, feeling a ping of recognition, as if my breastbone was a bell, and he had just chimed it. "The only catch being that we weren't drinking."

"Yeah. Well. When the crazy behavior is all there and the only thing missing is the booze, we say the person is 'dry drunk'."

"Do you think I'm a dry drunk?" I asked Paul, anxiously.

"Revelle, I've known you what, eight years? I've never known you to be violent before, drinking or not drinking," he replied. "I don't see a pattern. This is really new, so I'm inclined to think this might be more about Sonny than it is about you."

"So are you thinking I should go to A.A.?" I asked anxiously.

"No, I'm not thinking that. I'm thinking you should go to Al-Anon. It's for the families and friends of alcoholics."

⚜

"This is Marlene from Pathways To Growth. I'm calling to extend an official job offer," a singsong voice announced. Marlene sounded positive her news would make her popular. My heartbeat quickened and my hand tightened on the receiver.

I was in my parents' kitchen, drinking instant coffee that was already tepid on top of being tasteless. When the phone rang I'd been wondering if Mom could tolerate my buying and bringing real coffee and a French press into her kitchen.

"That's wonderful," I said to Marlene, tossing my vapid beverage into the sink and starting to pace the kitchen as far as the curly phone cord would allow. I'd heard about Marlene's organization from a woman I'd met at my first Al-Anon meeting a few weeks ago. When it was my turn to share, I'd said, "I know this isn't a jobfinders' club. But what I really need is to find a job. I'd love to network with people after the meeting and hear about any leads any of you might have. Being unemployed really brings out the worst in me. I just attacked my boyfriend, and I feel terrible about it. But I was never violent before I got into this relationship." That part was a lie. But the rapist I'd sent tumbling down the bleachers at 16 was a memory so silent and deep it was like the tree in the forest that fell soundlessly because nobody had been there to hear it.

A stoop-shouldered man at the Al-Anon meeting had actually frowned at me when I'd said I needed help in finding a job. He'd shaken his head, the long ends of his waxed, oversized mustache waving around like seaweed underwater. I had dropped my eyes, my face burning, feeling like I'd woken up in the wrong life.

Everything I was doing was wrong: saying inappropriate things, being unemployed, living with my parents and almost braining my boyfriend with a bottle of wine. I had rapidly wrapped up my sharing. Some meetings since then had been better, partly because I could see everyone had problems, and I wasn't the worst person in the world. But right now the best benefit of Al-Anon felt like the networking and job leads I'd found.

"This position would be supervising and teaching the adolescents in one of our detention cottages in central Los Angeles." My heart sank: Los Angeles would mean a godawful commute into the most barren concrete environment imaginable.

Marlene was continuing to sing her cheerful song. ". . . swing shift, three p.m. to eleven p.m., Tuesday through Saturday. The job pays four ninety five, with full medical benefits after a six-month probationary period."

"Four-ninety-five a week?" I said, trying to sound neutral rather than disappointed. I had been making significantly more than that at Prentice.

"No, four-ninety-five an hour."

"Even with a master's degree?" I asked faintly.

"Well, yes. If you'd only had a bachelor's degree, our scale would put you at four sixty an hour," she said briskly. "Also, you'll be working every holiday. Sorry, but that's how our seniority system works." I closed my eyes and leaned my forehead against the wall. Since Sonny worked days, swing shift meant I would almost never see him. The commute would be as grim as a coal mine. And four-ninety-five an hour was wildly depressing.

"Marlene, I really appreciate this job offer. I need to think about it. Let me call you back tomorrow with an answer." Her good-bye was cool in tone. I'd ruined the fun part of her day, the generous offering of jobs to people in need.

Three days later I returned to the Al-Anon meeting at St. Agnes church, breathing in the smell of stale Folgers coffee, grateful for the 16 pairs of ears and eyes giving me their full attention. "I turned down a job offer that was for really bad hours and pay," I reported. "I think that substitute teaching around here could work, though, so I've registered for the test." It puzzled me that people in Al-Anon seldom talked about work or other ambitions. I could have talked about mine all day.

"I've been practicing more acceptance of Sonny, and putting my focus more onto myself. I haven't been getting angry. The program is really helping." I didn't add that Sonny had been horrified by the idea of me working a swing-shift job. "I want you to be my full-time playmate!" he had cried. "Tell that Marlene person, not no, but hell no!" Repeating all that would be focusing on the alcoholic, which I wasn't supposed to do. Plus it would make him look childish, which he generally wasn't. Not really. I wrapped up my sharing by stating that I was finding some experience, strength and hope in Al-Anon. I'd keep coming back. I got some nods and smiles in response, which was all the feedback these meetings allowed. I tried to feel grateful. These well-meaning, constrained people were the only tribe I had now. My real tribe was beyond my reach up in Portland.

❦

The candlelight flickered across Sonny's strong-featured face. It was Valentine's night. I looked at the remains of our dinner: canned cream of mushroom soup, Ritz crackers, and carrot-raisin salad.

It was late, past ten, because Sonny's initial, exuberant idea had been to take me out to a fancy dinner. We had spent the evening driving around to half a dozen good restaurants, to find each of them packed, reservations only on Valentine's night.

"Where is this relationship going?" Sonny asked. His tone was flat, elbows planted on the table.

"My career is stalled out," I said. "That makes it hard for me to commit." I had taken the CBEST test a week ago and was waiting for the results so I could finish my applications for substitute teaching. Subbing itself was fairly pathetic, though neither Sonny nor anyone at Al-Anon seemed to think so.

"You're just between jobs," Sonny said. "That happens to everyone at some point. It's our relationship that's stalled out."

"No. We're in love." That was true. I loved Sonny deeply. True but unspoken was how unhappy I was. I miss Oregon, I miss my tribe, I thought dully.

"I need for this to go somewhere. I need for us to be going somewhere," Sonny insisted, slapping his hand on the table. I remembered he had had a break-up before I'd met him because the woman hadn't wanted to get married or have children. In front of me, the golden beeswax tapers in the wooden candleholders Sonny had carved by hand had burned down to stubs that flickered dubiously. *I am the tapers*, I thought. The face of a little girl, my daughter, appeared in my mind, dimly lit like the room. "I see us getting married, eventually," I said, without conviction. But my would-be daughter's face became more visible with those words.

"I don't want to talk about getting married," Sonny said, his voice low and even, "unless you set an actual wedding date with me." All his playfulness was gone. I'd never seen him like that before. I was fatigued from our long, disappointing search for dinner, and my blood sugar had plummeted so low that the soup and crackers I'd finally eaten weren't making much difference.

"What can I say?" I said. We both knew I was stalling, but he was obviously prepared for this conversation, while I wasn't. I had broken our informal engagement months ago, and the topic of marriage had been on hold ever since. I considered asking him light-heartedly now if he was sure he wasn't currently engaged to anyone else. But I knew that joke would go over poorly.

I slumped at the table, poking at the limp carrot-raisin salad on my plate. I couldn't imagine life without Sonny at this point, couldn't envision a better option for the weeks and months immediately ahead of me than marrying him. My old life in Portland was over. I had to work with the options I had now. Sonny would break up with me sooner or later if I didn't marry him. At our ages, that was to be expected: I'd broken up with Mike for the same reason. I looked up.

"We both want children, right?" I said, watching his face carefully.

"Absolutely." His handsome face was still as a photograph, watching me with that purity of focus that told me I was the center of his universe. It was his signature expression, the one that bound me to him.

"I can't picture myself raising a child in this godforsaken place," I said honestly. "Back when we met, you said you loved Oregon. Would you consider moving there with me?"

Sonny's face registered surprise, then excitement. "I have the kind of skills that can find work anywhere."

My spine straightened, energy flowing into my body. "So if we got married, you're promising we would move to Portland? And we would have one or more children." I could feel my daughter's spirit quickening there in the room, urging me forward, wanting to be born.

"Yes. And I'll help you start your own dance studio." His face and voice were quietly confident. While Sonny had voiced this intention back in the fall, I'd intuitively known it was linked to being married, and for that very reason I'd been passive: no dance studio and no engagement, either. Parts of Sonny's character scared me, but the prospect of being without Sonny, without the bright, warm light of his love, scared me more. "Let's set a date," he said now, pointedly.

I looked above Sonny's tousled head to a calendar tacked onto the wall behind him. L.A. Landscape, it said at the top. I rose, took it from the wall and brought it back to the table. I flipped from February past March, April and May, with photos of cactus gardens, jacaranda trees and beds of bright impatiens, to June. The June photograph was of bougainvillea, brilliant crimson flowers on vines clinging to a white adobe building that held it upright in space. *I am the bougainvillea*, I thought, unable to stand on my own. At least right now.

"Let's get married on June 20th," I said, finger on the glossy white square that was becoming the portal to my future.

"June 20th is the eve of the summer solstice. The longest day of the year," he replied, intrigued. "The most daylight. That's a great date."

"We've got plenty of time for planning. I want my Oregon friends to come."

"Of course. I'm eager to meet them. *Where* are we getting married?" he asked urgently.

"Definitely somewhere outdoors."

"Mrs. Chapman's big garden!" He slapped the table with excitement. Mrs. Chapman was his latest remodel client. She adored him.

"Perfect," I said, instantly embracing the idea. I had seen her garden. The lovely lawn was bordered by sage, lavender, and fountain grass all flowing together in the wildish way I loved. "We take our vows at sunset!"

"Dancing at the reception, led by you!"

I pictured myself choreographing a dance that would involve the people I loved the most. Then the dance would spread to the audience, plugging them into their own joy and ability to dance, like the magical night of the Electric Parade. Sonny's face across the table was avid, transformed from its earlier grimness. The room itself now vibrated with energy.

"We got engaged on Valentine's Day," he grinned, pleased with himself. Then he looked down at the Ritz box, cracker crumbs and Tabasco bottle on the table. "Sorry it wasn't more romantic," he added.

"I forgive you," I said, putting the dinner debacle behind us. "I'm so excited I can't stand it." I stood, raised the back of my hand to my forehead and swooned showily, falling backward in a limber faint to show he had swept me off my feet, and I was ecstatic we had gotten engaged. Sonny rose on cue and caught me, one arm at my waist, the other cradling my neck, and bent to kiss me, the picture of a knight in shining armor rescuing a damsel in distress.

Chapter 12
Wedding

"Elly, aren't you supposed to be sequestered somewhere, so that nobody sees you until I take you down the aisle?" Dad looked a little flustered.

"That's the old-fashioned way." I kissed his smoothly shaven cheek. "Your new-fangled daughter wants to socialize as much as possible."

We were in Mrs. Chapman's lush garden. My abundant hair was piled high and pinned loosely, with curls cascading down. My earrings were real fuchsia flowers, picked that morning from my mother's hanging basket. I felt so excited and anxious for everything to go well that I was breathing in tiny puffs, like when I'd taken CPR training in college and worked on the infant doll. I could have a genuine faint if I kept that up. I pressed my palm against my belly and breathed into it so that my hand moved outward.

I introduced myself to Sadie the florist, a pretty girl of about 21 with a dramatic mane of dark brown hair and darty eyes of the same color. She was arranging a big, rowdy bouquet of eucalyptus and sunflowers on the altar with rapid little movements. When I asked her how long she'd been in the flower business, she confided happily that she was not really in the flower business. But she wanted to be.

"I just met Sonny six days ago at a gas station. He was pumping his gas on the next island over, and he struck up a conversation with me." She cut her eyes over at me to see how I was taking this. She must have seen interest rather than jealousy, because she continued. "You know how friendly he is, so I started telling him how I hate my bookkeeping job, and he was, like, really sympathetic. You're marrying such a great guy," Sadie gushed as she snipped the bottoms off the ends of three particularly huge sunflower stalks. "I told him that I'm a gardener, actually a grower is the word, since I'm into edibles as well as flowers." She held up two thorny artichokes that I hoped wouldn't be occupying the altar as I took my vows. My brother Rick walked up and stood next to me.

"I said to Sonny, 'I'm trying to get the hell out of bookkeeping. I'm trying to get a break as a designer who grows her own natural materials.' And right away, he said, like, 'Well, why don't you design the arrangements for my wedding this Saturday?' So, like, here I *am*!" she beamed, mercifully moving the artichokes away from the altar into a large basket bristling with natural materials. "I'm hoping he'll give me a good reference so I can get more work like this."

"I wonder if she checked Sonny's references," Rick muttered. I mock-cuffed him on the ear. He enjoyed Sonny but didn't put a lot of stock in his reliability.

Paul joined us, huge and freshly haircutted. He wore his only suit, a navy blue one, with a peacock feather patterned tie. I hugged him.

"Revelle," he said, looking a little stricken. "I've never seen you look more beautiful."

"Gosh. Thank you, Paul," I said. He had never been one for effusive compliments. And with so much on my mind, I'd forgotten I looked any different than I usually did. We stood in the slanting late afternoon sun looking at each other for a slowed-down moment. His kind brown eyes helped me breathe deeply, like a dancer, instead of shallowly, like Scarlett O' Hara with her strangled, cinched-in waist. I loved Paul, with the kind of purity I loved Mary, and wide open spaces, and God.

My life had changed dramatically after Sonny and I got engaged for real, that second time. I had direction and purpose, waking each morning with my head humming with happy plans for the wedding.

I spent my spring days carrying those plans out while substitute teaching. I only subbed for grades K-6, and I found I loved it, managing the classrooms easily, leading the children in song and dance games as rewards for doing their assignments. It paid well, about a hundred dollars a day, which further shored up my confidence in myself.

"Planning my wedding is one of the best jobs I've ever had," I had told Vicki and Frank in April as they had helped me with the wedding invitations.

"It is?" Frank said dubiously, affixing a stamp to an envelope corner with the care of a fine jeweler.

"I actually get to *do* things, instead of trying to convince people to *let* me do things. That's the problem with looking for work, that's why recessions are such a bummer. You go around begging to be allowed to work. When it came to wedding planning, I'm already hired. I get to do all these creative things. It's such a relief to be creative again." I had been a little manic, even to my own ears, as I addressed an envelope to Shasta with a calligraphy pen. She'd been getting more involved with tree-sitting, which I thought was great.

"You are so Type A," Vicki had said. "I am so not. I'd be fine with not working if we could afford it. But what will you do after the wedding is over and you're out of work again?"

"I'm going to become self-employed, like Sonny," I said, enthused. "When we move up to Oregon I'm going to own and operate a dance studio."

"Wow," they said in unison, their hands becoming still over the envelopes and stamps.

"If Sonny can pull off being self-employed being as disorganized and flaky as he is, I know that I can pull it off."

"You've got a point." Vicki nodded. "Yeah," Frank said thoughtfully as he resumed stamping envelopes.

My bond with Sonny deepened in those months. The marriage commitment and the promise of a child were trust-builders and aphrodisiacs to us both. I even bonded somewhat with his mother,

Jane, as dour and anxious as she was. I reminded myself she'd been wounded by an alcoholic husband and then being widowed abruptly. Sonny himself never seemed tempted to drink, which I thought was wonderful. I no longer felt a need for Al-Anon. Every hour of my time had become golden to me again.

⚜

The sun was setting at my back as my dad walked me slowly down the grassy aisle. I felt his body's warmth in my hand, tucked into the crook of his elbow. I heard the wedding march, the notes sweet and clear as clarion calls, as Rick played it on his trumpet. Many guests turning their heads to watch me were my parents' friends, and friends of Sonny's mother. A well-tanned contingent, hands plucking now and then at their shirt-collars, were carpenters and tradesmen who were colleagues of Sonny's. Little Carmenita was already at the altar, having strewn my path with rose petals brought down from Portland, the city of roses. She, my three bridesmaids and Sonny's three groomsmen all watched me raptly as I approached. Nobody was dressed alike. There was a story behind that.

⚜

"I'm designing and making my own dress," I informed Marisol in early May, holding the phone to my ear with my left shoulder as I ironed the bodice.

"You're so artistic. I bought mine off a rack," Marisol sighed. "Honey, please don't eat the hamster food," she added, without missing a beat.

"Why?" I heard Carmenita challenge her.

"Because Izzie doesn't take your food, so it's not fair for you to take hers. If you'll put it away, you can talk to Auntie Elly when I'm done."

"OK!"

"I'm gold," I said smugly to Marisol. "So my dress is off-white, and it's a halter that goes to the ground, but the skirt has floating panels of different widths, so that my legs show through when I move."

"Whoo-hoo!" Marisol said.

"And the panels are mingled with ribbons strung with beads of wood and colored glass. Listen, I want Carmenita to be my flower girl."

"Only if she stops eating hamster food. Nita, Auntie Elly wants to talk to you."

I got Carmenita's excited buy-in on being the flower girl, then talked with Marisol again to plan Carmenita's dress.

"Who are my fellow bridesmaids?" Marisol asked. "Liz, I hope?"

"You and Liz and Vicki," I confirmed, shifting the phone to the other ear. "But I'm creating a progressive dress policy."

"You mean you won't force us to get ill-fitting dresses in some faux satin material of a horrid color that we'll never wear again?" Marisol cried hopefully. "With overpriced pumps dyed to match?"

"I'm liberating you from all that! Free dress code!" I crowed. Marisol and I had been bridesmaids together years earlier for the same girlfriend from Pitzer. As much as we'd liked Sharon, we'd shared plenty of pithy commentary about the costly, wasteful shoe and dress debacle.

"You're a Goddess-send!" Marisol breathed worshipfully. "Thank you, thank you, thank you. I'm sinking to my knees as I speak." I pictured Carmenita taking advantage of that and stepping in for a hug, the grainy smell of hamster food on her breath.

"Now, who's paying for all this hoo-haw? Your parents?" Marisol asked briskly. She sounded to be standing upright again.

"They're paying for the reception. Sonny is paying for everything else, like the invitations and flowers and photographer. And I'm doing the work, the management, the sweat equity. I'm making the cake, besides my dress. I'm stretching everyone's dollars."

"You're good at that. Do the groomsmen have to rent penguin suits or do they get free-dress code too?"

"Free-dress for groomsmen. I've declared it so," I said grandly. This role of benevolent queen was really working for me.

"I want phone numbers for Liz and Vicki, please," Marisol announced.

"You want to enlist them as partners in crime. I'm going to find hamster food in my nuptial bed!" But I gave her their numbers. I loved Marisol. She and Carmenita were my heart. And now here they were, part of my wedding. I had never felt happier in my life or more complete.

Sonny's eyes held mine as my dad released me, and I joined him at the outdoor altar. He was wearing the shirt I'd sewn for him, billowing-sleeved and open-necked like a Renaissance man, made of the same off-white material as my dress. Mary smiled at me, an ethnic-style minister's stole around her neck reaching almost to the ground, vibrantly hued as Joseph's coat of many colors. I smiled back, my eyes full with tears. Mary, along with Sonny, made my year of exile in southern California worth all the pain and confusion.

Out of loyalty, I had originally asked Pastor Rachel to marry us. I'd remained a member of Fideles House, and would soon return to it. Also, Rachel's praying for my marriage would be a powerful thing, like a female Moses recreating the burning bush for us there in hedonistic Southern California. But she declined, because she'd be in Alaska with relatives on the summer solstice.

One Saturday morning in late March I was packing boxes with Mary at her house. She and her husband were moving to Claremont. I had spent the night, after helping her with a square dance, a chaplaincy outreach event for students that I'd suggested. We had stayed up late afterward, curled up on her couch with the lights low. Talk turned to our childhoods. Without knowing I was going there, I had found myself telling her about the carnival and Palomino model horse and sick man. Her face turned from a picture of horrified tenderness to fury at the man, then love and sorrow. She had held me close. I hadn't told her, though, about my guerilla attack. I'd never told anyone about that. I was too ashamed.

"Mary, I need to ask you something," I said that next morning as I stacked books by Henri Nouwen and Thich Nhat Hanh into a stout box. "It's kind of big. Would you preside at my wedding to Sonny? Marry us on June 20th?"

Mary stopped wrapping newspaper around a hand-carved African mask, emptied her hands, and waited until I stopped too and gave her my full attention. "I'll be honored to marry you," she said, looking into my eyes in that way she had where you felt like her body and soul and just about every minute of her history since her birth were showing up there in front of you. Her presence was that strong. Or, maybe God's presence was that strong in her.

ॐ

Now, in the garden with all the people I loved around us, Sonny and I looked into each other's faces. I felt pure adoration, both for him and coming from him. When Mary led us in the vows we'd written and we put the rings on each other's fingers, I was in a trance as absorbed and joyful as the times I had done ecstatic dance. Then Sonny was kissing me, and Mary was presenting us to everyone as Sonny Champagne and Revelle Jones Champagne. Everyone cheered, as if we'd finished presenting a play with the most jubilant of endings.

The food that Mom had arranged with the caterer was dazzling: brie and bleu cheeses, slim mango and melon slices from deepest orange to palest green, baguette bread heaped in hand-woven baskets, and clusters of red and green grapes spilling around and over everything like friendly hands that couldn't stop touching their friends. Organic mesclun salad sat leafy and fluffy in great wooden bowls. The entrée and wines were Oregonian—blackened wild salmon ringed by roasted hazelnuts and Chardonnay and Pinot Noir from the Willamette River Valley.

"I wish Grandpa Joe could be here," I said to Mom, my memory of him piercing me like an arrow released from beyond the veil. She looked at me and nodded, her brown eyes gone still and soulful. But a second later she was greeting a friend from her church, no longer holding the remembrance with me. I suddenly realized Grandpa Joe had been her only living tie to her girlhood, to Palestine. How much had she given up by becoming American? Because she'd made her past opaque to all of us, I had no way of knowing.

Sonny and I mingled and talked with people, sometimes together, sometimes apart. Mom urged a plate of food on me, but all I ate that whole evening was five grapes. I was too fed by joy to take in anything else. I did see Sonny drinking the Pinot Noir, his strong throat exposed and lit by the last beams of sunlight as he upended the goblet. I said nothing. It was his wedding.

After dinner we awarded two of Sadie's oversized, bristling bouquets, to the longest-married couple and shortest-married couple. I held them gingerly, hoping the winners wouldn't get pricked by their prizes. Longest marriage was my family's long-time friends, Gerry and Lee Whitson, at 51 years. Shortest marriage was Mohammed and Leslie, who I knew through Vicki and Frank. They had gotten married just two weeks earlier.

"And people said it wouldn't last!" Leslie cried, raising her bouquet triumphantly, which sent a couple of thistles flying through the air. One landed in Sadie's dark hair as she was looking in the other direction. My dad quietly removed it without her noticing.

I led off the dancing with a bold, out-there solo to "When Love Comes To Town," the bluesy, rocker song by U2. I'd pulled on midcalf leggings for modesty's sake, and of course kicked off my heeled sandals so I could dance barefoot on the wooden dance floor under the big, open-air tent. Sonny joined my dance toward the end, as planned, except I hadn't planned that he'd stumble so much. He was buzzed and bleary-eyed. I refused to be alarmed and took my bow with him to big applause. Then Wolfman Rick switched to "Elmer's Tune," and my dad and I swing-danced, happy and laughing, before I beckoned my mom to take my place. They looked great; I'd coached them for three weeks in advance, recovering their body-memories from decades prior when they'd originally danced to it. Their peers followed their lead and took to the floor eagerly, and I clapped for all of them, for their joy in their long-forgotten dancing. The Mexican Hat Dance was next, which Carmenita led with a big sombrero, after I'd urged and cajoled everyone on the grounds onto the dance floor, including the Latino food servers. "I talked with your boss!" I assured them. The hat dance was a hit across all ages and ethnic groups. The revelry under the white tent in the garden only rose with the hours, as the moon rose in the eastern sky. It was the solstice, the longest day of the year, the beginning of summer and the beginning of my marriage.

My favorite photograph of our wedding is one that Liz snapped spontaneously at the end. My mother, Rick, Paul, Marisol and Vicki are around me, chatting with each other, and I am holding Carmenita. Her legs are around my waist, and my legs are showing a little through the streaming panels and ribbons of the dress. Sonny is not there. I learned later from my dad that he was on the other side of the grounds, arguing with Sadie, the first-time florist, who grew increasingly furious as he refused to pay her what they'd agreed on earlier in the week. Sonny had been unfazed. "It was as if this kind of thing happened all the time, and it was water off a duck's back for him," Dad told me. He had taken Sadie aside and quietly written the check to her, himself. When I learned that, I reimbursed Dad.

In the photo of wedding's end, my head is bowed toward Carmenita and hers is raised up so that our foreheads are touching, the curves of our throats making a heart shaped space through which soft light is shining. We are absorbed, as intent on each other as lovers, while my new husband was off-camera, intent on a conflict with a woman who had been charmed and excited by the opportunity he had presented to her, a woman to whom Sonny had broken his promise.

Chapter 13
Honeymoon

It was well past midnight—"the witching hour," as Mary had called it with a twinkle—when we drove south to a hacienda-style bed and breakfast in Laguna Beach where we stayed three nights. It sprawled, lush with vegetation and hospitality, and we sprawled within it, ready to rest after the intensity of the wedding and the work that led up to it.

We made love, made friends in the group breakfast room, and made plans for our move to Portland. We would rent a U-Haul and drive it, plus my little truck, north. Rick used some vacation days to help us, stopping to see Oregon Caves and Crater Lake on the way. We'd find a house to rent, unload the van and the men would fly back to California while I unpacked, nested, nestled back in to Portland, looking for space that could be my dance studio. Sonny would finish the Everett job in about three weeks, a month at most, saving money by living with his mother, and then he'd drive his truck up to join me.

As we strolled through art galleries, took long walks on the beach and explored its elaborate netherworld of tide pools, my body was vibrating with something new. I asked myself what it was, and got a humming answer: I love my husband; I adore my husband; I am a wife. I remembered having thrummed with the first part of that inward chant soon after Mike and I had broken up, prior to meeting Sonny, in the absence of any husband or lover. It seemed that archetypal wife energy, Hera energy, had been alive in me for some time, sculpting me from the inside, so that I was shaped to hold Sonny when he arrived and be filled by him. I was so intoxicated with being married, with being loved rather than rejected, that it didn't matter that I didn't have a job and had earned less than eight hundred dollars over the past two months. I was confident that I would find dance students and build a successful business.

Near the tide pools, the rocks were so big they appeared like small cliffs that dropped straight into the waves crashing twenty feet below. Sonny happily climbed up onto them, long limbs at dramatic angles, and found places to wedge each of his feet, and extended his hand down to help me up, but I could see the boulders offered few footholds for me. They were smooth, slippery with spray.

"I'll stay down here, sweetie," I said. "I'm not comfortable coming up."

"Trust, Revelle!" he said passionately. "Marriage is based on trust."

"The tide is coming in," I pointed out. "It's not a trust issue. Nobody can turn the tide."

"But I won't let you fall. I'll protect you." He bounced his hand up and down, urging me to take it. I was nervous, even more than usual, but took his hand and climbed up. Sonny held me from behind, my back to his chest, as I stood awkwardly on my arches on the too-round, too-smooth boulder, my feet without purchase of their own. "Isn't the view beautiful?" he enthused, and I nodded because it was, but the foamy surf was roiling beneath us.

The day we left the hacienda and drove up the coast to the boat-launch for Catalina was dazzlingly bright, breezy, about 78 degrees. After we boarded we wandered the boat hand in hand, chatting with fellow tourists and then with a young Latino fellow who was polishing one of the boat's sparkling white surfaces.

"*Limpio*," I said admiringly. He nodded.

"*Muy limpio!*" Sonny chimed in. The fellow smiled.

"*Limpioso!*" I cried, raising an arm heavenward for emphasis, making the worker laugh.

"*Hay un telefono aqui?*" Sonny asked unexpectedly. I hadn't known we had any phone calls to make.

"*Aqui, no,*" he replied. "*Alla, si,*" he explained, waving to the dock and office area.

"I told my mother I'd call her, so I'll do that now," Sonny announced cheerfully.

"*Vamos in cinco minutos,*" the boat worker said pointedly. He was telling us the boat was leaving in five minutes, and his tone implied there wasn't time to leave the boat, make a phone call and re-board.

"How about calling her from the island?" I suggested to Sonny. "There's really not time now."

"It's just a quick call," he said over his shoulder as he trotted away.

The minutes ticked by. The boat's engines started with my husband nowhere in sight. Trust him, I told myself. Your stomach doesn't need to be clenching up like this, I told myself. Sonny was an adult, in charge of his own schedule, and if he wanted to call his mother, that was his choice. I strolled to the part of the boat farthest from the dock since that implied the most trust and the least worrying. Then we were in motion, the water opening between the land and us as if an artist were painting it, brushstroke after brushstroke. I tried to keep breathing. It was quite possible Sonny was on the boat. It would have been just like him to have orchestrated a flying leap from dock to deck at the last possible second, attracting attention, playing to whatever crowd was available. He would probably find me any minute now in the wake of his little adventure, face flushed, high on adrenaline.

But the boat motored on over open ocean; the coastline disappeared from view, and I was alone. This was the last boat of the day to Catalina. The worker had said there was no phone on the boat, and cell phones would not come into any of our hands until years later. I flirted with two little towheaded twins and made small talk with their parents to distract myself from what was happening. My stomach was roiling with anxiety. Sonny had had full knowledge of the chance he was taking when he decided to de-board to call his mother. Did a part of him really not want to go to Catalina with me? Why could calling her right then have been so urgent? I said good-bye to the young family and went to the prow of the boat to watch for land. The wind whipped my hair. I scanned the sea wishing to see dolphins, but did not. After a long time the tops of the island's palm trees and hotels started coming into view.

"*Donde esta su esposo?*"

I turned and saw the young Latino boat worker looking at me with concern. He was asking me: where was my husband?

"*Estara conmigo manana,*" I replied with fake composure. "*Su madre esta enferma.*" The kind, dark brown face nodded, and was gone. While I was fairly sure Sonny would join me tomorrow, I had lied about his mother being ill. I just hadn't known how else to explain his behavior.

At the dock, I managed to find and compile our luggage, and then realized that even though the hotel was walking distance from the harbor, I couldn't carry all the bags by myself. I could do it in two trips, but then someone might steal the bags that I temporarily left behind. Why wasn't my husband with me? I stood flustered, fighting back tears. I tucked my chin down so my hair tumbled forward to drape my distress.

"Taxi, miss?" I looked up to see an older man addressing me.

"Um, yes, please." At the hotel a perky, fresh-faced lass checked me in and congratulated me on my wedding. They must have made a note when taking our reservation. She produced a message from Sonny, who had called to say he'd be on the first boat tomorrow and to call him at his mother's house.

I thanked the girl, then promulgated the tale of my mother-in-law's illness that had detained Sonny back on the mainland. When she mooed in sympathy I felt the need to elaborate.

"She has lymphoma," I heard myself report in a grave, confidential tone, pulling from a movie made for TV I had half-watched a week ago while hemming my wedding dress.

"What a dedicated son he is," the clerk said feelingly.

"Indeed," I confirmed, the brave bride soldiering through a honeymoon night alone.

Up in the room I pounced on the phone and called Jane's number.

"Hello," Jane said.

"Jane, it's Revelle."

"I can't believe you let the boat leave without him," she said.

"What?" I didn't think I'd heard right.

"Let me have the phone," I heard Sonny say to her, followed by the sound of his footsteps. In my mind's eye I saw him taking her phone from the kitchen to the back patio.

"Elly, I am so sorry." His voice was rich and warm in my ear. I was quivering with pain and anger and didn't respond right away. "Are you there?" he said.

"I'm here." I was at the crossroad. I could either express my true feelings in their native language, which would mean crying and screaming, or discipline myself into rationality.

"Why aren't you saying anything?" He sounded anxious now.

"I'm so upset it's hard to talk." My throat ached. "I'm wondering why you didn't do what it took to be here with me."

"I thought I would make the boat," he said. "Of course I want to be there with you. May I please explain what happened?"

I gazed dully out the window at the Pacific ocean. "Sure."

"Here's what happened. I'd promised my mother that I'd call her once during the honeymoon. But I completely forgot while we were in Laguna Beach; I was so caught up with you and with being your husband and making love to you and planning to move to Oregon. And when we were on the boat I suddenly remembered I had to call her, but I knew that once we'd get to Catalina, I'd get caught up with you and the island and I'd forget all over again."

I believed that.

"So the only way to keep my word was to call her right then, and the fact the boat was leaving in five minutes actually seemed like a good thing, because she talks too much, and I'd be able to say I had to catch the boat and run. But I would still have called her like I'd promised."

"It all feels so crazy," I said. "Besides missing you, I feel humiliated.

People ask about you. I feel too embarrassed to tell them you missed the boat, after actually getting onto it. So I start making up fibs, and then I hate myself for that."

"I don't expect you to fib for me. I promise I'll make this up to you, Revelle. How can I make it up to you?" Again, the warm, husky voice compelling me to closeness, making me feel like the most important thing in the world to him. I pictured the sound of him travelling from my ear canal into my brain stem, triggering endorphins that travelled out and soothed the nerve endings in my heart and womb that were throbbing with pain. I started to feel a little more like myself.

"How can you make it up to me? You can tell her it was your fault, not mine, you missed the boat," I said.

Sonny hesitated, then said: "OK."

Silence. "I'm waiting."

"You mean right now?"

"Yes." The pain was flaring up again, breaking through the cloaking endorphins. I could hear the phone travelling back into the house, where a television commercial was nattering in the background about the wonders of a clothing detergent that restored soiled and troubled households to harmony. *You are so full of shit*, I silently advised the detergent-besotted actress.

"Mom, just in case I wasn't clear earlier, it was my fault I missed the boat," I heard Sonny say. "There. I told her," Sonny said, directly into the mouthpiece again. I felt limp. It hadn't helped.

"I guess I'll see you tomorrow," I said faintly. He was launching into another declaration of love as I hung up the hotel phone. I don't care how you feel, I thought. I care what you do.

He arrived in the hotel lobby just past noon the next day, handsome features set in a childlike expression of remorse, proffering a pretty bouquet of blue and pink statice. The perky clerk said:

"Welcome, Mr. Champagne! How is your mother feeling?"

"Oh, she's fine," Sonny said distractedly, keeping his gaze trained on me. The clerk looked baffled at his casual dismissal of her lymphoma. Earlier that morning, when asked for an update, I had solemnly announced that she had moved into hospice. Maybe the slightest tinge of wish fulfillment on my part.

The honeymoon didn't regain its stride during those last two nights on Catalina. I felt closed off from the hotel staff because of my lies, closed off from Sonny because he'd abandoned me. I felt little confidence in our lovemaking, and Sonny resented my lack of passion, complaining that I carried a grudge.

"Maybe it takes time to rebuild trust," I said.

"Maybe you should practice forgiveness," he said.

If I wasn't practicing forgiveness, I would annul the marriage, I said to myself, the silent thought feeling more real to me there in the airy, sunlit hotel room than Sonny's physical body, which had been so jarringly absent from me the prior 24 hours. My library of unspoken thoughts and feelings was growing.

Chapter 14
Autumn

Tom Petty's voice was raspy and the hardwood floor smooth under our bare feet as I led my rock 'n' roll dance class in Portland's Hawthorne district. It was late October and I had five students tonight. We all faced the mirror covering the wall as we jumped, shimmied, boogied and whirled. At six dollars per class per student I wasn't even beginning to make a living. This was despite subletting the space to a yoga teacher, a career counselor, a rather wild-eyed judo instructor and a flowing-clothed practitioner of healing arts so numerous and esoteric that I wasn't really sure what she was doing in my studio on Wednesday mornings. I hoped that it was all legal.

But I was deliriously happy as I led my fellow dancers. I had been right about changing careers: I loved teaching dance to people who wanted to be there, instead of teaching English to people who did not. The joy of moving freely and fiercely to music, muscles and tendons extending their full length and then curling back in to the body, was a rush. Tonight I noticed that all six of us were breathing in different ways, at different rates, some deeply like me and Deirdre, and others faster and more labored.

Deirdre was in her late 20's, worked as a barista in a nearby coffeehouse, and had moved here from Ireland with her parents as a teenager. Her dancing was riveting, a force of nature as strong as her Celtic ancestors and the wailing bagpipes they played in ancient days while going to battle. Her long arms, waist-length chestnut braid and lean, flat-bellied body all scythed through the air with incisive passion, with never a hint of indecision or ambiguity. I considered her a better, stronger dancer than I was. A momentary observer could have taken her for the teacher in any given dance class, her body language was so clean, emphatic and compelling. Even I sometimes got distracted watching her. But deeper observation would show that she never made eye contact with fellow dancers or smiled, as the rest of us tended to do. Deirdre wasn't dancing with us, but just among us, being witnessed by us. She was in communion with her own private pantheon of demons and angels, exorcising some of them and being exhorted by others of them. I liked her the way I liked being around half-wild horses, with more respect than any sense of being comfortable.

The Tom Petty rocker ended and "Best Of My Love" started, the long, leisurely Eagles ballad I used for our warm-down in this routine. I had created a dozen routines since returning to Portland, some of them excitedly conceived in my mind during the move north a month after our honeymoon. My brother Rick had used a week of vacation to help us, and the three of us had done a two-vehicle caravan north, with the U-haul carrying our furniture and household possessions, and my little truck carrying our camping things, overnight bags and ice chest for picnic lunches. We had left Sonny's big truck at his mother's house since he would be flying back down to finish up Mrs. Chapman's remodel. We traded off driving alone and driving with each other, like playing musical trucks: sometimes Sonny and I side by side, forearms on each other's thighs, while Rick drove alone, then Sonny riding shotgun with his new brother-in-law while I drove alone, the ocean and sky on my left a great expanse of variegated blue hues that fed the expansiveness I was feeling about my new life. I was delighted the two men liked each other and a little surprised given their differences: Sonny ever ebullient and carefree, his wide, strong jaw typically smiling or relaxed, Rick so self-contained, with care and responsibility written into the geography of his narrow, thin-lipped face.

When alone I played my favorite tapes, loudly. I went into rapturous trances of concentration as Richard Thompson's passionate voice, then Joni Mitchell's silvery sound, then Paul Simon's lyricism filled the little cab. Dance routines composed themselves in my body and mind the way that birds flocks create great, shimmering formations in the sky when migrating north for the summer. I danced with my butt in place on the truck's black bench seat, or mostly in place, trying to keep my right foot steady on the accelerator. Shoulder-shimmies worked well, as did arm and hand movements, as long as they were with the arm and hand not on the steering wheel. Body waves and undulations were more dangerous because they tended to kick my right foot forward. When I almost rear-ended a red Jaguar just south of the Oregon border, I sighed and dialed the volume down as well as the intensity of my movements.

Tonight in my dance studio, most of us hung out and chatted after "Best Of My Love" ended. We sat the floor, sweaty and complete, some of us stretching languidly, noses to knees, toes pointed. After everyone finished collecting their things and went out into the cool autumn night, the studio was absolutely quiet. I missed Sonny the most at these times, when things became still. I stayed another two hours, working at my desk with stacks of bills, my checkbook and a calculator. Money was always on my mind when I wasn't dancing.

The phone was ringing as I walked into the house a little after ten p.m. It was Sonny. "My darling! La la la la la la la la!" I trilled happily to him, plopping onto the couch. We talked almost every day, but I still got excited over it every time. Being married felt wonderful.

I loved our house too, despite living alone. We had looked at three houses our first day in Portland, including a huge farmhouse-style, fixer-upper in Southeast. It was built in 1929, and Sonny thought it a marvelous place, seeing its possibilities like the carpenter he was. But I had been repelled by its sagginess and smell of mildew. I would be starting a business, fixing up a dance studio that wouldn't be a studio to begin with, and living alone for the first month, and I wanted my home to be a refuge from projects and problem solving, not a site for more of those. I found and then championed this two-bedroom craftsman's house near Forest Park in Northwest Portland. It was set back from the street and had so many tall trees surrounding it that I felt we were in our own small forest. I loved it, Sonny less so, because it was relatively new and didn't cry out for his own craftsman's abilities.

"No wonder Californians want to move here," Sonny remarked at the price. He had paid first and last month's rent plus a $500 security deposit in cash, which had sent our landlord's eyebrows into his forehead. But she'd accepted the thick wad of bills when we'd explained we didn't yet have a local bank account.

When we unpacked I'd practically worked circles around Rick and Sonny, placing dishes in kitchen cabinets and sheets in closets with fast-footed, fevered eagerness. By the time I took Sonny to church with me for the first time we had great stacks of flattened cardboard boxes to be recycled, and our first household as husband and wife. That night I made love with Sonny in our new bedroom inside our private forest with even more ardor than usual, feeling silky and abundant as a goddess.

"How was your day?" Sonny asked me now.

"Good, but hard."

"You always say that," he said. I could hear him smiling a thousand miles away.

"Yes I do. The sub-letters are on me again. They lose their keys; they want new keys. It's too hot; it's too cold. We need more fans; the fans are in the way. We need more space heaters; the space heaters are in the way. Where did their yoga mats go? We need a lost and found; why isn't there an official lost and found?" Before I was done, Sonny was laughing. But I'd barely gotten started. "I'm starting to think it might be better to rent to talky-type groups, like writers' circles or twelve step groups. You know, people who don't need to keep so much weird judo junk and New Age healing equipment lying around. I love all these creative types, but they're really high maintenance. Plus they sweat, and they say, 'why don't you get a shower installed?', and I say, 'Uh, be*cause*, it'd cost 7,000 dollars that I don't *have*.'"

"People always want more. They'll always ask for more," Sonny said sympathetically. "A lot of it isn't doable on the budget you've got."

"Keep talking. I need advice," I said, going to the kitchen. I picked up an apple and bit into it. Meals on any steady schedule were a thing of the past.

"A flat 'no' never works. It just makes people argue with you," he said. "You have to give them choices, let them see that they're choosing one thing over another."

"So . . . they're choosing low prices over getting to take a shower?"

"Exactly! You're a quick study!" I was laughing along with Sonny.

"I love you, sweetheart. I do," I said after we'd settled down. I remembered the work-party Sonny had led in order to convert the Hawthorne retail space into a dance studio, how his corded, ropy-muscled forearms had looked as he'd hammered nails into wood. "Men love to help," Marisol had remarked as she set up colorful screens to create a small office space. "Yep!" Sonny had happily agreed. It was true. Sonny loved helping me.

"I love you too. You give good phone," Sonny said. His voice was a deep purr in my ear.

"Thanks. But I'm looking forward to not giving you any more phone soon." I was alluding to his moving. Sonny had finally finished the Chapman remodel, after two unanticipated delays and extensions.

"We're going to be looking at a little more phone," Sonny said in a different tone. My stomach went acid. I set the half-eaten apple down. "I got offered a new project. It's another kitchen. Mrs. Chapman's neighbor liked my work so much when she saw it that she hired me on the spot. We can't turn this down, Elly; we need the money. But I'll come visit you before I start the job. I promise."

I ground the tip of my big right toe into the kitchen floor until it hurt. I felt immensely tired and was fighting back tears, but I didn't want to complain when Sonny was working so hard to support us, and support my dancing.

"What are you thinking?" Sonny finally asked.

"I'm thinking that some people are single mothers," I said. "But I seem to be a single wife."

Chapter 15
Intimacy

"Horsey, go there!" my former housemate cried into my ear. Gaylin was riding on my back and pointing imperiously to the large living room of Fideles House. Sonny stood beside me. It was the Sunday between Christmas and New Years. We were having a party now that the evening worship service was over. Gaylin's mother Jenny and her Canadian husband were visiting Portland for the holidays, and Sonny and I had hosted them for dinner the night before. I was able to feel deeply happy for Jenny now that I was married too. It was my goal to become pregnant within the new year of 1993.

"Honey, you've been riding this horse for ten minutes," I said, turning my head to nuzzle his face. "You're a lot bigger than you used to be."

"New horse!" Gaylin cried. He raised his arms to Sonny like a Pony Express rider seeking a fresh mount. Within seconds, they were galloping into the living room, Gaylin shrieking with delight. Sonny was a taller, much stronger horse. I smiled and went to the kitchen to help Marisol and Sister Sandy set the food out. Sister Sandy had hulking shoulders over skinny hips and legs, and wore a tousled brown 1950's style wig. She towered over Marisol in her tottery black pumps.

"I'm so poor, I can't even pay attention," she declared in her deep, agitated voice. The poverty was credible, with runs in both the legs of her flesh-colored stockings and her aura of good-natured distress. Marisol nodded sympathetically as she cut spinach and kalamata olives for quiche. I mixed hot chocolate, the real kind with pure cocoa, sugar and a pinch of salt. The kids would get candy canes as stir-sticks. The adults could spike theirs with Peppermint Schnapps. Sister Sandy arranged Christmas cookies haphazardly on a platter as she launched into a tale.

"I was riding the Max train downtown and this man had had one too many. I mean, he was sloshed, and so was his friend. They sat down on either side of me since those were the only two seats left. That seems to happen a lot when I ride Max, don't know why that is. Anyway, they were talking across me and practically falling into my lap. I'm thinking to myself: how do you spell irritating? So after a little bit of that I said, 'Here, let me trade seats with you so you can sit together.' And we did. And this drunk man said, 'That's so nice of you. I love you!'" And I said, "Right back at ya, honey!"

Marisol and I laughed. Sister Sandy was an original. When Sonny had initially seen her on his first visit to Fideles he was puzzled as he watched her from across the room. "Oh. She used to be a he," he then said with sudden clarity. I had nodded, glad for his neutral, accepting tone. Paul, standing next to me, had remarked, "We have a high tolerance for weird around here."

"Me too," Sonny had replied. "That's why I'm feeling at home."

He and Pastor Rachel had taken a liking to each other when they first met in July. My tall lean husband had crouched down on his elbows at the dinner table to be eye-to-eye with the forty-something black woman who was almost as wide as she was tall. Rachel's partner Christina, fair-skinned as Snow White but with aviator glasses like Gloria Steinem's, had also seemed drawn in by Sonny's charisma.

Rachel's sermon tonight had been about intimacy. She said to think of the word as into-me-see. "It's risky to let someone see into us," she said in her gravelly, androgynous voice. "That person will see before very long that we are riddled with flaws, just like dogs have fleas and lawns have weeds. We can't hide those flaws. And it might be too much for them. Yes: we might get rejected—that's the cold reality of intimacy." I had met eyes with Paul across the room.

We both smiled wryly. Lena, his former wife, had finally left Portland altogether, after reuniting with him briefly in the fall. I knew Paul was hurting, which felt unfair. He was probably the best man I knew, full of love, full of fire, full of humor.

"But God has built us to be close to each other, and to yearn for God. God and the Son want intimacy with us, they want to see into us and to be seen by us. But we tend to turn away. We feel we're too ugly to be seen into and still be loved, after being seen like that. We run away a lot from intimacy. I've run away a lot from intimacy." She smiled at Christina to her left, who winked at her. They had celebrated their fourteenth anniversary while I was in California. "But the good news, part of the gospel that Jesus brought, is that we can build our capacity for intimacy." Rachel's dark, expressive face radiated hope and confidence. "It's the same way that athletes build their capacity to run marathons. When you keep running farther, you gain the ability to keep running farther still. You feel tired, but the tiredness doesn't dismay you. You can push back against it." I nodded, knowing that feeling. "We can build our intimacy skills so that we're equipped for the hard times, the way that expectant mothers train to give birth in Lamaze classes. Giving birth is hard, and being well prepared for it makes you less overwhelmed by it, and more successful at it." I felt like she had written this sermon just for me.

"We're frightened to be close to each other more than briefly," Rachel continued. "Into-me-see? Scary! Risky! We chase after material riches instead. We buy stuff. Does anyone here know what the biggest predictor of human happiness actually is?"

"Having the most toys?" Luke called out.

"No, having the biggest toys!" Sister Sandy said, rolling her eyes to show she was being silly, too.

"It's the number and quality of relationships in our lives," Rachel said. "Our relationships with each other. Our ability to be in community and to be intimate with each other, these are the biggest factors for our happiness. We distract ourselves from relationships by being busy." She paused to sip water from a clear glass. "Having a million things to do is the classic excuse for not having a steady prayer life, for not being intimate with God. It's also the most common excuse for not being intimate with our families. It takes time to sit still and really listen to our child or spouse." She was pacing now, the energy building. "I'm telling you, intimacy is hard. And insisting that we're needed elsewhere is our culture's favorite way to avoid it." She paused, and her gaze rested neutrally on Sonny, sitting next to me. I turned to look at him, too. He tucked his chin down and looked up beseechingly at Rachel at the same time, the classic face of the repentant bad boy.

"But the truth is that we are needed right here!" she shouted, actually jumping up and thumping her considerable weight back down on the floor. "In the house of Christ. Here! We! Are! Christ is calling us into intimacy with him. Into-me-see." She was on a roll, speaking in cadence, her voice and arms flowing like water. "Christ wants us to come to him exactly as we are, wanting to forgive us for our flaws and sins. We just need to offer up our brokenness to be mended. We don't have to stumble around in our aloneness, our lack of closeness, our lack of intimacy. No! No!" Her movements and voice slowed down now, became softer.

"When he taught us to take communion, Christ was saying: please be intimate with me. He is saying this very night to us: Please: into-me-see." Rachel now stood stock-still. We watched her, barely breathing. "As we take communion," she almost whispered, "I ask that you reflect that Christ is saying, personally, *to you*, into-me-see."

Christina played the guitar as we sang "One Bread, One Body" and formed a circle to take communion. I thrilled to the lovely, river-like melody and looked sideways at Sonny. He was riveted on the chalice and platter holding the big, rustic loaf of bread. His face, deeply tanned from the southern California sun, stood out among us pale northerners. His eyes blazed bright blue, and he looked about as fully alive as a person could be. I was flooded by love for him.

My turn came and I stood in front of Rachel, who was even

shorter than me, broad-shouldered and barrel-chested in her man's black dress shirt and colorful minister's stole. She eyed me with a joyful gravity.

"Revelle, this is the body and blood of Christ, given for you." I looked fully back at her, nodded, then tore a piece of the thick, fleshy bread from the loaf and dipped it into the chalice of grape juice that Luke had made by hand. Jesus was whispering in my ear, *Into-me-see.*

"Amen," I replied, then put the juicy piece of bread into my mouth.

⚜

Paul came to my dance class the following morning since school was out. I hugged him close when he walked in the door, grateful that I had actually arrived on time, and he hadn't had to wait outside in the cold. Since Sonny had arrived a week before Christmas, I had already missed one of my own dance classes and been late to two others. If he felt like making love or making an elaborate meal when it was time for me to leave for the studio, he detained me, dismissing the idea that I had a set schedule. "You're not a wage slave anymore," he laughed when I protested. "You're the boss now. You get there when you get there." Seeing as little of Sonny as I did, I generally yielded to him to avoid conflict, despite my resentment. But my students and sub-letters were starting to give me funny looks. I'd become someone they weren't sure they could trust. The eczema on my hands flared up during Sonny's visits, and I tried to ignore that, too.

One student that never gave me funny looks was John, dancing this morning between Paul and Deirdre. He was my best student in December, if I defined best by attendance. John was a gaunt, almost bald fellow in his late fifties who came to my morning classes like clockwork. He was the first person to buy a month's pass of unlimited classes for $60 up front. He turned out to be the only person who would do that until March, which made me like him very much all winter.

John danced, or rather flailed his way through the songs like a marionette puppet operated by a drunken sailor. I frequently worried he would fall on his face or careen into a fellow dancer who couldn't muster evasive action quickly enough. My first thought upon seeing him stumble around ecstatically to music had been that the Candid Camera crew had crept into my studio. The premise of the episode was clear: How would a dance teacher respond to a spectacularly bad dancer? Would I call the paramedics to put them on standby? Maybe take him aside to tutor him on balancing techniques? Or would I just rush to raise the limits on the studio's liability insurance? His awkward love for dance was touching. Sometimes it almost moved me to tears. Other times it triggered laughter that I quickly converted into coughing.

This morning we did spinning turns during the chorus of "Baker Street," John perambulating in his happy, haphazard way and Paul moving across the floor in his big-bodied, dignified, tuba-like way. On the third reverse of direction he sustained a minor collision with John, who appeared to have completely lost track of where he was in the universe. Paul stayed on his feet and even caught the smaller man's hand, keeping him from falling. John apologized profusely before launching into more impassioned spins. Deirdre eyed him warily and kept a prudent distance on the other side of the room. I laugh/coughed and kept going, remembering what Rachel sometimes said before communion: "All are welcome here."

Paul lingered after class to visit. We sat in my little office behind the colorful screens and propped our feet on my bill-strewn desk.

"We need back-story on John," I said. "I think that he used to be a monk. I think he lived for decades in a secluded order in the Oregon countryside."

"OK," Paul nodded, rubbing his beard. We were playing a favorite game from grad school. "I can see the monks keeping bees and selling honey. The jars have good, plain labels that radiate integrity."

"Yes! Then John visits his relatives in the city, and some lively young niece introduces him to rock music. And he has an epiphany.

He discovers that he lives in a *physical body*, a body that can move and produce pleasure, pleasure that God would *actually bless*."

"Oh, yes," Paul picked it up. "And so he abandons his solitary monk's cell for the music-riddled city. He lands, disoriented but ecstatic, at Dancing Fool, where his niece had suggested he might find relief for his new condition."

"And relief he has found," I said soberly.

"The other monks understand he has a new calling now. And God loves John."

"More than ever," I said, feelingly. But the moment needed more. "Amen," I nodded with conviction.

"And the people said—" Paul cued us, raising his arms—

"AMEN!" we shouted in unison, raising our hands high and clapping them together. After Paul left, I worked on my bills. There was the Home Depot credit card on which the studio's renovations had been built, my student loans, the large, lingering dentist bill from my root canal of three months ago. The heating bill for the studio was frightening. A stern letter advised me that my undergraduate student loan from Pitzer was supposed to have been paid in full within ten years after I graduated. That was laughable. I added everything up. I was $9,058 dollars in debt and sinking farther every month, even with Sonny paying the rent on the house.

On New Year's morning a group of us went for a hike in Forest Park: Marisol and her family, Jenny and her family, Paul, Sonny and I. It was overcast and in the low 40's, but going uphill on the Wildwood Trail warmed us. Sonny, Gaylin, Carmenita and I felt frisky and forged ahead, the kids periodically coaxing us into being their horses, since it gave them better views and helped them keep up with us.

"Those ferns are growing right out of that tree!" Gaylin exclaimed from Sonny's back. "That's weird! That's cool!"

"Wow!" Carmenita said from my back. Gaylin's observation was true: ferns were growing, startlingly, from the massive trunks of the Douglas fir trees. They waved gracefully at us in the chilly breeze like celebrities from floats in the Rose Parade.

"The ferns have an unexpected home. Kind of like you, up in British Columbia," I noted to Gaylin, remembering how worried he had been about having to move from Portland.

"Yeah, kind of," he said cheerfully. Jenny had told me that he and his new best friend were inseparable. "Things came apart, then came back together for me, like you said they would."

"Like they did for you, too," Sonny said to me. He leaned over and kissed me on the lips.

"Don't do that!" Carmenita exclaimed, squirming on my back. She grasped my face on either side and pointed it to the left. "What kind of ferns are those?" she asked me, pointing to the lush, thick growth on the steep hillside.

"Those are sword ferns," Sonny began.

"Not you!" Carmenita protested. "I asked her!" She had never liked Sonny, for some reason.

"I think I see three different kinds of ferns," I said. "Sword ferns and some deer ferns. And those delicate ones with the dark stems are called maidenhair ferns."

"I like the maidenhair ones the best," Carmenita declared. I could see Marisol's emphatic nature in her daughter, feel the strength of her will through our joined bodies.

"I like Revelle the best," Sonny said, a little too loudly, then glared at her. He was irritated by the child's dislike, but I didn't try to smooth things over. I could feel myself pulling away from him. He'd leave tomorrow. At one time I couldn't bear to sleep without him. Now, I resented that he came and went on his own terms. I was eager to be on time every morning to my studio again. Sonny hadn't even pretended to look for work during this visit. It seemed that our Portland house was his vacation spot, and his mother's house in Anaheim was his home.

The ferns growing from the tree, supported by the thick trunk, made me remember the bougainvillea in the calendar-photo the night I'd agreed to marry Sonny. The crimson-flowered vine had covered most of a wall, and been wholly supported by the white adobe building. Back then, I had been the bougainvillea and Sonny the solid building.

I was in love with Sonny as much as ever. But that New Year's Day in Forest Park, I gazed at the ferns growing on the hillside and thought, I am not the bougainvillea any more. I am the maidenhair fern, with my own roots in the ground and fellow ferns all around me.

Chapter 16
Dancing Fool

"OK, I know it's chilly in here," I told my group one winter evening. "But in ten minutes we're going to be really warm." These pep talks were a nightly necessity. Some people had their arms wrapped around their bodies. Deirdre was jumping up and down, stiff bodied as a pogo stick. I didn't recognize the towering young fellow with shaggy blonde hair.

"I'm Revelle." I smiled at him. "What's your name?"

"Taylor." The man had a lilting voice and pronounced his name with absolutely no 'r' at the end. He was the biggest person I had ever seen in my studio. His large white teeth, golden tan and cheerful scruffiness made him look like Hawthorne's version of a Hollywood movie star. But no Portlander had a tanned face in February.

"Glad you're here. Where are you from, Taylor?"

"New Zealand," he grinned.

"Cool," I said. "Portland needs more Kiwis."

"Oh right on," he said, beaming bigger and displaying a faceful of dimples. Deirdre had stopped jumping up and down and was holding still, watching him like a cat. I hurried to start the music.

"We've got a beach theme tonight!" I announced from the stereo in the corner. "Let's free-dance for the warm-up." The Beachboys' "Little Surfer Girl" flooded the room with its wistful, dreamy sounds.

I started doing deep stretching lunges. In the mirror I saw Taylor's huge body in sky-blue sweatpants and raggedy t-shirt, moving his arms above and around his head in wavy, floaty, feminine motions. I struggled not to stare. Deirdre was striding around the perimeter of the group with her usual intent expression, long auburn braid swishing like a horse's tail. Taylor started mincing and twirling amongst the other dancers, then leapt into the air to execute a sudden pirouette, arms akimbo. He was a parody of a prototypical he-man doing ballet. Laughter bubbled dangerously in me, and I turned away from him in order to quell it. I was grateful for every paying student who walked in the door, and didn't want to offend one of them for a second. I kept dancing.

⚜

"Taylor is hot," Deirdre said flatly. We sat at the Oasis Café after class, warm from our dancing. She was eating pepperoni pizza and I had a glass of Pinot Noir. I'd decided it would be codependent to keep joining Sonny in not drinking when he lived a thousand miles away.

"I could see that," I said in a neutral tone.

"But weird," she added.

I shrugged. "I've got a high tolerance for weird." I sipped my wine. Earlier in the evening I had watched Deirdre arguing with a man in a suit outside the studio. He evidently thought Deirdre had taken his parking place. "I don't think so," she retorted. "Well, I do," he replied. "Well, I'm not impressed by your designer suit," she shot back. "*And*, I'm not afraid of my *anger!*" she bellowed, leaning toward him. He had shaken his head and walked away, muttering something about anarchists.

"That's so great you can have one glass of wine and not want a hundred more," Deirdre said now. "I've been clean and sober for seventeen months. It's a hard road. People make assumptions about you. Like, everyone always thinks if you're in recovery you fucked everyone in sight when you were drinking."

"Really? My friend Paul's in recovery. I never assumed that about him."

"He's a guy. Nobody cares if they fuck around or not. There's a stigma when you're a woman." She wiped her mouth with her napkin. "But drinking never made me horny," she continued. "I went straight into anger. I'd have a few drinks and start in on anyone who pissed me off."

"What got you into recovery?" I asked.

"I had the choice between ten years in prison or getting treatment. I'd gone after a cop with a baseball bat," she replied, popping the last bite of pizza into her mouth.

"Whoa." I could picture her, hot-eyed, her lean body in attack mode, the embodiment of a she-warrior, only going after the wrong enemy. My thighs felt a rush of warmth from the alcohol; I was drinking on an empty stomach.

"Mind if I join you?" a lilting, half-familiar voice said from far above our heads. We looked up to see Taylor's tanned face dimpling at us. Deirdre gave me a panic-stricken look, a Celtic lass caught in the headlights. I decided she was mute but not endangered.

"Sure," I said cheerfully. He sat down next to me with a glass of amber beer, and I scooched my chair toward the wall to make the needed room for his shoulders. "The more the merrier," I added, to make up for Deirdre's silence. He glanced at her hands and mine, which were all resting on the table. I rubbed under my wedding ring, where the skin tended to itch from eczema.

"So, wow, great class! And you're quite a dancer," he said to Deirdre, who responded by looking out the window. I tried to ESP her a message: this is where you say thank you. It didn't work; she said nothing. After an awkward silence, Taylor tried again.

"I heard about *Dancing Fool* at the youth hostel down the street. That's where I'm staying while I get my feet under me. Just arrived two days ago." He drained half his beer.

"Oh, I stayed in the hostel when I first got to the States, too!" Deirdre suddenly perked up. "I'm from Ireland."

"Oh right on!" Taylor returned to his default expression: a delighted, dimpled smile.

"The coffeehouse where I work loves our kind of accent," Deirdre disclosed further. "They don't expect you to have a green card either."

"No!" Taylor leaned forward, fully encouraged. By now, Deirdre had visibly relaxed. There was no longer a hint of femininity in Taylor, and it was hard to believe he danced as he did. I sipped my smoky wine and glanced at the door as they chatted. A man in a trench coat and red scarf entered, letting in a rush of cold air, and I went as still as Deirdre had gone earlier on her first sight of Taylor. High cheekbones, olive skin, eyes large and luminous. It was the man I'd seen coming in the door on what had turned out to be my last spring at Prentice. My stomach tightened, for no reason that made sense, and I tried not to stare at him as he ordered. He was smiling, maybe joking with the woman behind the counter. He looked as good in profile as he had full on in that brief, devastating moment in 1991. Why was this man so compelling to me? The man I knew-but-didn't collected his pizza and left with another influx of wintry air.

I finished my wine and told Deirdre and Taylor goodnight. They were still chatting as I walked back to tidy the studio for the wild-eyed judo instructor who had it the next morning at 6:30.

ॐ

"Revelle, your feet are brutal," Paul said. "I want to take another go at them."

We were sprawled in Marisol's living room—Marisol, Ruben, Carmenita, Paul and me. I was almost horizontal in the easy chair with Carmenita lying on me face-up, eyes closed like a person who had peacefully fainted. It was a Sunday night in March, and in church earlier we had done the foot-washing ritual, each of us kneeling at the feet of the person to our right with a low plastic tub of warm water and a towel before allowing the person to our left to do the same for us. I had felt devastated by Carmenita's little-girl feet, so dainty and firm and sweet in my hands that I had wanted to bend over and kiss their heels and arches and tiny toes. Her feet had sent me into such a wave of child-hunger that it hadn't occurred to me that Paul might have had any particular reaction to washing my own feet.

"What do you mean, my feet are brutal?" The weight of Carmenita's body felt wonderfully heavy on mine, like the palm of God holding me in place, keeping me from floating away with fatigue. Whatever Paul was proposing, I had no intention of moving.

"Your heels are cracked. Your toenails are overgrown. They're like the feet of a homeless person." Paul's voice was indignant. Carmenita stirred, looking up into my face as if for an explanation. I shrugged, not knowing what to say. Marisol met my eyes, smiled, and resumed mending a pair of socks. We'd always shared a strong work ethic, and not been overly concerned about how we looked.

"There's a tub and some towels under the kitchen sink," Ruben said mildly. Paul disappeared. Minutes later my feet were in deliciously hot, soapy water, and he was clipping my toenails. I loved the feel of his hands on my feet.

"I invited Sonny to join my men's group," Paul offered. My eyebrows shot up with interest. I loved the idea of a group of men confronting Sonny, holding him accountable for his actions. It would be much more powerful than a single wife bringing things up to him.

"And?"

"He said it sounded great," Paul replied. "Then he changed the subject. Then he went back to California."

"So he does that with you, too," I said lightly, staring up at the ceiling. "Can I make a confession about my *Dancing Fool* studio?" I asked the room in general.

"Confessions are welcome here," Marisol said, suddenly at my side. She gave a green bottle to Paul. "Lavender lotion," she stated, like an operating room nurse, and retreated to the couch.

"I had no idea I would be spending most of my time being a businesswoman, just trying to keep the studio going," I said. "I got into this whole thing for the dancing. But I only spend about 10% of my time actually dancing. The rest of it's the bills and the marketing and the crazy sub-letters."

"A little worse than teaching," Marisol mused from back on the couch. "80% of our time on the bureaucracy and the classroom management, 20% on the actual subject we're teaching."

"I think I'm hitting 22% by now," Paul said. More rubbing of my arches, more sighs of pleasure from me. Presently he said in a speculative tone, "Ruben, I think you should consider joining my men's group."

After a minute, Ruben said in his slow, thoughtful way, "I think I need to go back to California."

Everybody laughed except me, Carmenita cracking up in a sudden, convulsive way that hurt since she was on my stomach. Paul kept massaging my brutal feet, which felt fabulous, even as Carmenita had almost knocked the wind out of me.

※

"When are you going to move up and live with me?" I asked Sonny. My tone was wrong, though, too negative, and I wanted to kick myself. The phone was cold in my hand while I paced the studio in my bare feet. It was late. Everyone was gone and the lights were low. I could feel grit and other tiny detritus on the hardwood floor, and it crossed my mind to mop the floor, as I often did during phone conversations. I was getting a cold silence.

"Let me start over again," I said. I felt a headache coming on. I held my forehead, trying to remember the syntax the self-help books taught for expressing negative emotions. "When you keep visiting me instead of moving up and living with me like you promised," I began carefully, "I feel like I'm your mistress instead of your wife."

"You want to know when I'm going to move up? As soon as you get a job," Sonny said unexpectedly. I stopped dead in my tracks.

"I *have* a job. I've been working my ass off!" I said hotly.

"So have I. I'm the only one making any money though. If you would get a B-job with an actual paycheck to cover the rent and bills, I could move up and have a chance to get my business off the ground in Portland."

I paced the floor again, pausing now and then to rub the irritating grains of dirt off the soles of each foot onto the top of the other foot. I loved my dance studio; I had never felt so alive and excited and challenged as I had since starting it. Getting the business off the ground occupied sixty hours a week. Being responsible to a paycheck-job would sabotage its success. But Sonny did have a point.

"I'm willing to get a part-time teaching job once you move up here," I said. "I'm not willing to both put my dance career on the back-burner and *also* keep living by myself."

"You have to trust me," he said, voice turning silky. "You're not trusting me, Revelle."

That's because you're not trustworthy, I thought. But a person couldn't say that to her husband.

"Why haven't you ever looked for work while you're up here in Portland?" I said. My tone was tinged with anger, devoid of the healthy detachment that Al-Anon taught. I hadn't been to a single meeting since returning to Oregon.

"When I'm in Portland I'm on vacation," he replied. "It's the only time I have with my wife. I'm not about to work 60 hours a week down here and then pound the pavement up in Portland looking for a job, and then ricochet back to Anaheim to start all over again. I'm not a slave."

We went back and forth, Sonny wanting me to get a paycheck-job in order for him to move up, me countering that we could budget our money and save for him to move up, at which point I'd be willing to get a paycheck-job and do *Dancing Fool* part-time. He argued that budgets had never worked for him, that his work was too unpredictable in nature for that.

"No," I said, "*you're* too unpredictable in nature for that."

"OK, you're right, Revelle," he said. "I'm too scatter-brained for a regular job. I show up late, I lose good tools, I get mad at the wrong person, they fire me. That's why I've got to be self-employed. I don't have a choice. But you have a choice. You're able to pull off a regular job. You just don't want to."

"My last regular job ended very painfully," I reminded him. "I'm only willing to risk all that again if I have a husband who chooses me over his mother."

"You need to get help for your jealousy," he said in his patient, saintly voice. "If she weren't willing to let me live here for free, I wouldn't be able to pay the rent on the Portland house every month."

We kept circling round and round. We both thrived on being self-employed, the creativity and autonomy of it. We both said we wanted to live together in the Portland house. But the more we talked, the more I got a mental picture of his Anaheim life being quite pleasant for him, and his potential Portland life being just plain harder. And he didn't want the harder life.

"Let's talk another time when we're both calmer," I finally said, choking back tears. After we hung up, I sank to the dance floor, grit and all, and tried to soothe myself by stretching.

The phone rang. "Are you OK?" It was Marisol, with lots of noise in the background.

"Barely."

"Did the judo instructor raid your cash drawer, tie you up with leggings and leave you for dead?"

"No. I had another fight with Sonny."

"You'd told me you were meeting me and Paul here at the Laurelthirst tonight," she said. "You were supposed to be here at nine, when the band was starting. It's quarter till ten."

I smacked my forehead. "Marisol, I completely forgot. I'm so sorry."

"Can you come over now?"

""I can't. I've still got more to do here. I'm really sorry." Silence ensued. "I seem to be saying I'm sorry a lot, don't I?"

"Yes, you've been saying that a lot," she said. "It started after you married Sonny."

"Then maybe I'm sorry for that, too," I said, a throwaway remark to appease the friend I had stood up. After we said good-bye I finished cleaning the floor, balanced the checkbook, and paid the bills that were keeping *Dancing Fool* afloat. I got home after midnight. By five the next morning, I was wide-awake with adrenaline, anxious that my husband might never live with me, and anxious about getting more paying students through the door of *Dancing Fool*. I had more control over the second thing than the first, so that was where I decided to put my energy.

One rainy, gray afternoon at the beginning of April I got out of my truck to lead my 5:30 class and noticed the door to the Camelot Theater was open. It was just 4:45, and I remembered my recurring vision of doing an original show in a small theater. My feet had traveled through the door into the small lobby. A man, tall and pencil-thin in a bright purple sweater and skin-tight black jeans was standing in the middle of a ladder, taking down posters in a rather haphazard manner. He was reaching too far to the right, trying to avoid coming all the way down and moving the ladder over. I worried he would fall.

"May I help you with that, sir?" I reached up to take the posters that were flopping and waving under his left arm.

"Oh, hello," the man said, handing the posters down, as a tired parent might hand rambunctious children over to their babysitter. I organized the floppy, willful posters into a straight stack while he got down, moved the ladder to the right and took down the remaining two. I added these to the stack, rolled them all together neatly and handed them to him.

"Travis Dekum, at your service," he smiled and extended his hand. "Or rather, you've been at my service, most kindly. Thank you!"

"Revelle Jones Champagne. I'm your neighbor at *Dancing Fool*, a couple blocks down." I shook his hand. "Pleasure to meet you. I take it you work here?"

"I fear I'm the manager. Actually responsible for the place, but don't tell anybody," he whispered dramatically, eyebrows raised in mock alarm. He was clearly gay. I liked him.

"I shan't tell anybody. But there is something I shall tell you." He leaned in with an attentive expression, and I spoke in a confidential tone. "I appear to be a standard-issue, thirty-something female Portlander. But that is just my disguise. I am actually an innovative dancer, gifted at both choreography and performance. Some have compared me to the young Isadora Duncan. I suggest I do a show in your theater," I concluded boldly, looking him in the eye. I had no definite plan for what this show would contain. My heart was beating fast and my breath was short. Travis's smile widened. His face said he was interested.

Two hours later I had secured my show. Travis had followed me to my studio and watched me lead the first half of my class, exuberantly joining in on "YMCA" when we started shaping the letters with our bodies. We watched each other across the room, playing off each other's campy moves, cracking each other up. Before he left he caught my eye, winked, and gave me the thumbs-up sign. I smiled hugely, pressing my palms together in front of my heart before bowing in thanks. Later I joined him in his chaotic office, and we shook hands on four shows starting on August 7th. I watched him write them into his big desk calendar in bold, extravagant handwriting.

That evening as I drove across the Willamette River to my empty home, my body was bursting with energy, my head with ideas. All my memories became suffused with joy in the radiant light that landing my first show cast on my life. All my memories became suffused with joy in the radiant light that landing my first show cast on my life. I remembered Disneyland, and Baroque Hoedown. I wanted to create dance contagion in my show's audience like I'd done that magical night. What was it Sonny had said after I'd won little Cammie's trust and gotten her reunited with her mother? His words had felt like a key of some kind. It had related to my instincts.

My eyes fell on a sign that warned against air-borne diseases. Born! Sonny had said I was born for that, born to be a mother. I screamed with excitement in the truck like a winner of a grand prize. The name of my show would be *Born For This*.

Chapter 17
Betrayal

"This is a real mess," I said, my voice low since not everybody had left yet. Paul and I were washing the pots and pans side by side after church one Sunday evening. Sister Sandy, who really shouldn't be allowed to cook even under Pastor Rachel's supervision, I felt, had let the split pea soup burn. I was scrubbing at the hard brown stuff on the bottom.

"You mean your marriage is a mess?" Paul said.

"No," I said, irritated. "This soup pot that burned."

"Oh." He didn't sound at all apologetic, just kept scrubbing the bottom of the similarly charred rice pot. We had all discussed pitching in for Kentucky Fried Chicken when the damage to the dinner had become evident. We'd finally decided that only the soup and rice at the bottom were burned and inedible. Our eating the unburned parts for dinner had surely spared Sister Sandy's feelings. But Marisol and some others had headed out with purposeful body language soon after the service was over, and Paul and I were pretty sure where. "When is Sonny's next visit, anyway?" Paul asked.

"Next weekend. I think."

"You think." Paul made an exasperated sound. "You know, lots of guys would treat you better than Sonny is doing. Why are you still with him, Revelle?"

"You know those vows I took that day last year?" I said sarcastically. "They didn't include 'until a better offer comes along.'"

"The vows didn't include either that you'd permanently live in separate states and . . ."

"We're not permanently living in separate states!" I pushed the hair back from my face with my upper arm since my hands were wet and soapy. I felt frustrated and misunderstood. "Look, I like being married. I'm at a time in my life that it feels right to be married. I don't want to be single."

"But you *are* single. The marriage license and adding Champagne to your name aren't making any difference."

I stopped scrubbing the pot and glared at him. "You're just cynical because things didn't work out with Lena."

"No, I'm smarter because things didn't work out with Lena. Remember, you're the one who said Jenny had been a single mother, but you're a single wife."

I felt slapped. Tears sprang to my eyes. "Why are you being such a jerk?" I said. Or maybe I kind of yelled it.

"I'm on your side, Revelle. I'd rather be married than single, too. It's wonderful to go to bed every night with someone you love, and cuddle and talk about your day. But that's not what's happening for you."

"But I think it still can!" I cried. We had both abandoned the burnt-bottomed pots and were facing each other, wet hands dripping onto the floor. "You didn't see what Sonny was like in California! He loves me like a . . . like a rock!"

But Paul had been at the wedding. He had seen what Sonny was like. Now he just looked at me steadily, his brown eyes hard and soft at the same time as my face burned with humiliation. He thought me pitiable.

"OK," Paul finally said with a shrug, turning back to the rice pot. He might as well have said, "Go ahead, keep playing the fool." I wanted to smack him in the face and throw myself into his arms and cry, all at the same time.

⁂

"Your dancing was excellent. Innovative indeed," the tall Asian fellow said in an incongruous British accent. We were at the

University of Portland, and I had just led a sample dance class, trying to lure people from the stately red-bricked campus in North Portland down to the funky Southeast world of *Dancing Fool*. This fellow had not danced, but instead had peered through the door, and then stepped in to watch for the last ten minutes. He looked both dignified and young in his clean jeans and corduroy sport coat, so I couldn't tell if he was a professor or a student who dressed well.

"Thank you," I said, still breathing a little hard. He was clearly making a point of meeting me. I was conscious that my dance camisole left my throat and neck exposed, so that I was partly undressed, at least compared to him. I smoothed my wildish, ever-challenging hair away from my face.

"My name is Jason," he said. He extended his hand and I shook it, a strong, gentle hand. Neither of us was in a hurry to let go. "I'm the captain of the rugby team," he added, as if I'd asked what he did.

"Ah, rugby," I nodded with interest, though not at the rugby. Our hands continued to connect us.

"'Elegant violence', we say of our sport," Rene said with a shrug meant to be self-deprecating, but that didn't fool me. "I'm from Malaysia, and rugby is popular there. You and I are both athletes, I suppose, just of different types." We finally released hands, light brown fingertips trailing across light brown fingertips. I felt an opening in front of me. If I told him I'd love for him, in particular, to come to one of my dance classes, he probably would. With this kind of animal energy between us, one thing could easily lead to another. And I wouldn't be so damned lonely, for at least one night.

"Well, Jason," I said, taking a step backward to break the spell. "It's a pleasure to meet you."

"Likewise," he nodded, head inclined like a courtier. I could almost believe that he could make violence elegant. I felt his eyes on me as I turned and walked away.

"That was great. It's always great with you," Sonny murmured, his lips against my hair as he held me from behind, two spoons nestled together in the springtime night. He had arrived in his truck at nightfall with an air of heroism, just one day late this time. He'd wanted to make love right after showering and I'd followed his lead, famished for love, touch, sex.

"I landed my first show," I murmured in our warm haven, our nest of two. "I'm super excited about it. It's at the Camelot Theater off of Hawthorne. In July."

"Congratulations." He kissed my neck. "I'm looking forward to it."

"Thanks." That had been the easy part. I summoned my courage now. "At some point we should stop using condoms and see if I can get pregnant," I said softly. The profusion of daffodils, crocuses and rhododendrons were filling the air with birth and fertility, and the jarring talk with Paul and the temptation that Jason had represented were prodding me to start our family. Waiting passively for Sonny to initiate wasn't working. Men had decades in which they could get around to having children, while I, 34 now, had a biological time-clock ticking. Sonny remained silent though, and he wasn't meeting my eyes as I twisted around, trying to engage him.

"We agreed from the beginning that we're going to have children," I reminded him, working hard to keep my voice calm. I knew Paul would scoff at me, but my intuition really told me that if I got pregnant, Sonny would be motivated to move up and live with me.

He rolled onto his back, breaking our embrace, and stared out the window beyond the foot of our bed. I followed his gaze to the tall rhododendron bush outside, silvery grey in the moonlight.

"I already have a child," he said.

The room shape-shifted and I was mute as I tried to find my own shape in the strange new space. Were my toes and fingers all here? Was my waist still narrow, my hips curved?

"Did you hear me?" the stranger said after some time.

"Yes." I felt frightened. "When was it born?"

"Ten years ago." Sonny shifted, turning onto his side toward me. He was suddenly eager to talk, as if I were a counselor who had warmly invited him to unburden himself. "My roommate had had a girlfriend and I had gotten to be friends with her over the months. But then they broke up, you know, the thing where the guy isn't ready to settle down yet. She was lonely and invited me to come over and hang out."

I didn't want to hear this. My body was flooding with shock and fear like it had when I'd gotten the news of my father's cancerous kidney almost two years earlier. But I had to hear this.

"She was Puerto Rican. Her name was Celia. Still is, I guess," he smiled a little. "I'd just gotten dumped myself, so we were drowning our sorrows with beer. Cheap beer, PBR. We got drunk. Then we thought it would a great idea to play strip poker. You know how beer makes every idea seem like the best one you ever had?"

I really didn't. My body was inert as stone next to him, in the dimension I shared with him, but in my heart's dimension I had crashed up against the bedroom wall, thrown there by the news from the soft-voiced stranger.

"So, with most of our clothes off, it seemed like the obvious thing to go ahead and do it, even though we didn't have a condom," Sonny shrugged. "It was the worst sex I ever had. And we never did it again. But she got pregnant and didn't want an abortion. Just my luck."

The understanding came, like a miner's forehead lamp shining into the dark room, why Sonny had always been religious about using condoms with me.

"What about child support?"

"She gave up on it eventually. I didn't have steady work back then. For the first couple of years I helped out. I built them some furniture, and once I bartered to get them a washing machine. I brought groceries over once in awhile, and dolls and toys. I always felt good about helping. But Maria said it wasn't fair for me to do whatever was convenient, when she had to do everything for the kid twenty-four seven, whether or not it was convenient for her. We had words. We haven't talked in years."

"Why didn't you tell me you had a child before we got married?"

He sighed, rolling away onto his back. You knew I wouldn't have married you then, I thought. There isn't an honest bone in your body. My library of unspoken thoughts and feelings now had books tumbling off the shelves, spines broken, pages breaking out, a place in chaos. If I had spoken my mind from the beginning and filled no books with the dishonesty of my silence, could I have avoided the appalling mistake that was my marriage to Sonny?

An hour later I dragged myself through the door of the old Baptist church like a cat someone had kicked to the curb. I hadn't eaten anything since coffee and toast in the morning, but the idea of food was nauseating. I saw no sign to tell me where the meeting was but the sound of feminine voices led me downstairs to a lounge-type rumpus room. I looked around at the outdated red and yellow beanbag chairs on the orange-brown shag carpet. They created images in my mind of horny teenaged members of the youth group getting it on with each other after the long-haired youth pastor who led their Christian rock band left their Wednesday night meetings and went home to his sweet-faced, petite wife. The youth pastor and his wife had both been virgins when they married during college, and whenever one of them now got a lustful crush on a good-looking congregant or coworker, they talked about it. They prayed together to God to make the misplaced lust go away. This actually worked for them, so I hated them for having the problem-solving skills that Sonny and I didn't.

I sank into the corner of a sagging sofa covered with some elderly tweedy material, looking daggers at the mostly middle-aged women sitting peacefully around me. A pretty thirtysomething with a great haircut that framed her face led the meeting. She actually has time for a haircut, I thought with bitter accusation. No way was she self-employed and working 60 hours a week like me.

"My name is Erin," she said. "Hi, Erin," we all said, like empty-minded Stepford wives.

We went around the room with introductions, and I used my real name, after briefly considering an alias. Everybody always remembered Revelle. What if one of them showed up someday at *Dancing Fool*, knowing the sorry state of my life? I tried to stop grinding my teeth.

Erin of the enviable haircut read the twelve steps aloud and the plump woman next to her read the twelve traditions. I was almost twitching with anger.

"The theme I've chosen for tonight is acceptance," Erin announced. Then she shared about how she was accepting that her husband, who was often out of town on sales trip, continued to drink off and on. Sometimes he went to his A.A. meetings, and sometimes he didn't. "Of course I want him to not drink at all, and to go to his meetings and work his program. But my program teaches me I can't control people, places or things. So I'm accepting that this is where he's at in his own recovery," she concluded, settling back into her yellow beanbag chair. "The floor is open for sharing."

The room fell to silence. I broke it. I could have broken a million things that night in the Baptists' basement.

"Acceptance," I began. Maybe my voice was a little sarcastic. "OK. I accept there's no changing the fact that my husband had a child ten years ago. I 'accept'"—my fingers slashed the air with quote marks—"that he abandoned that child, and I *accept* that he didn't even tell me the child *existed* until tonight. But accepting it doesn't help me know what to *do*." I paused. "Since we're supposed to be honest here, this acceptance thing isn't quite doing it for me."

The women's faces regarded me soberly. A couple of them actually nodded a little. People didn't usually share like this, but I couldn't help it.

"Maybe I should get divorced," I said. The ugliness of the word relieved me because it matched the ugliness of a father abandoning his child. "I cannot trust my husband. I was clear during our courtship that I wanted a family, and he said that was what he wanted, too. But now that we're married he doesn't want to get pregnant with me, or even plan for it. He doesn't even live with me. He lives in Southern California and visits me when he gets around to it."

The women's faces now looked baffled. The prohibition on crosstalk didn't mean that you didn't get feedback on their thoughts. My situation confused them. It confused me, too, and it exhausted me to try to explain it to people. I took a deep breath.

"Without a ton of details that would take up a lot of time, I'm not convinced I should accept things I find unacceptable. When I was an English high school teacher, accepting crappy behavior from kids meant I'd get more crappy behavior from them. Being a wife doesn't seem all that different." I paused, feeling I could talk for hours, but knowing the other women had their own problems they'd come here to talk about, too. "Thanks for listening," I concluded.

An hour later, after we'd said the Serenity Prayer, Erin surprised me by offering her phone number.

"I liked how honest you were," she said, looking straight into my eyes. "If you ever want to chat or have coffee, give me a call." I thanked her and reflected that God might want me to forgive her for having great hair.

When I got home, Sonny's truck was gone, and so were his clothes and duffel bag. A note on the dining room table read:

> Revelle,
> I'm not proud of my past, but I thought you had a right to know. If you're willing to get a real job, I might be willing to have a child with you. I'll call you from my mother's house when I get there.
> Love, Sonny

His use of the word 'love' was bullshit. I got furious all over again that he was dangling the idea of having a child as a possible reward if I would give up my dream, my dance career. Plus, he had no record of keeping his promises, regardless of what I did or didn't do.

I sat at the dining room table, glad this time to be alone, and wrote and sketched into the night. First I was hurling emotional vomit onto the pages, sick and agitated. Then, as always happens after vomiting, I felt better, and I found myself moving around freely in my inner library of stifled thoughts and feelings for the first time since meeting Sonny. I was taking books off the floor, reading their strewn pages, being informed by their words instead of shoving them back into their shelves and turning my back on them. In my private library I studied and worked in a trance, oblivious to time, feeling in my body what words, images and motions resonated the most. What I created was like a slim new volume: detailed drawings of dance movements for my show, *Born For This*. It was far past the witching hour when I finally curled up, composed as a cat, in a sleeping bag on the couch, rather than reenter the bed of the chilling stranger who discarded his children.

The dining room table held in the dark, alongside my voluminous notes and dance drawings, a soft, deliciously irregular piece of handmade paper I had gotten in a trade with a local artist. It was scripted with my calligraphy hand.

Betrayal

Here, my love, is what betrayal means:
Blood running black
The moon gone to red
The cosmos ripped open at its seams.

Chapter 18
Kyle

"Hello, is Travis there?" I said. The male voice that answered the phone was not Travis, the exuberant theater manager. I was foraging in my refrigerator one morning in early May for some lunch to take into the studio. I wanted to talk with Travis about my show before I got caught up in the classes and meetings I had scheduled for the day. My list was always too long. I liked to do a top-priority item in a preemptive strike, without even adding it to the list.

"Travis no longer works here," the voice said, calm and professional. "This is Kyle Roanhorse. I'm the new theater manager. How can I help you?" I slowly turned away from the refrigerator, closed its door, and faced the window over the sink. I remember that the morning sun was streaming directly through the window, and noticing that the window was smeared, dirty. Cleaning the windows of the house had never made it onto any of my lists, at all. I stood up straight, lifted my head, pointed my right toes and took a step forward, as if stepping onstage.

"My name is Revelle Jones Champagne." I emulated his confident tone. "Congratulations on your new job!"

"Thank you." He sounded slightly amused and slightly friendly, which gave me the beginning of a good impression of him.

"I'm the dancer who owns and operates *Dancing Fool*, the dance studio a few blocks west of your theater," I said.

"OK," Kyle replied neutrally. If he had heard of it he would have told me so. My stomach tensed. I didn't want to lose my show.

"Travis told me in March I would do a show in your theater starting July 13," I said. "Do you see it on your calendar?"

"Well, Travis's calendar and my calendar aren't necessarily the same things," Kyle replied. I could hear him smiling, trying to say it nicely. "Tell you what, why don't you come in and let me see the kind of show that you have in mind, and we can go from there."

"You're asking to see me dance. At your theater. Like an audition," I said. I wanted to make sure we were on the same page.

"Given that you're a dancer, that sounds like a good plan to me. If it's all right with you, Miss Dancing Fool," he added in a playfully courteous tone.

"I'll be happy to do that," I replied. "I understand. You're wanting to make sure I'm not excessively foolish," I said slyly, zinging him back.

He laughed, and I felt 60% sure that my show would still happen. We decided I'd come in at three the next day. At the top of my day's list I wrote, "Call Travis to confirm July show." Then I crossed out Travis and wrote "Kyle" above it. Then I crossed out the whole line with bold strokes of my pen and left for the studio, the lunch I had meant to pack forgotten.

✼

As I walked into the theater, a familiar anxiety built in my stomach, but I maintained the head-up, long-necked, graceful walk that was equally familiar, the one that defied the anxiety. A black-haired young man was leafing through papers in the manager's office. "Revelle?" he said, standing up and extending his hand. I started. He was the Native American man I had shared the brain-battering glance with at Prentice two years ago. The man I'd seen again at the Oasis.

"Have we met before?" he asked, reading the recognition in my face. Attraction was buzzing in the air between us like the way the bee bushes had vibrated with sound in elementary school.

"Not exactly. Good to meet you." I shook his hand, two lean hands meeting in the air, testing the other for strength and finding it as bone and sinew pressed bone and sinew. Neither of us was smiling, which I appreciated. We both had something at stake here and it wasn't a social occasion. There was the full, sensual mouth, the large hazel eyes with thick eyelashes. The high-cheekboned, olive-toned face was both the same as I remembered it, and different. He was slim, medium height, with bone-wide shoulders and narrow hips.

"Thanks for coming in," he said.

"It's a pleasure." Give me back my show, right now, I wanted to say, but I knew I could earn it back. I was wearing a tiny vintage cardigan, cobalt blue, over my strappy black dance-camisole, and leggings under my fitted skirt that flared and stopped above the knee. Kyle was wearing black jeans and a blue Oxford shirt with the sleeves folded above his elbows. A white t-shirt showed at his neck under his shirt.

"Let's go over to the stage and hear a little about your concept before you show me some of your dancing." I nodded agreement. "Can I carry that for you?" He took my tape deck and led me into the theater.

"OK! There are three acts that create the story-arc," I told him, hopping backward up onto the stage and wagging my butt backward to get my body situated. He followed suit, just not needing to hop as far. "The first act is called *Bliss*, and it's analogous to innocence, but not necessarily childhood. The dancing reflects steady ascent in life. Lots of pleasure, with the obstacles that arise being overcome pretty easily. An example of the music in it is the 'Pachelbel Canon.'" Kyle nodded readily, his expression open. He seemed to be with me so far.

"The second act, of course, messes all that fun stuff up. It's called *Betrayal*. It's about loss and descent, coming face to face with the shadow. An example of the music in it is blues, not the good-natured-grumbling stuff, but the really gritty sounds. Pain. Also, I'll use Pink Floyd's 'Dark Side of the Moon.'"

"A classic," Kyle nodded. "I like it." I felt encouraged.

"I do some writing, besides dancing. Here's a short poem that speaks to the core of the second act." I showed him the handmade paper on which I'd scripted "Betrayal" that awful night a few weeks earlier. He read it thoughtfully, fingering the paper that was dense and soft as wool felt. The air thickened with something beyond the two of us. Or maybe it was between the two of us. I felt it as a chill that went down my spine, and a warmth that crept into my thighs.

"I get it," he said simply after a minute, releasing the poem back to me. "And how does the third act resolve the tension?"

"With a lot of energy," I smiled. "The final act is called *Born For This*, which is also the name of the show. It's about breaking through the pain of betrayal into joy and finding life-purpose. One of the music pieces is "When Love Comes To Town." But the joy in the final act is a lot more textured and soulful of a state than the earlier bliss.

"OK. I don't have any problem with your concept. I have a question for you, though, and it's one I always ask the people I work with," he said. "What do you want to get out of this show? Because it'll be one hell of a lot of work." The large hazel eyes looked at me expectantly.

"Good question," I nodded. "First, I like to work hard. No worries there. And, I want two things from the show. I want to become a better-known dancer, known for doing expressive things with the body that move people, that help them get unlocked inside themselves. And that ties in with the second thing: through the show, I want to attract new students to my studio and build my dance classes, my clientele." I could have said more, but I stopped myself. His face told me he was satisfied with my answer, and anyway, it was really time to dance.

I put the tape I'd mixed for this audition into the tape player, and took the stage while he sat in the front row. "I'll have other dancers in the show, of course," I told him. I hadn't asked Deirdre and Taylor yet, but I was sure they would do it. And a few others would appear, too.

"Of course," he replied.

At first I made some eye contact with Kyle while I danced. But his eyes and face were sending so much energy back that it served to increase my nervousness. So I did as the performance coach at Pitzer had taught, shifting my focus to a seat in the middle of the theater, pretending a person was sitting there who loved everything I was doing. That put me back in my zone. When I danced a segment to "Dark Side Of The Moon," spinning, staggering in circles, then collapsing and doing floor movements that expressed more struggle, I closed my eyes briefly. I saw Paul's large, honest, workman's face. He was the one who loved me unconditionally, the stuff with Sonny notwithstanding. He was there on the floor with me, witnessing my pain, yet not drowning in it. I got that lively, activated feeling in the base of my spine that all my life I'd linked with joy, and when Pink Floyd faded out and U2 faded in with "When Love Comes To Town," I rose from the floor and danced as I probably never had before. I used steps from the solo I'd done at my wedding, but found whole new movements coming through my body that surprised even me, jump-kicks flying in all directions and fluid undulations that started with my neck and snaked through my spine to my legs, my facial expressions flowing from curiosity to surprise to radiant happiness. When the music faded out like a road disappearing into the distance and I moved off the stage with it, I heard applause and cheers from my audience of one. I had re-earned my show.

A few weeks later I was hiking with Erin one sunny morning on Mount Tabor, the forested park just east of the Hawthorne district, after joining her at an Al-Anon meeting. Her husband, who traveled a lot in his work, had relapsed spectacularly, running up their credit cards for thousands of dollars while in New York City on a three day drunk. I felt slightly guilty that it felt so great to see her frustration with her marriage become more equal to my own. Her beautifully angled haircut was even growing out and needing a trim, an imperfection I found endearing.

"What's going on with you and Sonny?" she asked me, after she'd wound down a little from describing her husband's drunkalogue and her efforts to cope with it all.

"Well, we've been writing letters lately instead of calling," I said slowly, considering my answer. "To be honest, I've been so excited about my show I haven't really been thinking that much about Sonny," I admitted.

"You're working your program!" Erin said, enthused. "That's what we're supposed to do, focus on our own lives instead of obsessing about the alcoholic's ups and downs."

I laughed. "I think it's a coincidence about working a program. But I've stopped asking Sonny to move up. It's a lost cause. Plus, my work kind of goes to hell when he's up here, anyway."

"Well, that's crazy," Erin said indignantly, shaking her head so her smooth, glossy hair danced in the sun. I laughed again; I liked Erin. She was smart, kind, and much more vulnerable than the Stepford wife first impression I'd gotten of her. As a real estate agent she was self-employed, which was another thing we had in common besides living on our own a lot of the time. Before we said good-bye, she'd written down the date of my opening show in her calendar, and promised to come. I hugged her, elated.

Down at the theater I worked with Kyle on the set and lighting. He had never stood me up or been late, not once, despite a heavy, complicated schedule that involved developing several other shows besides mine. The choreography for the show was revealing itself the way a forest becomes slowly visible at sunrise, first with general forms and outlines against the horizon, then the finer branches, leaves and needles becoming clearly etched as well. Elation was my steady state that summer, with my desire to eat and sleep diminishing as I was fueled by excitement over my show. The Hawthorne district felt like a creative person's Disneyland.

"I didn't know you could get two flavors instead of one," Kyle said. We sat at the Oasis Café on Hawthorne. He was referring to the Italian soda I was drinking, which had both peach and vanilla flavoring, while his had just blackberry. We were both a little nervous. He had suggested taking a break together away from the theater.

"You can have two. You just ask," I said.

"Great. I'll ask something else. What kind of a name is Revelle?"

"It's an old family name. From England. My dad's side."

"Oh. I'd been thinking maybe it was the French version of revel, as in, revel in abandon. As in the way you dance," he said, looking fully, steadily at me. I dropped my gaze, flustered. I needed to shift focus.

"So, Mr. Roanhorse," I said lightly, "How long have you been in theater?"

"All my life," he said. "But professionally, this is my first year. I'm a refugee attorney."

"That's a new one," I smiled. "In that nomenclature, I'd be a refugee English teacher."

"But you know what Tom Petty's advice is," Kyle grinned back.

"*Don't! Have! To live like a refugee!*" I sang in my best raspy Petty imitation, rising from my chair and pulsing my arms above my head to the beat.

"Very good!" he cried. "You can sing as well as dance." I executed a deep curtsey, arms fully extended and head dramatically inclined, then sat back down. We merrily regarded each other. Attraction was buzzing louder in the air than it had a year ago with Sonny at Disneyland.

"So what's your refugee story?" I urged.

"Well, my parents had pushed me to be an attorney, and I went along with their program. But after I got the J.D. and had worked in a firm for a year, I hated it. I'd always loved theater; I did it all through high school and college. So when I found out Travis was leaving Camelot, I jumped on it. And half the job is doing grant-writing. That's what holds the theater together, financially, the grants. Having a legal background makes me good at landing them." I nodded. I could see him competing for grants and winning.

"So, what's your tribal background?" I asked him. "I've been wondering." His face flickered briefly, the way a shadow appears and disappears from the corner of your eye.

"My father is Apache," he said, "But I call myself a mutt, because my mother has Jewish, Gypsy and Spanish ancestry. Even though she's blonde, like you."

"You're eclectic. Cool," I said. "Blonde doesn't mean anything. Did you get any folk dances handed down to you with all that good ancestry?"

"I'm not a dancer," he demurred. "I like to slow-dance, but anything other than that I'll leave to the experts like you."

"Big mistake," I teased. "You're missing out on all the juicy stuff. Folk dancing is famously kind to people of all coordination levels."

"Spoken like a true dance instructor," he inclined his head in a graceful nod of acknowledgement.

"That was a dance move. That was a head bow!" I exclaimed. "See, you can't escape your heritage. There's a dancer in you," I said with playful intensity, leaning down and across the table. He leaned forward in response, slim brown forearms on the table.

"Tell me something you don't tell most people," he said.

"I'm half Palestinian." I was half hypnotized by the luminous hazel eyes.

"No kidding!" he said with interest. His face lit up as if I'd handed him a wrapped present. But I shrugged. The other person's non-whiteness was always more interesting.

"What does your husband do?" he asked after a few beats, trying to sound casual. His mouth worked on the straw and the blackberry soda lowered itself obediently.

"Sonny is a carpenter. In Anaheim, actually. California." I lowered my mouth to the straw but did not trust my coordination in sucking and swallowing, and skipped doing them. I hoped he wouldn't notice my unlowered soda level and my rising anxiety.

"Anaheim is a long way from here," he remarked presently.

Truer words never spoken, I thought. "Yep," I said after another few beats, feeling my mouth do the crooked-smile thing. I wished I knew better how to explain an absent husband. It wasn't as if we had million-dollar jobs in separate cities and flew to see each other every weekend. I turned my head to look out the window onto Hawthorne. A tall, skinny young fellow, bearded like Jesus, was riding west on a bicycle, wearing nothing but grey underwear.

"I'm sorry. I don't mean to pry. It's not my business," Kyle said, lifting and waving his hands in apology.

"It's OK. Everybody wonders. Southern California seems to be where the best carpentry work is," I dissembled.

"I mean, you're here, Revelle." Kyle was smiling a little, as if I didn't already know what he was talking about, as if I hadn't been struggling with the pain of this for the eleven months of my marriage.

"He visits me. My dance studio and church community are up here. His business contacts are still down there. You could say we're in transition. So," I said, sitting up straight, "what does your wife do?" Kyle didn't wear a wedding ring, but I wanted him to show his own hand.

"I'm not married," he said in a helpful, clarifying tone. "I have a girlfriend, Jewel. Right now she's living with me. Well, actually we're both living with my sister. But we're not good for each other. I'm trying to gently encourage her to move out. So . . . is your husband . . . Sammy, is it—?" He had changed the subject back to me.

"Sonny."

"Is Sonny coming to your show on August 7th?" His full lips drained the rest of his purple soda, eyes staying locked on mine.

I felt my straight spine weaken, my height diminish. I sensed it mattered how I answered. This smart, sexy guy was closing in on me, like a loving predator. Or maybe the loving part was my imagination. It was confusing to be both single and married. I broke eye contact again and looked out the window for a sign. A man on a unicycle was pedaling busily toward me on the sidewalk, actually playing a bagpipe as he balanced on the tiny, flimsy contraption. The plaintive, wailing notes sailed through the summer air into the cafe, making me think of Deirdre and her Celtic ancestors. They had played bagpipes going into battle. But there was no battle going on here. Just a flirtation. I smiled at the fabulously coordinated musician, wanting to put dollar bills into his bagpipe case, or something. Kyle smiled, keying in on my change in mood. He expected me to say something. I remembered that Mary had told me once, "When you're in doubt, say something that's true, anything at all that's true. It will bring you back to center."

"I don't know," I said to Kyle, my tone clear and confident now. "I don't know if he's coming up for the show." It was true, and I also knew it, in that moment at least, to not be my problem. "Thank you for the soda." I got up, my spine supple and strong again.

"My pleasure. It's good to get to know you a little better," Kyle said, rising more slowly.

When we walked to the door, he rested one hand briefly on my lower back before he reached in front of me to open the door with the other. I felt his hand, even through my hip-yoke skirt, like a lick of fire reaching into my root chakra. I yearned for more of his touch, and then felt my face burn with humiliation at that need, and by the fact that it was landing in this moment with Kyle, when I'd intended for that need to land only with my husband, who was a thousand miles away.

Chapter 19
Born For This

"It belongs in the final act," Taylor said stubbornly. We were at Deirdre's place, a narrow, skylit loft above a warehouse, rehearsing there because the judo instructor had my studio tonight.

"No, it belongs in *Betrayal*," Deirdre countered. We were talking about Taylor's Maori dance, a fierce spectacle that he performed shirtless, muscles rippling, brandishing a staff. It was as far from his ballet persona as a Doberman Pinscher in attack mode was different from a Persian kitten.

"A warrior is born to be a warrior," Taylor insisted. "He's protecting his tribe. He's not betraying anybody. It's the opposite; he's proving his loyalty. A Maori is born to do this dance!"

"But *excuse* me, you're *white*, not Maori!" Deirdre wailed.

"Entirely beside the point! I'm a New Zealander!" Taylor cried in a crescendo, waving his arms wildly. I laughed. The three of us enjoyed this hashing out of the show, the drama behind the drama. "All of our ancestors were warriors at one time, including yours."

"That's true," Deirdre conceded. "The Celts were fabulous warriors. They used to charge into battle naked. Hey, can I do a solo to bagpipe music?"

"YES!" I shouted, jumping up and down. "I love bagpipes. Hey, have you seen the guy who rides around on Hawthorne on his unicycle while he's playing the bagpipes!"

"Oh, that guy rocks!" Deirdre cried. And so it went. It was past midnight before I left, sweaty, exhausted and happy. Taylor said good-bye at Deirdre's side.

"You know, U2 is a Christian band," I told Kyle. He had remarked on the intensity of the lyrics and my dancing in "When Love Comes To Town." We were in the theater, working on the set for the show. It was warm, and the air smelled of paint and turpentine.

"It is not," he said immediately. I got the mental image of my foot kicking at age ten when Dr. Watson first tapped my knee with a rubber hammer.

"Oh yeah. Christian," I replied, stepping cheerfully into the fray as my brother Rick and I had always enjoyed doing with each other. It was a fact, and I wasn't going to defer to him. "They're just not fundamentalist, so it doesn't make the news."

"Are you Christian?"

"Yes. You didn't know that about me?"

"I don't know any artists who're Christian."

"Well a bunch of us are. I guess we have trouble coming out of the closet." I tossed him a look, and he grinned at me.

"So, do you have a support group? Like, 'My name is Revelle, and I'm a Christian artist'?"

"No. But we need one." We laughed. "You know, I feel betrayed that you don't like Christians," I teased.

"Wait! I like you. So I must like Christians."

"Bad line, bad delivery. You're a better actor than that. Try again." I felt drawn to him. He was just as compelling as I'd found him in that first meeting of eyes when he'd held the door for me that day at Prentice.

"But I'm not acting!" he protested. "I do like you. Don't feel betrayed. OK, let me tell you something. It's serious."

"OK," I said readily. We set down our paintbrushes and got more comfortable on the floor.

"When I read your poem *Betrayal* that first time, I got shivers down my spine," Kyle said.

"Really?" I was intrigued.

"'Here, my love, is what betrayal means'," he said, holding my eyes with his. They were a tractor beam locking me to him, only hazel instead of blue, and everything else in the world dropped away. "'Blood running black, the moon gone to red, the cosmos ripped open at its seams.'"

"You memorized it," I said, almost whispering. His delivery of it was so natural and heartfelt that it took us down into a moist, dense place.

"It spoke to me," he shrugged. "Plus, it's short. That helps." We laughed a little, rising a couple of feet from the depths.

"How does it speak to you?" I said, diving right back down. "Or if that's too personal, we can drop it. We could talk about something else."

"No," he said slowly. "I'm glad you asked. It was a long time ago. When I was nine, my uncle molested me. He kept molesting me off and on, whenever he was in town, until I was twelve."

"That's an enormous betrayal," I said softly. "I'm sorry that happened." My eyes were full. I hesitated, then felt guided by God to go ahead. "I was assaulted, too, when I was little." Telling him was a type of gift, like my mother helping the crippled woman by carrying the cake to her car. It was a refusal to leave the other person standing out there all alone and vulnerable. "By a stranger. Maybe less of a betrayal. But it leaves a scar."

Kyle was watching my face, listening closely, his high-cheekboned face taut and thoughtful. Then he said something I've always remembered. "We know each other," he said. That was all.

※

My heart was pounding as I sat up in my old flannel-lined sleeping bag to answer the phone.

"Darling! I found you! Are you actually sleeping at the studio now?" It was Sonny.

"It makes the most sense," I mumbled, rubbing at the crusty

things in the corners of my eyes. The 'darling' thing felt like an act. I was keenly attuned these days to drama.

Sleeping in the studio on stacked yoga mats had become my solution to the thirteen to fifteen hour days it took to prepare for the show while keeping the studio afloat. Driving across the river to the empty house in Northwest every night would have just wasted my time in that final ten days where every waking minute was packed with urgent activity. I washed my underwear and camisoles in the bathroom sink, rolling them in towels to pre-dry them and then running the fan on them overnight. And it got light by 5 a.m. in July, waking me in plenty of time without an alarm clock.

"I'm going to move up," Sonny was saying.

"I've heard that before. I don't believe it," I said, slowly sitting up, like a child waking from a lovely dream back into reality.

"This time I'm really moving up. It's not just a visit. I'm going to be there in time for your show."

My show! It was less than a week away, I had loads of work left to do on it, plus my morning class was starting in half an hour. My body flooded with adrenaline, making me bolt up out of my sleeping bag. "Sonny, I'm not sure your coming to my show is the best idea," I said. I remembered his disastrous appearance at my aerobics class in California. "It makes me nervous to think about it, and I'm already nervous enough about the show as it is."

"But I would be coming to your show to support you," he said. He sounded hurt.

His supporting me felt laughable, except for the fact he was still paying the rent on the house. I paid all the rest of my bills, which were in a frightening stack on my desk three feet away. I'd felt for months that I was on my own in Oregon.

"Sonny, it's better for me to not get any promises from you at all. It's too upsetting when you break them," I said, yanking a stretchy skirt over my hips with my free hand. I needed to go to the bathroom but the phone tethered me to the office.

"OK, then I won't promise. I'll just be there," he said boldly.
"I have to go," I said. "Good-bye."

※

"Onions in your omelet? Black olives?" I asked Mary. I was making breakfast for her at my house, where she'd spent the night after driving up from California. Her cousin Teresa in Beaverton, the suburb just west of Portland, had been diagnosed with breast cancer, and Mary had come up to help her for several weeks. Happily, she'd also be able to come to my show.

"No vegetables, just cheese and salsa, please." I rubbed pepper jack cheese briskly against the hand grater, ecstatic that Mary was with me, yet also antsy to get back to the studio to work out the kinks in the second act.

We had stayed up late talking last night. Mary had been appalled to learn that Sonny already had a child that he'd abandoned years ago. She hadn't indicated, though, that she thought I should definitely end the marriage. And I was leery of suggesting that, myself. Vows were vows. I served our omelets and toast and we said grace and started eating.

"Are you going to let go of Sonny, or not, sweetheart?" she asked me, in her warm, frank way. I almost asked her if she'd been talking with Paul, but it would have sounded paranoid.

"I've been working so hard on the show I haven't thought a lot about Sonny. But the theater manager and I have been hitting it off. As friends, of course." I tucked my face down into my coffee mug.

"What's his name? What's he like?" Mary was all over it, eating without letting her eyes leave mine.

"Kyle Roanhorse. Well, he keeps his word. He's not some wild child careening around like Sonny is. He's there for me. Kyle is . . . kind," I told her.

"What has he done that's kind?" Mary asked.

"He's helped me with my show." I'd stopped eating.

"That's his job, not kindness. Try again."

"He took me out for an Italian soda. And a glass of wine the other evening."

"That's courtship behavior. He wants you. I'm not feeling the kindness yet."

"But I do feel it. He just looks at me and kind of oozes it."

"No, I think he's oozing desire. I think you're interpreting that as kindness."

I burst out laughing. "How can you be so certain? You haven't met him. You don't how how he treats me."

"That means his charm has no impact on me. Not meeting him makes me more objective. I know how beautiful you are and how you look when you dance. I can guess the rest."

"And I don't have any right to be going down that path, because I'm married." I spoke preemptively, to keep her from saying it.

"The letter of the law would say that," Mary agreed. "The Spirit of the law, capital S, that's more nuanced. I don't think it would be healthy for you to get romantically involved with Kyle right now. At the same time, I don't think you really have a marriage."

"But what am I supposed to do about that?" I shot back. "I can't make Sonny move up here to live with me. I don't trust him anymore, anyway. And I'm not moving back to southern California. That would be like death for me." Mary nodded agreement.

"So I don't really have a marriage. But I'm a married woman who has to both fend for herself on a daily basis, *and* practice celibacy. I'm angry!" I said, standing and starting to pace the kitchen.

"Well you should be! This is ridiculous!" She stood up too, like a civil rights activist ready to desegregate a bus with me. I regarded her, holding still for a minute.

"I want to have sex so badly I could scream," I said quietly, pressing my hand against my flat stomach. "And I want to conceive."

"I hear you," she said feelingly. "Let's scream together." So we did, and her screams were almost as loud as my own. It was a primal release, deeply satisfying, like the next best thing to making love and having an orgasm.

When I went out to my truck ten minutes later to drive up to the studio, my elderly neighbor Bob was looking at me from his front porch.

"It's just a new kind of therapy, that screaming stuff," I called to him. "Nothing to worry about." He raised a weary-looking hand before turning to go back into his house.

ॐ

"Do you like sushi?" Kyle asked me a couple of days later. His hands were in his pockets and he was leaning against the studio wall. He had shown up to watch the last ten minutes of my 6 p.m. dance class.

"No, I actually don't like sushi," I said, loose and limber from dancing. "I don't like jazz music, either. I'm uncool," I said happily.

"It doesn't make sense for you to not like *jazz*," Kyle said. His tone implied he could concede the sushi, but the jazz was too much. "You live outside the box, and jazz wrote the book on outside the box."

"Things don't always make sense. My dad's a conventional straight arrow guy and he loves to go hear jazz. It irritates the hell out of me; I can't dance to it. It wobbles around and doesn't know what it's doing." I was waving my arms like a castaway sending SOS signals. "Give me rock, give me folk, give me blues and gospel, give me indigenous music, I can relate to all of it. But don't give me jazz."

"But you told me you used to go to some place called Heaters with your dad to hear jazz." Kyle's arms were now waving like mine.

"Well that was to be with my dad!" I pointed out. "And it's called Steamers."

"You're always changing your mind!" Kyle cried, exasperated and laughing. "'No jazz for me, never, anything but jazz' and then it comes to your dad and you're, 'Yeah, jazz all the way, I'm there, you bet, anything for Dad.' Women like to break rules."

"Well, rules only exist to serve people!" I wailed, enjoying our dramatics. "Of course you break them when they fail to serve! You mean that's not self-evident to an educated person?"

"Women only break rules when it serves *them* to break the rules!" Kyle fairly shouted. His smile was as wide as the Columbia. We ended up sharing a Hawaiian pizza at the Oasis. I declined on sharing a pitcher of beer. The opening was just two nights away.

Kyle was intrigued that I'd chosen little Carmenita to be in the show, and that she had natural performance ability. "She's like a niece to me," I explained. "I've more or less helped raise her."

"Carmenita's lucky. I wish I'd had a mentor like you when I was a kid," Kyle said. "But no. My family had this idea I was born to be a lawyer. And I bought into that. I built my life on that. Then I finally realized *no*. I was really born to do theater."

"Amen to that." I raised my glass to him.

"It's fun to watch you work with Carmenita, you're so loving and encouraging. You'll be a great mom." The topic of motherhood was as loaded for me as a rifle in deer-hunting season, so I didn't touch it. After a minute he filled the awkward silence.

"So, it seems like most of your friends are married."

"I guess that's true," I said. "Marisol, Vicki. Mary. Liz." We had finished our pizza, and the sun was setting in the window that looked toward the West Hills.

"Most of my friends are single. Don't you feel like a third wheel when you hang out with married couples?" Kyle asked me.

"No. Not at all. I feel good when I'm around them. It's like they're showing me how to do it, how to have a happy marriage and be a good parent."

"I've always just assumed I can have a happy marriage and be a good parent. But not with Jewel. We bring out the worst in each other. It's just that we both like being in a relationship and don't want to be alone."

I wondered what the worst in him looked like, and what he did that brought out the worst in Jewel. I couldn't ask those things, so I asked something else.

"Is your dad like that? Preferring to be in a relationship?" I knew his parents had divorced when he was 13.

"I've never known him to be single. So, yeah, I guess he is. Right now he's in New Mexico. He wants me to join him down there, reclaim my Apache heritage or some bullshit. I'm taking a pass on that." He finished his beer with a swift upward motion, and planted his glass back on the table in a firm downward motion. My face must have shown my skepticism about glib dismissal of one's ancestors.

"What, you think I should take him up on that?" Kyle challenged my silent thoughts. "Try to reconstruct the glorious powwow past of the People?" His voice was laden with irony. In the past month he'd made several suggestions for ironic notes in *Born For This*, most which of which I hadn't accepted. I liked nuance and depth more than irony.

"No. I've done some reading and I don't have romantic illusions about the Apache. Yes, the whites stole their land. Which was wrong. But before the whites ever arrived, they tortured other tribes and enslaved them. They weren't just victims. They were also first-class victimizers."

"You're right!" Kyle said cheerfully. "You're the first person who's dared to point that out to me. Thank you for not having white guilt."

"You're welcome. I'm not standard-issue white, anyway. The Palestinians are warriors from way back. I shouldn't be criticizing the Apache. Nobody's hands are clean. Nobody's." That last part must have come out a little strong, because Kyle shot me a surprised look. My guilt over my revenge on the rapist had been coming up inside me, a visceral force at times, as I'd been rehearsing for the show. I hadn't expected that to happen. But the creative process was like the holy spirit, something that had a life of its own, and that you couldn't control.

In my sleeping bag in the studio that night, I couldn't help imagining Kyle lying beside me, kissing me, legs locked behind mine. I tried to imagine Sonny instead, since he was my husband. But that mental picture wouldn't materialize at all. My eye traveled to the painting on the wall, barely visible in the low light: *Him, Her, Him Dancin'*. I'd bought it in Santa Fe when I was 19, and it had traveled everywhere with me since then. The bold way the three figures leapt and moved spoke to me of fierce vitality, of people being both free inside themselves, and warmly bonded with each other. I lay there, my body exhausted from my own dancing, 16 hour days and lack of sleep. Tonight I saw something in the triptych that was different than I'd seen before.

Two men and a woman wasn't the most stable configuration in the world. In fact, it had been known to lead to violence.

Chapter 20
The Show

"I'm raising the curtain in two minutes," Kyle said.

The six of us were backstage, fidgeting, bouncing on our toes, pulling our arms across our bodies to stretch and loosen them. John, the oldest of us, was pacing. Carmenita's small, pretty face brimmed with excitement, but her body was still. I was impressed by her eight-year-old composure. I touched her hair with affection, then nervously checked my own. It was held high with combs, with a few tresses cascading down in their trademark ripples. Then I touched my dress. Even Carmenita hadn't recognized the core garment as the one I'd made and worn for my wedding. I'd had to take it in since I'd lost weight. I had different camisoles and overskirts for each of the three acts.

I was wired, sleep-deprived, almost breathless from excitement. Preparing for the show, the 70-hour workweeks and practically abandoning my home for the studio had been a trial by fire. Doing the show tonight, though, felt like a proving ground for my life. I needed people to witness this expression of myself, this in-depth take I had on what it was like to be in the world, in my skin. And I needed them to respond. A passive, polite audience would be a damning thing. By the end of the last act, most people should be dancing along with my little troupe, in whatever way their bodies naturally danced. If they were not at least moved by what happened tonight, I would have failed. John caught my eye and smiled. I smiled back. He'd been thrilled when I'd asked him to be in the show.

But the first time Kyle had seen John dance, Kyle had taken me aside and said, "Uh-uh. We're not putting this guy on stage."

"Excuse me," I said evenly. "This guy has a name. It's John. And the audience will end up loving him more than anyone else on the stage."

"He stinks," Kyle hissed quietly.

"He's the counterpoint to the technically good dancing. He carries the soul of the show. Trust me on this one." I touched Kyle's bare forearm and looked calmly into his eyes. John had stayed.

Now, Kyle said to all of us, "Don't put too much pressure on yourselves. It's normal to hit your peak in rehearsal instead of in the performance. There's always less at stake then, and you're looser, less nervous. Just pretend you're rehearsing tonight."

We all nodded, then fidgeted faster as he walked away to the curtain pulleys. At my nod, Carmenita went to the center of the stage and laid down since the curtain would open to her. John crossed to the other side for his eventual entrance. Taylor, next to me, took Deirdre's hand, bent and kissed it. I would normally have looked away from a passionate gesture like that between a couple, to give them privacy. But our hearts and bodies had all become so interwoven in the endless hours of rehearsal that I held their joined hands in mine, bent and kissed them both. Deirdre followed suit, her cheek brushing mine.

Then the airy violins of "Pachelbel's Canon" started as the curtain lifted to the first act. Pale gold light fell on Carmenita as she slowly sat up, stretched, and looked around as if waking to the world for the first time. After a minute I stepped softly out to join her, and my body finally became calm, focused. I was now doing the show instead of thinking about it, which was a much happier state. In this first act I was Carmenita's whimsical mother, playing hide-and-go-seek with her in flowing movements among the set pieces, periodically lifting and carrying her so she floated like a bird.

Presently Taylor tiptoed down the aisle of the theater, seeming in his street clothes like someone who'd simply arrived late. But then, as Kyle trained a spotlight on him in profile, his face registered intrigue at what we were doing on stage. Carmenita took notice of him, stopped dancing, beckoned him to join. He demurred. I coaxed him next. More bashful resistance. The audience was curious and amused. Finally Carmenita and I reached down and each took a hand, and Taylor made a great show of clambering clumsily onto his belly, legs waving wildly, until he was standing upright on the stage. As the music switched to "Dance of the Sugarplum Fairy," Carmenita and I sat down to watch him. Taylor went into full ballet mode, prancing and pirouetting, completely unfazed by the audience's laughter at the incongruity between his masculine bulk and effeminate demeanor. Presently the lighting became softer, warmer, and the golden sound of "Baker Street" came on, drawing a dreamy, passionate solo from me that culminated with Taylor lifting and carrying me into flight as I had done with Carmenita.

And so it went, alternating between songs, solos and ensemble dancing. By the end of the first act, Deirdre and John had also joined in so that all five of us were interweaving merrily back and forth across the stage, all different human sizes and gaits, to the Beatles' "Norwegian Wood," each holding high over our heads six wide pastel-colored ribbons that caught the pale gold light and became woven together by the paths of our bodies.

The applause sounded to me a little better than obligatory as Kyle slowly lowered the curtain. Carmenita slipped beneath it at the last minute, carrying the riotously interwoven ribbons out to the audience, trotting up and down the aisles handing out ribbons like a flower girl run sweetly amok who wished to marry her dance-troupe to the audience. It was innocent and unexpected, like Taylor's entrance had been, and peeking from behind the curtain, I could see it engaged people. My wish to dissolve the nagging, traditional barrier between performers and audience, between doers and spectators, could conceivably work.

The second act, *Betrayal*, was where we were most likely to lose people. Though it began and ended with Pink Floyd's popular "Dark

Side of the Moon," it asked the audience to sit with pain and the shadow. The climax of this act was my solo to Janis Joplin's "Piece Of My Heart." I had choreographed and practiced this piece to an extreme. I used all of the stage, jumping onto and off the low walls of the set with hitch-kicks, expressing the anger and anguish that can travel with love. When Kyle had seen me in rehearsal making great circles with my upper body, arms extended and my hair unbound so that it moved in crack-the-whip style, he'd said, "That's great! Your hair is like having another whole dancer on stage. I'm going to backlight it. You'll look like an angel fallen from grace."

"Finally, a use for my crazy hair!" I cried, smiting my forehead then reaching my hand to the heavens.

"What are you talking about, I love your hair!" he exclaimed. In rehearsal I'd always used emotional memories and experiences to fuel my dancing in any given number, and my fuel for "Piece Of My Heart" had been my rawness around my marriage, how rejected I felt by Sonny. On stage now, though, the pain I found myself dancing was that of not being a mother. Sonny didn't even exist for me in this moment. I was born to be a mother, and it was ripping my heart out to not be one. I surrendered to that, holding nothing back, letting the emotion inhabit my face as well as my body. I heard applause when I dropped to the floor at the end of the song, which I hadn't anticipated. I smiled in the dark created by my arms. Their being *with* me when I danced like this was the best kind of love. It was just one notch down from God's love.

John started the next piece as I lay there, Leonard Cohen's "Bird on a Wire." This number had sprung from my once seeing him noodling around to this song in the studio before class started. His boniness, bald head and awkward body language matched the lyrics and melody with a surprising ping, like the way your body welcomed a coarse-grained bread for breakfast the morning after an expensive French dinner of over-rich, creamy sauces. Now, after a searching type of solo to the first verse, he knelt and roused me and we moved in a duet, soulful and fast and slow in turns, me doing most of the dancing, John holding down the basics in his earnest way, like a bass player new to his instrument jamming with an experienced guitarist doing first one riff, then spinning off into another. "This song makes depression interesting instead of boring," Kyle had remarked during rehearsal. "It makes you keep reconsidering what sadness is." Deirdre and Taylor joined for the last third of the song, our ensemble using the whole stage to dramatize one aborted attempt at freedom after another. John went into his signature spinning, broken by occasional staggers (no acting needed there). The frustrated, doomed energy built until Taylor finally grasped my waist and started to lift me over his head at a right angle to himself. I extended my arms and legs behind me, toes pointed, chin raised in hope, a bird needing desperately to launch. Taylor straightened his arms to their full length—then started trembling. Kyle had had to coach him endlessly on this part. "I could lift two of Revelle!" he'd cried in protest, and Kyle had calmly kept saying, "I know you're able to lift two of her. But this part is acting, not dancing," until Taylor had finally submitted to failing at lifting me.

Now, after lifting me fully over his head and then trembling, Taylor slowly buckled his legs and went to his knees. As I fell in chaos, Deirdre and John half-caught me and, without breaking motion, lowered me to the floor. We had rehearsed this part about a hundred times on the thick martial arts mats in my studio. It was the riskiest move in the show, because small as I was, Deirdre and John were slight, too, and it needed to look like a true fall, an uncontrolled one. Head down and shoulders hunched, Taylor jumped off the stage and skulked down an aisle as "Dark Side of the Moon" closed out the second act.

Performers traditionally stayed backstage during intermissions, but I felt that sociability trumped tradition. I quickly changed into a sky-blue sundress and sandals and joined people in the crowded lobby. Marisol was holding court at a card table covered with a brilliantly colored silk sari, serving snacks, wine and bottles of microbrew beer with an air of happy authority. Here was Erin, all smiles and hugs, and over there were Pastor Rachel and Sharon, holding hands, so dark and so light. Across the room John was talking animatedly with a redheaded woman whose back was to me. Next to her, Taylor greeted with high-fives a group who looked to be from the youth hostel down the street. A tall fellow, garbed all in black with a mask and long cape like Zorro, stood across the room by himself. Given this was Hawthorne, he didn't look wildly out of place, but I didn't recognize him. Maybe he was an artsy fellow barista of Deirdre's.

"It's going great," Kyle said, suddenly at my side. "Everyone's nailing it. You look fantastic."

"I'm not so sure," I replied, not wanting to jinx it. My uncertainty and eagerness created a tightrope inside myself, making me sharp, alert, wildly alive. I wanted to keep dancing on my inner tightrope. I maybe wanted to keep living on it. Paul came over, caught me in one of his solid, grounding hugs, and introduced me to a rapid succession of smiling people who drummed with him, went to men's group with him, sponsored him, used him as a sponsor or were partners or children of those people. "Did you invite everyone you ever met?" Kyle teased Paul.

"Pretty much," Paul said mildly, then left for the card table because Marisol was signaling she needed help serving refreshments. The lobby was small, teeming with hubbub, and in the crush of people my right side pressed into Kyle's left side. A body-memory of how it felt to make love flashed through me, followed by longing, and I wondered if it was Kyle's desire or my own I was feeling.

A middle-aged man I didn't know with large white teeth and an expensive looking sport-coat approached us. He was smiling big and talking fast. "Samuel Roth. Kyle and I go way back; I'm a friend of his uncle's." I glanced at Kyle, whose mouth opened, but who clearly didn't stand a chance of getting into the conversation. "I'm visiting from New York; I produce things off Broadway. I'm always looking for new stuff, new concepts. And I've never seen anything quite like what you're doing here."

"Hello, Samuel," I said, shaking his hand. I noticed it wasn't as strong as mine.

"I say this with all seriousness," he said, releasing my hand and fixing me with hooded brown eyes. "I felt like I was watching Janis Joplin, reincarnated as a dancer. The emotion was that raw. The theater was vibrating there for a moment." He offered me a business card. "I'd like you to call me sometime." I took it, thrilled, then stood helplessly, with nowhere to put it.

"Here, I've got a pocket. I'll keep track of that for you," Kyle said. I gave the card to him, relieved. The New York producer gave us a little salute and turned to go. "Breathe," Kyle murmured into my ear, and then called out, "Five minutes to curtain!" Marisol started putting corks back into wine bottles, and I trotted backstage and changed back into costume, dizzy with feeling.

Our final act, *Born For This*, started with me in a heap on the floor, the same way *Betrayal* had ended. "Pachelbel's Canon" played softly as Carmenita made her way onstage, searched around and finally found me, in a reversal of the first act. She managed to stir me, and we embraced, then danced a duet, relieved to reunite. Then bagpipes sounded in the far distance, ancient and stirring, and we sat expectantly on the low wall at the back of the stage. Deirdre walked softly onto the stage in baggy sweatclothes, cupping her ear and looking around, curious, enchanted. I saw some faces in the audience light with enchantment in turn, like a lake's surface reflecting a sunrise. Then she slowly started moving to the bagpipes, which became a little closer in our ears. Her dancing quickened, her big sweatshirt coming off to reveal a crisp tailored shirt, and then the enormous sweatpants to reveal a plaid kilt, tights and tap shoes. She looked down, amazed at her native garb, and the bagpipes swelled as she found her way into a Celtic dance, arms close to her sides, feet stamping emphatically, heels and knees kicking high, face rapt and focused.

Taylor's Maori dance, performed to Paul's drumming, was yet more moving. The lead-in was ominous music and lighting effects that suggested Carmenita, Deirdre and I were in danger of attack. We crouched in fear, and Taylor leapt onto stage, reassured us, then launched into warrior mode, displaying his strength to the unseen enemy. He wore just blue and red face paint, below-the-knee pants, and a necklace of teeth and claws. His dance of protecting his tribe was primal and fiercely skilled, something most people would never see in their lives, yet recognized, once it was in front of them, in their DNA, their limbic brain stems. Nothing could have been clearer to anyone in the building than that Taylor, shirtless and ripple-muscled, the same guy who'd merrily minced around earlier, was born to carry the energy of a warrior.

Kyle had said wryly of this number, "I'm not a very tribal kind of guy. This kind of thing sets me on edge. But I can see he's effective." We had talked about the *Born for This* concept again a week ago. Kyle thought that whatever you had the most fun doing was probably what you were born to do. "If it makes you happy, you were born for it," he said. "I disagree," I said immediately. "Fun is easy. By itself, it's cheap. Even happiness is fleeting. Nobody's going to be happy all the time," I declared. "What you're born for, though, comes from digging deeper." Kyle's face opened with interest, so I went on, using my hands like an Italian chef talking about his food. "What you're born for, it's like your vein of gold, something you have to prospect for. You might have to, I don't know, walk through a fire and come out on the other side to find your life's purpose." Kyle's eyes were soft and he was half-smiling at me. It was the almost trancelike expression Sonny's face had used to have when we'd lie in bed and I'd talk about dancing. In that moment I wished I were married to Kyle rather than Sonny. They both got who I was and they both wanted me, but Kyle handled it all in a way that I could trust, rather than a way that led me on and let me down, over and over, like a bird thinking it was free and being stopped by the wire again and again. It crossed my mind that just one core thing was what attracted me to both Sonny and Kyle: they were each helping me work my way toward who I was.

"When Love Comes To Town" was my biggest solo besides the Janis Joplin piece. It had morphed in the past year from the straight-ahead dance I did at my wedding, to the more intense piece I did for Kyle in order to land the show, to the version tonight that was both more subtle and more wild than either of the prior ones. I was crawling in great prowling movements on the floor, then up on my feet to slink bent-kneed across the stage, then turning two rapid cartwheels that ended in the splits, then rolling sideways onto the floor, spinning on my bottom and spiraling back up onto my feet again. I heard applause, but I screened it out, because I was living inside the song. I used to feel that dancing to it was letting me work out my pain over being victimized, both by the rapist of my childhood and later by Sonny's betrayal. But I had come in the last weeks to see myself as maybe having betrayed Sonny, too, by marrying him when I shouldn't have. And God knew the rapist had ended up being not just my predator but also my prey. Weirdly, I now loved the guilt implied by U2 when they sang about being there at the crucifixion of Christ, and greedily throwing the dice for his clothes. My favorite lyric in any song, ever, was the clincher that they'd seen love conquer the great divide. I did a flying deer leap off a low wall at those words, and Taylor, who had been sitting onstage watching, rose to catch me at the waist and extend the leap. Then we ran three paces together, gathered ourselves and I launched a final leap, Taylor this time lifting me over his head and keeping me there, my arms and legs outstretched and head raised triumphantly, in a reversal of the earlier act's failure. The audience cheered and applauded, and I learned later a number of them rose to their feet.

As the U2 song faded out, "The Elephant Stomp" faded in, and Kyle and Taylor pulled the set pieces all the way back so the stage became wide open. I'd chosen this song for its big, fat, celebratory sound, the kind of sound that loosened up your neck and hip joints and made you grin. My little troupe and I got down from the stage and danced down the aisles, beckoning the audience to join us.

People smiled and nodded along in rhythm, but there didn't

seem to be any takers. They looked comfy in their seats, comfy with the old division of: "I'm a spectator, you're a performer." My gut clenched with fear, like it does in those dreams where you show up at school or work naked, a laughingstock. But then somebody in the other aisle, near Carmenita, was on her feet, pumping her arms toward the sky in an exultant raising-the-roof motion. It was the redheaded woman whose face I couldn't see at intermission. Wait a minute. That was Shasta! She'd come up from California. I whooped with joy, and then other people started following Shasta, standing up, raising the roof, bobbing and swaying, joining us in the aisles. I clapped and jumped up and down; the party was on. Within minutes most of the so-called audience was sprawled along with the troupe like a living, pulsing organism onto the stage, in the aisles, a few children standing on their seats to dance. The hugely gregarious music had what I called the equalizing effect, because it discarded any notions of "good" dancing, and invited dorkiness, instead. The wailing, blatting saxophone led you to take big, fat, jolly steps, and flap your elbows and move in all directions—forward, backward, sideways—and that's what everyone was doing.

Rachel was hamming it up, shimmying her immense shoulders, mugging at children who mugged back at her. Carmenita was trying to lead some dancers in The Wave from atop Taylor's shoulders, but couldn't get people's attention because she was as far above everyone's sightline as she would have been on an African elephant. Deirdre and John danced with the Kavanaughs from my church, and two kids from the hostel got another group going in a grapevine-type step that looked Eastern European.

Still seated in the middle of the theater, smiling and nodding along, were two women in colorful headscarves. It was Mary and her cousin Teresa, and I realized Teresa's scarf was due to her hair falling out from the chemotherapy she was getting for breast cancer. Mary's scarf was empathetic, a gesture of support. I skipped to the seat in front of them, stood on my knees and addressed Teresa over the drumbeat. "Thank you for coming! How are you feeling?"

"I've been better," Teresa smiled wanly. Then she said, as if done with herself for the moment, "I love your dancing. And . . . I love your hair."

"This old stuff?" I touched a tumbled-down tress. "I've got too much of it. If I cut it off, could you use it?"

She laughed, startled. "Well, maybe I could!" Mary and I laughed too, not because the idea was foolish, but because it made us happy. We all clasped hands for a minute, breathing and looking at each other, and then I kissed their hands like I had done with Deirdre's and Taylor's at the beginning, and rejoined the throng on the stage.

When "The Elephant Stomp" ended, Paul and two of his drummer friends took up almost seamlessly with their drums. They had already been set up, playing along with the taped music. When Kyle stopped looping it and let it fade out, they took over. All of our dancing hitched for just a few seconds and then locked into the more ancient, straightforward beat the drummers made. It felt like a trance to move to in a group, but the kind of trance where you were deliciously awake.

People's faces, all open and radiant, told me something was happening for them, too. Shasta and I looked at each other knowingly, sharing the secret of our fire dance by the Klamath River, back when my being a dancer was just a dream, and she had believed in it with all her heart, without hesitation. I steepled my hands and bowed my head to her in a little prayer of thanks, and she nodded merrily to me before Marisol's and Ruben's bobbing heads moved between us and they were dancing with me. The Zorro man was striding around the margins and perimeters of the stage, moving his cape in whooshing circles, just dangerous-looking enough to suggest he was holding space for betrayal, lest we forget it in our joy. Perfect.

A portal opened for me that night like the ones that had opened a few times when I'd been in wild places and when Pastor Rachel led us in communion. It was as if Jesus stepped into me and gave me his eyes. I saw clear through John's clumsiness to his core of grace, and straight through Deirdre's belligerent, cop-bashing anger to her core of tenderness. My marriage, a failure in any human eyes, was in Jesus's eyes blameless and part of a greater good, and my being fired from Prentice was a part of the grand design too. Being raped as a child was something from which God had healed me, as surely as maple trees grew back from winter skeletons into thick green summer glory. Everything broken felt redeemed, made whole that night. That made the universe a different place, no matter that this feeling, like all feelings, couldn't last. Abundance could flow toward need in this fallen, scarred world the way that my oversupply of hair might transform Teresa's baldness. All human suffering, past and present, awful as it was, had hope of redemption, of joy. The end of my show, my dance, our shared dance, stitched the cosmos back together at its seams for a short, shining moment.

We had all been born to do that together.

Chapter 21
Prodigal

"Is this everyone? I thought we had more men," Rachel said. She, Marisol, Ruben and I were sitting outdoors on the side patio of the Fideles House. We were here for a clearness committee, a way for me to get people's advice, in the wake of getting a startling phone call from Sonny. He'd announced that he was now in Portland for good, and he was staying at the youth hostel on Hawthorne. He hoped to move back in with me as soon as possible. He had been hired on as lead carpenter by a newly forming construction company. Oh, and he loved my show. He had been the man at my opening night in the Zorro costume. My dancing had been amazing; he was so proud of me. His tone was as blithe as if he were describing a vacation he'd recently taken. Listening to him, my body had felt as Erin had described feeling when learning her husband had gone on his three-day bender: pounding heart, clenched stomach. I was barely able to breathe. Sonny had been at my opening night, but disguised. It freaked me out.

I'd told Sonny I needed to think things over, then called Rachel. She had suggested I have a clearness committee, which was a Quaker custom designed to help a person in a dilemma discern the best path to take. Rachel and Fideles in general borrowed customs from a number of spiritual traditions.

"I invited more men. But Luke is at a pottery show in Seattle, and Paul 'recused' himself from the committee," I reported, rolling my eyes a little. Marisol and Rachel exchanged glances. I thought recusal sounded like something a pompous politician would say.

Paul had a real bee in his bonnet concerning this topic. "And I asked Mary to come, since she would be perfect for this. But she's taking her cousin to chemotherapy today."

Rachel nodded and opened us with a prayer, hands joined, that asked for God to be present, and God's will to become evident to us as we looked at a marriage covenant that was in trouble. We unclasped hands, raised our heads, and Rachel started right in.

"I should let you all know that Sonny called me yesterday," she said in a neutral tone. My eyebrows went up. "He was asking for my help. He said he'd do anything to save the marriage." I realized I was glaring at her, because she sat back and raised her hands to her shoulders, palms facing me. "I'm just reporting. When I suggested marriage counseling as a possibility, he said he'd do it."

"Sonny has said a lot of things," Marisol said dryly. "They don't always pan out." Ruben nodded.

"Thank you," I said pointedly to Marisol and Ruben. Rachel was already pissing me off.

"Revelle, let me be honest. We get, or I should say I get, mixed messages from you about your relationship with Sonny," Pastor Rachel said.

"Really?" I said. "I thought it was obvious my marriage is messed up."

"Not really, not to me. I've always thought you two were deeply in love with each other," Rachel replied, and her face was so open and warm that I suddenly felt warm toward her again, as I'd usually felt before learning Sonny had been lobbying her. "When Sonny has been in town you always seemed excited and happy to be with him. When he's gone you seem independent, but still pretty happy."

Ruben nodded, agreeing with Rachel.

"You see me when I'm at church," I pointed out. "Church makes me happy, the community makes me happy. But I'd never intended to live alone, with my husband a thousand miles away."

Above and behind Marisol's head a hummingbird with an iridescent green throat hovered like a miniscule helicopter at a bright red feeder. Marisol leaned forward to speak and he disappeared. Had he even been there in the first place?

"Well, sweetie," Marisol said, "I do think your marriage is messed up. Your dance career makes you happy—it's not just this community that makes you happy—and Sonny has supported your dancing. I think that's the reason you haven't left the marriage yet. But he's let you down in every way."

Kyle's never let me down, I thought, with a pleasure so private it was like a curling inward toward myself. But it would have been presumptuous to bring him into this conversation, as if he were some kind of an option. To speak of him at all would make me look like a wife considering an affair with the first guy who'd paid some attention to her. The notion was immoral, foolish. The attraction would probably go nowhere. Yet Kyle symbolized the kind of marriage I wanted, and that emboldened me a little.

"I've never been able to depend on Sonny. And we're powerless over people, places and things. Al-Anon at least has that much right. I haven't had any choice but to accept the way Sonny is."

"I think a person always has choices," Marisol said.

"But sometimes all those choices are bad ones," I replied, frustrated. "The choices I'm seeing are to continue in a bad marriage or . . . divorce someone who loves me more than I've ever been loved before. And that divorce would likely mean giving up my dance career."

All three of them shook their heads at that last.

"It's easy for you to shake your heads. But just for one example, where would I live, right now, if I left my marriage?" I asked them evenly.

"I would love for you to live with us," Marisol said without missing a beat. Ruben nodded again. Marisol had always spoken for both of them. "The problem is that we've got Angel and Luis staying with us while they're looking for work." These were her younger cousins who had been getting involved in a gang in East Los Angeles. Her small, pretty face was clouded, troubled.

"But they will move out at some point," Ruben said slowly. "It's just hard to know how soon." I smiled fleetingly at them. Their desire to help me was as strong a presence on the patio as Kyle was a presence in my mind these days.

"And I have to say, Revelle, I don't think it's about finding a new place to live," Rachel said. "I know you don't like hearing that. But I do think it wouldn't hurt you to give Sonny a final chance to do the right thing," she went on. "Why not get some counseling with him? Men can be very slow to change. But—" she leaned forward, speaking slowly and forcefully as she often did at the climax of a sermon—"when they're finally ready, men often change all at once."

I felt a little hope add itself to the tension in my chest, like a guitar string being tightened after someone with a good ear had declared it sounded flat. After a thoughtful silence, Ruben stirred and spoke. "I have seen some men change all at once," he allowed. "It was always either Jesus or a woman that made them stand up and see the light and smell the coffee."

"That's a mixed metaphor, *carido*," Marisol said, smiling, and I burst out laughing, the tension in my chest breaking up in a way that felt wonderful.

"But you all knew what I meant," Ruben said.

"Yes, we did," Rachel said. "People can change and grow, and the sacrament of marriage can help them do it. So can counseling."

"And I haven't tried that yet," I nodded. "I probably do owe that to the marriage."

We talked awhile longer, and Rachel gave me names and phone numbers of two counselors she thought well of from her big black address book. We closed with a prayer, Ruben leading it this time at my request, since I felt Rachel had dominated the meeting somewhat. As Ruben asked God to guide me, thoughts of Kyle buzzed in my mind like the hummingbird that was reapproaching the bright red feeder.

"I thought our counseling session yesterday was great. I'm really glad we did it." Sonny said, enthused as a child after his first swimming lesson. I watched him chopping mushrooms at the picnic table of our campsite in Oxbow Park, feeling content and cynical at the same time. His tanned, striking, strong-jawed face was the same as when I'd met him two years ago, yet changed in the deeper structure to me now, like the way Ed Norton three years later would feel like a whole different person at the end of *Primal Fear* than he had in the beginning of that movie.

The sun was going down, and Sonny was making dinner on my decade-old camp stove. I'd offered to cook with him, but he had urged me to relax, let him do it all. He had moved in with me ten days ago, and this was his new modus operandi: pampering me. But I'd never needed pampering. I'd needed your basic loving husband. A stable marriage. A child. I should be a mother by now.

We had made love again moments ago in our tent, after swimming in the Sandy River and sunning ourselves on the river beach. The sex between us was as compelling as ever, at least in Sonny's eyes, and I wasn't about to turn him down, although I thought about Kyle most of the time that we were necking and snaking our bodies together. Why hadn't Kyle called? I felt like an addict jonesing for a fix.

"Didn't you?" Sonny prompted me now. "Think the counseling session was good for us?"

"Sure, honey," I said, meeting his eyes and smiling. By now there was a degree of theater in my interactions with Sonny. I was creating reenactments of the love I had originally felt for him as carefully as those eccentric history enthusiasts created reenactments of Civil War battles. They were no more eccentric than me.

Our counseling session had been bullshit, from my perspective. The therapists Rachel had recommended hadn't been available on short notice, but one of them had suggested Leah, who, yes, could see us immediately.

Leah was a sweet-faced woman with an adorable ski-jump nose

who couldn't have yet seen her thirtieth birthday. She had asked us—in far too perky a voice, I felt—what we'd wanted from counseling. I'd eyed her tailored, dusty rose business suit suspiciously. If she put that much stock in appearances, she would probably like Sonny just fine.

"I want Revelle," Sonny had replied with disarming honesty. Leah smiled.

"I want a stable marriage and two children," I told her. "I want my dance studio to flourish. And to raise my children close to nature, in a community. With a man I can trust." My emphasis on the word 'trust' was a little caustic. Her face was getting cloudy, confused. I doubted she knew much about betrayal.

"I can give Revelle all that," Sonny stated confidently.

I stared stonily at the terra cotta colored wall above the too-sweet woman's head.

"Then why have you landed here?" Leah asked him nicely. I smiled a little. Maybe she hadn't just fallen off the turnip truck, after all.

"Oh, because I've been late to grow up, really," Sonny said, bowing his head humbly as a penitent. "But now I'm here. I'm a week into my new job, working for a construction company. It's going great! I should have done this ten months ago."

The session had gone on like that, Sonny all stirring sincerity and direct eye contact with the young woman who seemed riveted by his performance, while I thought about Kyle. I missed working with him, solving the show's problems with him, our smiles and the in-jokes we'd developed about dumb blondes (my jokes) and dumb Indians (his jokes).

"Revelle, you seem kind of checked out." Leah finally addressed me. "What's going on for you?"

"There have been a lot of words in this relationship," I said slowly. "They haven't helped. Words aren't actions. They're just smokescreens. They get in the way and don't change anything."

She blinked twice. A silence hung in the room.

"OK," Leah finally said. "Well, then, what action would you like from Sonny between now and the next session?"

I had talked myself blue in the face over the past year on what I was asking of Sonny, and I wasn't about to rehash it at this late date with Leah. "Sonny's actions are up to him," I said with icy serenity, getting up to signal I was done.

"I'm going to be the husband and father I promised to be," Sonny said feelingly, getting up and looping his arm around my waist. I was mute, expressionless.

"Good luck," the sweet young thing said. "Call me if you need me."

At our campsite now, Sonny presented me with dinner: fresh, crusty bread with garlic butter, sliced heirloom tomatoes and a mushroom risotto that had drained the very last of our propane as he patiently simmered it for practically an hour on the battered little stove. But it tasted wonderful, the flavor earthy and wild as an ancient forest. Dessert was a cobbler of Oregon blackberries that he had baked at the house before we left. "This is delicious," I said, as politely as I would on a first date, wiping the corners of my mouth with a none-too-clean bandana.

"I want to make you happy," he said, his face more in shadow than light because the candles had burned down low. But his expression was so grave that I realized he was not doing theater with me that night, as I was doing with him.

꽃

Next morning, Sunday, I went running on the little road, about two miles long, that went from the campground to the park entrance. I had butterflies in my stomach as I dialed the pay phone at the ranger station to check the voicemails on my studio phone.

Kyle's voicemail catapulted the butterflies in my stomach into doing cartwheels. My legs went so weak that I had to sit down on the pebbly dirt as I listened and then re-listened to it two times, my head twisting up awkwardly since the metal cord was so short, with no give or stretch at all.

Kyle's voice sounded friendly as ever. He said he was sorry to have been out of touch for a while, but he'd needed to take care of something. He wanted to get together to drink Italian sodas, or have dinner and see a movie. He said nothing related to work. He ended by asking me to call him, in the direct, frank tone I found so sexy.

I pulled myself up from the ground, replaced the receiver, spanked off the pebbles that were ground into my shorts, and slowly continued my run on my weakened legs. I was sweating into my black sports bra in the bright morning sun, and my sunglasses kept slipping down the bridge of my nose. I had no more eyes for the wildish Sandy River below me, where the salmon would soon be spawning, than if it had been a row of blighted city buildings, I was so flooded by my river of thoughts.

Dinner and movies were what people did when they were dating. I was no fool about this. You talked for a long time across a table. Sometimes you even sat side by side. It'd be dark in there, maybe candlelit. Conversation was invariably personal, and sometimes food got shared. With enough wine flowing, tidbits could even get fed to each other by hand. And movie theaters? Worse. Seats were notoriously close to each other. Whispered conversations amounted to nuzzling. There'd be knees and thighs touching, whether accidentally or not always being open to interpretation on first dates. It would be dark in there. There was the stressful question of holding hands. A whole bag of buttery popcorn had once spilled onto my silk-skirted lap due to a misread signal of my date's effort to hold hands versus the popcorn being passed to me. Movies' plots typically got crowded out of my mind by the issue of what would happen after the movie was over. Whole movies, some of them doubtless good ones, were completely lost to me because some sexy guy had taken me to it and then sat next to me during it. Kyle and I were so attracted to each other that a movie with him would be like sitting through a heart attack. I distractedly jogged the road there at

Oxbow, shuffling like a centenarian on mile 25 of a marathon, my fears and hopes were draining the blood from my legs so completely.

I rounded a curve on the narrow road to find a dusty Jeep coming straight at me. I jumped sideways into blackberry bushes as the driver swerved away from me, his alarmed face swiveling around as he slowed to look back and see if I was OK. I raised a palm to signal that I was, and his hand went to his face in a gesture of apology before he drove on at a slower speed.

Heart pounding, shaken and scratched up from blackberry thorns, I crossed the road and walked back toward the ranger station on the absolute edge of the road, watching warily ahead for large objects hurtling toward me. The dating thing had been nerve-wracking enough back when I was single. But now I was married, for God's sake. I had no right to date anyone. My head swam with buts, like a racer somersault-reversing every five seconds in a pool. I knew now that marrying Sonny had been a mistake. I knew that having a child with him would be a bigger mistake, a much harder one to recover from.

Kyle, on the other hand, was more of an adult than my husband would ever be. Working on my show with him had been a juicy, joyful chapter of my life, a heartful teaming, the way I had always pictured in my youth that marriage would be. And I was sick of being loyal to Sonny. It had gotten me nowhere. No, it had moved me backward, because another two years of my fertility were now behind me. Unrecoverable.

I trudged back to the payphone in the now glaring sun. "I'm not so big on movies," I told Kyle when he answered. "But dinner might be nice."

Chapter 22
Deception

"This is beautiful," Kyle said. He was stating the obvious, which made me realize he was as nervous as I was. We were sitting, close but not touching, on the grass of Waterfront Park, looking at the Willamette River, deep jade in the fading light. This was where the sprawling, funky blues festival was held every 4th of July, like Portland's modern answer to Woodstock.

"I love rivers. I love to swim in them," I replied, thinking of Shasta and playing with her in the Klamath River during my road trip to California. It felt like a lifetime ago.

"I did break up with Jewel," Kyle reported out of the blue, as if we'd already been talking about his girlfriend. We hadn't been at all.

"You did? How do you feel about that?" I said, my stomach leaping with excitement, my voice controlled so as to still qualify as a compassionate friend.

"A lot better than I did before. We weren't good for each other." He shook his head decisively. "She's moved out. I waited until she'd done that to call you."

Kyle and I hadn't touched each other tonight except for our fingers when we'd shared food at dinner. I was wearing a two-layered gauzy skirt that flirted with transparency, the maroon shot through with myriad shades of blue, and a turquoise camisole that picked up the lightest of the blues. A warm breeze was blowing the soft cloth against my legs so gently I felt I was being caressed. My desire for Kyle to caress me was an ache within me, the ache Mary had helped me scream about. I made myself focus instead on the birds flying over the river. I was a little tipsy from the bottle of Pinot Noir we had shared earlier at Jarra's, the Ethiopian restaurant on lower Hawthorne. The wine had gone down as smoothly as the dinner the delicate-featured, dark-skinned family had served us: lentils, spiced spinach and numerous other little dishes, mostly creamy in texture. We ate the food not with utensils but with our hands and the endlessly porous, flexible bread that we tore to hold each bite of food, and then used to soak up every drop of savory juice like an elegant, edible sponge. The whole business lent itself to licking one's own fingers, and I mentioned that doing that was considered good manners in some African cultures. "Then we're very polite," Kyle had said.

"Sonny and I aren't good for each other, either," I replied now, keeping my eyes on the river, where a sailboat was moving very slowly south, against the tide. Kyle looked at me with interest, inviting me to say more. Well, I might be good for him, but he's terrible for me, I thought. But saying that would bring a blaming, bitter tone into a civil conversation. And maybe when all was said and done, I wouldn't have been so good for Sonny, after all.

"What do you mean?" Kyle said after some beats of silence.

"I made a mistake in marrying him," I said.

"You made a mistake. What are you going to do about that now?" Kyle said, not letting go of it. I could see he would have been a good lawyer. He'd left the law to become a theater director, and now here he was, skillfully directing our conversation.

Sonny thought I was at an Al-Anon meeting right now, and then going out with Erin afterward because her husband had relapsed, yet again. This was fiction, but based on historical fact. Erin needed my support, I'd explained earnestly to Sonny, and the whole thing could run late, given the sorry state of her marriage and Erin's consequent fragility. Sonny hadn't questioned any of this, but just remarked on what a good friend I was to Dorothy. Dorothy was what I called Erin when I talked about her to Sonny, since in Al-Anon you were supposed to preserve people's anonymity. My deceptions were already becoming adroit and multi-layered, and I was only one evening into them. I didn't believe the old adage that the reason not to lie was the problem of remembering what you had told people. I knew exactly what I had told Sonny, and what I wasn't yet telling Kyle. Of course, prior to Sonny I had virtually always been a truth-teller.

"I need to end it with Sonny," I admitted. We both heard the lack of conviction in my voice. Silence ensued. I didn't want to drag him into my fears about how Sonny would react, or where would I live and how would I possibly support myself with my deeply indebted dance studio. "It's a lot easier to end a relationship when you're not married," I pointed out. Kyle's large hazel eyes stayed level on mine, not giving ground, and after a few seconds I had to look away, across the river. Alpha wolves stared down the other animals in their pack, I remembered. Sometimes they also stared at their prey, weakening their will to escape. I had stared Sonny down more than once, but it had been about calling him on his dishonesty, more than asserting dominance, I thought. I sensed Kyle was challenging me now to be honest.

"So when's the last time you saw your husband?" Kyle asked me. He clearly thought it was months ago.

"When I left the house earlier this evening." His eyes widened in surprise. I felt relieved, as if the wave that had been forming as a swell in the ocean, that I needed badly to ride in order to get to the shore, was finally breaking.

"Sonny moved up two weeks ago," I said. "He's working for a construction company. Eight to five, Monday through Friday." I stopped talking and watched the darkening river, trying to keep breathing.

"You didn't tell me that when I asked you out," he said after a moment. His voice was tense, and I knew even before I turned to face him that his eyes were becoming hard.

"You didn't ask. And anyway, you've known since we met that I'm married." My voice was low, but it had heat. "You've never said that we were anything but friends. Have you? *Have you?*" I was calling his bluff, making him explain the long flirtation of the past months.

"Revelle, I have to tell you something," he said, in a different, softer voice. "I really like you, and not just as a friend. I'm really attracted to you. You're right that I've been holding back about that." He reached for my hand, and my relief at finally being touched by him brought me off the crest of the wave where I'd been balancing on the surfboard. His skin on mine brought me down into the water, and the water was warm, not cold, as I had feared. The wave rolled on without me, the surfboard floated on the surface a few yards away, attached to me by an ankle leash, and I held onto Kyle's hand.

"I like you too," I said, almost whispering. It was an understatement, yet dangerous to reveal since I was married. But that was craziness. I was out in public with Kyle, with the whole world knowing I was married. I noted in the back of my mind that my life had become more crazy and more joyful, both, after everything had fallen apart that May weekend two years ago.

"I want to be close to you, I want to have a relationship with you," Kyle said, his high-cheekboned face urgent. "I've been afraid to say anything because you're married. But really, you've always seemed to me like you're on your own."

"Well, maybe both things were true." I wanted him to keep talking. I closed the two-inch gap between us so that my right side touched his left side, our hands joined on my gauzy-skirted thigh. My left hand with my wedding ring I kept beneath my skirt.

"Revelle, I'm 30 years old. When I was younger, in college and law school, I did a lot of running around. A lot." He waved his free hand in the air, dismissing a past he was telling me was now irrelevant. I didn't know whether it was relevant or not; I just kept listening. "Now I want something that will last. And you're not just beautiful. You're a woman I really respect. When I see you dance sometimes, it just—" he stopped and gestured at the eastern sky, where the moon was rising next to Mount Hood. "It sends me to the moon and back, it's so full of heart. Plus, you're so sexy." I liked that sexiness was the last thing he'd mentioned, not what he'd led with. "To be honest, I've had fantasies about marrying you and having children with you, but now you're telling me that Sonny is actually *living* with you?" He was visibly distraught. We both knew he meant sleeping with me.

"It's just been an experiment." That sounded terrible, and I shifted uncomfortably. It would be even worse to say I thought about Kyle when making love with Sonny. What would Mary counsel? "Say something different, that's also true," was what I imagined her telling me.

"I've thought about you a lot, too," I said softly. "When you finally asked me out, I was excited." I laughed a little, then Kyle laughed too. That triggered my laughing for real, from my belly.

"Well, I'm single and available," Kyle grinned. "What about you?"

"I'm leaving Sonny," I heard myself reply when I stopped laughing, and the solid, stable feeling I suddenly got in my lower back gave me to know I'd stated the truth. I didn't have the details or logistics in place yet, but I would leave Sonny. Pastor Rachel might not like it, and I even thought, myself, that Sonny's and my attempt at marriage counseling had been half-assed, too little help sought out way too late. But no amount of counseling could change people's basic natures, and Sonny was a child in a man's body. I felt drained. The light was gone from the sky now, the air cooler, smells of cut grass and river water in my nostrils. I bent my forehead to my knee to rest my neck for a minute, then raised my head again.

"Someone's got to be brave enough to get this off the ground," Kyle said. I held his gaze silently. I'd used up every ounce of courage I had to show up on this date in the first place.

"I need to kiss you. Is that OK?" Kyle said, leaning toward me. I parted my lips to say yes, but his mouth had already caught mine the way that dragonflies catch each other in mid-air above bodies of water in the summertime to mate. His lips were full, soft, warm. My left hand, with the ring I suddenly, but not at all suddenly, wished I could cut off, moved to cradle his face. It was so different from Sonny's, with a smaller jaw and smoother skin, that I felt the contrast as a reproach.

Kyle's kisses were slow, steady and increasingly deep, as if he had all night, which unfortunately I did not. I felt dizzy with desire and unrest. I was married to someone else, which put me in the wrong. But, after a year of Sonny's broken promises I was done with being right, done with being good. A part of me was ready to sin, was stepping up to it with a fierce joy, the way Deirdre got into it with designer-suited guys who wanted her parking space. My marriage had generated quiet fury in me because Sonny had let me down time and again. But Kyle, ironically the illicit one, had always done everything he'd told me he'd do. Never missing a beat, like Paul's drumming.

Kyle put his hands on my hips and lifted, scooching me to hold me as closely against him as possible. My heart was pounding as we wrapped our arms around each other. He was much slighter than Sonny, not dense with muscle, maybe halfway between Sonny's size and my own. Our bodies were so lean we were like two young whippets winding ourselves around each other, all bones and sinew with practically zero body fat. My trembling was as noticeable as the wide Willamette River sitting in front of us that divided Portland east and west, and that was probably why Kyle stopped kissing me to talk.

"Hey, I'm nervous too," he said. "But what's the worst thing that could happen here? What are we so afraid of?"

"The worst thing that could happen is that we'd fall in love," I replied. I didn't say it was that Sonny was still in love with me. I thought that was just the worst thing for Sonny. I wasn't thinking very well.

"No. It's worse to fall in love and not have it work out. Worst-case scenario here is a broken heart." Kyle was certain of this.

"My heart's been broken plenty of times," I said, thinking not just of Mike but of fellows I'd fallen for in college and high school. "It's always mended. I've always been able to love again." My certainty about the heart's resilience was a dead-even match for Kyle's pessimism.

"My heart's getting leathery," he grinned wryly, breaking eye contact, looking down and shaking his head a little.

"You're too young to have a leathery heart," I said, meaning it. Thirty was four years younger than me, and here he was talking like a survivor of multiple divorces. Our bodies were so closely entwined we would barely have filled up a single chair.

"Let me put it this way. I'm not looking to just have an affair with you, Revelle. Is that what you're looking for?"

"No!" I winced at the idea.

"Me neither. So we're on the same page." I nodded, his cheek smooth against mine, with not a hint of friction. The fantasy he'd mentioned of marriage and children with me was already sending *me* to the moon and back. He caught my mouth in his again, his hazel eyes dancey and shimmery like dragonflies. Somebody walking by whistled at us, making me jump, and my jitteriness reminded me I was on stolen time.

"I hate to say this, but I need to go home," I said softly. Kyle shook his head, opposed to that notion, and started kissing my neck.

It was a nerve-rackingly long time before I pulled my truck into the driveway of the house in Northwest. I was intoxicated, in an altered state, but no longer from the wine. I shed my gauzy skirt and crept into bed in my camisole and panties next to my husband, managing not to wake him. I dropped into a heavy sleep in which I was dancing in the air in a way that moved me from my bed in Portland out to the Oregon coast. I floated from the air down onto a yellow surfboard; the two haystack rocks in the near distance told me I was at Cannon Beach. The ocean and board seemed to have a pleasant will of their own, and I found myself surfing a large, long-breaking wave, the curl opening in front of me and closing behind me as if I were a magician willing that to happen. I was frightened I would wipe out, because I had absolutely no experience surfing. But I was learning quickly, and the board had a wonderful grippy texture on the soles of my feet, clearly wanting me to stay joined to it. I was getting the hang of the balancing act, using my knees as shock absorbers and making the little adjustments needed with my feet. I was thrilled to find I could surf without having had to shell out scarce dollars for lessons. I breathed the salty spray of the wave, exhilarated. Suddenly the board shot out from under my feet, sending me backward into the roiling ocean, which had turned from loving me to hating me in one instant. The leash linking the board to my ankle snapped taut, and teamed with the backlash of the wave to send the surfboard straight back and down at me, punching me in the stomach like a Poseidon-driven prizefighter. My breath left me as devastatingly as a popped balloon loses its air, the hard ocean floor banged up against my shoulder, and then I was taking briny water into my desperate lungs, more than a decade before a U.S. president would state, straight-faced, that waterboarding was not a form of torture.

Sonny told me later I screamed like a woman being murdered, but I don't remember making a sound. What I remember was the dark horror of drowning, of dying young, without having had the child I was born to have. That, and the guilt of having destroyed actually three lives with my need for revenge, because I knew that the rapist, the tall man with the Coke bottle glasses, had reached up with a long memory through the long-breaking wave to throw me off the surfboard and turn the freedom-giving waverider into the instrument of my destruction. Panicked, panting, I let Sonny spoon me against his warm body, holding me in a bed and a marriage that he, in his own mythological world, was imagining to be a haven, a refuge from his own fears and wanderings.

Chapter 23
Exodus

The next morning found me at an Al-Anon meeting, scared and fragile like a person with internal injuries. Erin, at my side, had gotten her beautiful haircut restored, and looked as strikingly put-together as when I'd first met her. The difference was that now I knew she had a messed-up marriage, too.

She reached over and squeezed my hand, oblivious to having been used as the body of last night's lie. The metal of the folding chair was colder than usual through my skirt; I hadn't found any clean underwear that morning, and was going without. I looked around at the serene-faced meeting attendees, feeling as if they could see the scarlet A on my forehead.

I had managed to hold myself together with Sonny as he'd gotten ready for work earlier. I'd ground up dark-roasted beans for coffee and squeezed fresh juice from rosy-red Texas grapefruits. I made toast and scrambled eggs, then didn't touch my food and let Sonny eat all of it. He asked me what my nightmare had been about, and I lied that I couldn't remember. I had been terrified. Into-me-see, Rachel's gravelly voice chided in my mind. I was blocking intimacy with him as completely as blackout curtains blocked the light from windows in World War II.

Sonny asked cheerfully how Dorothy was doing, then upended his rosy juice glass, exposing his strong throat like he had when drinking wine at our wedding reception. Wolves did that when they trusted each other. His trust in me had turned foolish overnight. Or, maybe not overnight. I stared at his handsome, confident face. I was glassy with lack of sleep and weighted like a cloudy old leaded window with the knowledge of the deception.

"Hello, earth to Revelle," he grinned. "How is Dorothy?" It finally came to me like sunlight through the unwashed kitchen window that Dorothy was Erin. Sonny thought I'd gone out with her last night.

"Oh, you know how it is when someone relapses. There's, like, no real resolution in sight, sometimes," I dissembled.

"But there is for us," he said brightly as he glanced at the clock and got up from the table. "We're solid. We're together. " He wiped his freshly shaven face with a blue napkin. Then he kissed me with his firm, supple lips and walked out the door at 7:30 on the dot as if he'd been executing all these leave-it-to-Beaver rituals for years. I stood leaning limply against the kitchen counter in the same clothes I'd worn the night before, and drained the last of my cold coffee. It hadn't gone like this one single morning in California when he'd been self-employed. It had been Sonny sleeping in because he'd stayed up late, the phone ringing with angry contractors asking where the hell he was, Sonny searching frenetically for keys, lost tools, items to return to Home Depot before he finally clattered out the door.

At the meeting I shared at the first chance after the opening readings, because I had never in my life needed so badly to talk. "My husband has been leaving for work on time every morning. I'm amazed by what he can do when he decides he wants to do it," I said. My head was throbbing and I felt it could shatter, like the bottle of wine I had hurled against the wall in California. The one Sonny had dodged, maybe saving his own life. "But then," I said more slowly, thinking it through out loud, "do we sit here congratulating ourselves because *we* didn't walk in late and interrupt the meeting? Is it really such a big accomplishment to be on time?" I saw a few smiles. "Well, if I'm dealing with Sonny, it's a big deal. I'm supposed to be grateful and jump for joy, as if now I can trust this man, now my marriage is great, it's kicking ass, it's a big rompin', stompin', can-do proposition." My arms sculpted the air with the grandiosity of my allegedly transformed relationship. "My minister Rachel probably thinks I'm not grateful enough for the fact that he's changed, that he's actually moved up and started living with me. But then, she has a partner who never did bizarre things to begin with. Rachel gets to take some stability for granted. I want to be able to do that, too." I paused and shifted my legs uneasily. It was hard to know what I could and couldn't say here. The breakable bottle that was me hadn't broken yet, so I kept going.

"My husband isn't drinking, at least not that I know of. That's another thing that's supposed to be a big deal. He's not getting drunk! He's holding down a job! He gets home on time!" My arms flew in different directions as if throwing crepe-paper streamers of celebration. "Well, big whoop!" Erin was smiling, but others were frowning. I stilled my forearms onto my gauzy-skirted lap: remember the audience. Plus, I needed to hold my precarious bottle-self safely in place.

I wanted to say that if I was dealing with Kyle, adult behavior was part of the baseline. It set the stage so that he and the people around him could do bigger things than just flounder and try to get by. Having a baby was a bigger thing. And I loved Kyle. But I'd never heard people talk about cheating in these meetings, at least, not their own cheating. I struggled to find my way back into Al-Anon parlance.

"I know that I'm supposed to have an 'attitude of gratitude.' And I do have a lot to be grateful for: my health, my church, my dance studio. I have plenty to eat, and that's more than most of the world has. I'm grateful for that." Approving nods from several people, boosting my flagging confidence. "But I'm not sure that an attitude of gratitude always works. Let's look at this morning. Right now I'm supposed to be leading my morning dance class. But I'm in 'emotional crisis—'" I mocked my own fragility with air quotes "—over my situation, my marriage, so I'm sitting here talking about that, instead. So I'm probably losing whatever new students I gained from the show I worked 70 hours a week to pull off. Why should I be grateful for a marriage that sets me up for all that? For a marriage that always lands me in crisis?"

I knew I was lying by omission, leaving out the incriminating fact that my cheating with Kyle was creating part of the crisis. Erin listened closely, chin tilted down so that her angled dark hair framed her lovely face, but the emotional temperature in the rest of the room was getting as cool as the chair under my thin-skirted bottom. I pushed on recklessly anyway.

"Maybe being grateful for a dry-drunk husband would just reduce my life chances and keep me spinning in circles. Maybe it would just keep me going to meetings instead of going somewhere with my frigging life. I mean, what about when an 'attitude of gratitude' means we're being grateful for crumbs?" I struggled for my next thought, which seemed to need oxygen in a room sucked dry of that. "I mean, if we have a choice in the matter, why have an alcoholic in our lives at all?"

My voice broke with frustration. The room became the Arctic. Even Erin stiffened. I slowly brought my arms back to my lap, the bottle of me close to breaking now. I hadn't just challenged one of the precious twelve-step platitudes; I'd stepped outside of the sanctioned Al-Anon narrative altogether. I'd suggested our whole reason for gathering might be misguided. A silence hung in the room, not the velvety kind you got when people were in accord, but the scratchy grain-sack kind you got when they weren't. When someone clearly didn't belong.

"Thanks for listening," I said limply, the words that always opened the way to the next share.

"My name is Mary Jo," a woman of about sixty said from across the room. Her first word landed so close to my last one that I realized she must have been desperately waiting for me to shut up. Her face was careworn, with deep lines between her nose and mouth that seemed to operate as brackets for her words. People turned their faces to her, eager to get back to warmth, to velvet. "I haven't been making conscious contact with my Higher Power lately. I've been starting to blame my son for being an alcoholic, blaming A.A. for not curing him from being an alcoholic. Basically, I've been doing stinkin' thinkin'. Whenever I do that, I know it's time for me to do a new Fourth Step. I need to take my own inventory. What are my own character defects? How have I been trying to control people, places and things?" She spoke on, her voice calm and clear, convicted as a born-again Christian, but I had stopped hearing her because the bottle that was me was breaking.

I got up and crept away, skirting behind everyone, toward the end of the fellowship hall. I was dimly aware of leaving my purse behind, next to Erin's. Once in the restroom I locked the door behind me and sank down to the floor, shaking and sobbing in gasps, the bottle shattering onto the floor into shards and jagged pieces. The space was small, cramped, and smelled of bubble-gum-scented soap. Hot tears streamed down my cheeks and snot poured from my nose. I was hemorrhaging fluids like the Pinot Noir had released itself onto the wall behind Sonny's head that wretched night in California. I slapped at the toilet paper and a rippling white streamer offered itself to me like a parody of a trailing bridal veil. I hugged my knees to my chest and the toilet paper to my face, but the thin stuff couldn't keep pace.

My crying was uncontrollable, like the projectile vomiting of my worst episode of childhood flu. What had felt simple and decided out by the river the night before with Kyle now felt heinous, criminal. Ending a marriage was like committing a murder, especially if the goal of it was to be with someone else. A different woman than the one I'd thought I was had set me on this crazy, twisted path. My sobs escalated with every scary thought that raced through my mind. They sounded unnatural even to me, like the panicked final breaths of an injured animal. The toilet paper mounted and trailed around me and the floor like a dutiful, never-ending bandage. A dull, hard ache was pounding in my nether-regions and it dawned on me that that meant my period was starting. It was only a week since my last period had ended. I was ovulating at double time. And, two more years of my fertility were gone since meeting Sonny, with no child in sight. I trembled and cried with a deeper frenzy, pawing furiously for more toilet paper. The jagged broken-glass shards of me might never get put together again. Maybe better to just accept that. The body of the rapist was there in the cramped bathroom with me, just as broken as I was. I had never gotten away from him. My revenge had only attached me to him across the years and miles as if with blood-soaked bandages. No wise God would award a child to a murderess. Of course my fertility was leaving me. Another hemorrhage.

Someone was knocking hard on the thin door, making it bump against my back.

"Revelle?" It was Erin's voice, worried, anxious.

I got up onto my knees, turned and let her in. She stared at me for just one second and then was in the space with me, locking the door behind her and getting down on the floor. She tossed both our purses into the far corner, and I realized I must have left mine behind as a signal to come find me here.

"Oh, honey," she said, and took me in her arms.

"I can't sleep with him again tonight," I gasped into her neck. My snot was getting into her perfect, glossy hair, but she didn't pull away. "I can't do it. It's sick."

"OK. You're going to come stay with me for awhile," Erin said. Her voice was decisive, confident, like mine was when I announced a new dance routine to my students. The tone said to the listeners that you'd already thought this thing through, and developed a great idea, one that would work for everyone concerned. Follow my lead, here we go, the tone said.

"Jason is in Boston on business. We'll have the place to ourselves," Erin added.

I nodded, my gratitude genuine now instead of a posture, her sweet-smelling hair tickling my swollen nose. It was a great idea. I'd stay with Erin for awhile.

"I'm thinking about you all the time now," Kyle said. His voice on the phone was low, understated.

"Same with me," I said. I was looking out the second-floor window at the red-bricked University of Portland campus two blocks away. Erin's house was lovely, glowing-floored, sun-drenched. Staying here made me feel like I could breathe again.

"Can I see you this afternoon?" Kyle asked.

"I wish," I said. "I have a commitment. Three weeks ago I said I'd make dinner for Fideles House." I didn't add that Sonny had made the same commitment. He'd actually insisted we sign up, as part of his splashing-into-Portland-life campaign.

Erin had driven down to my house with me after helping me get cleaned up in the bathroom. She helped me mobilize myself in the tree-shaded living room that still smelled of the morning's breakfast. I packed my toiletries and a few clothes—jeans, my swimsuit, running shoes and shorts, handfuls of dirty underwear I needed to wash—to take up to her place. I hurried, feeling like a fugitive in my own house. I wrote a two-sentence note to Sonny on the back of the first sheet of paper I could find, which happened to be a solicitation from the Democratic Party. I wrote that I was staying with a friend for a few days to get some breathing space. I'd be calling him at some point to check in. I signed it with just my first initial, and walked out of the house. I would have happily walked away from everything I owned in the world if that step could have taken away the fact I'd married Sonny.

I talked some more with Kyle, wishing I could get out of the dinner project and see him instead. But I knew that if I left matters in Sonny's hands, dinner would be so late the worship service would never happen. He'd also leave a huge mess for the others to clean up. As out of control as my life felt, I could still keep a commitment. Especially after revealing so much to the clearness committee (except for anything about Kyle) I felt the need to be visibly holding things together.

When he met me at the Fideles House, Sonny argued with me over what we should make. I wanted a simple menu, like tacos. I didn't say this, but the nice boxes of crispy pre-made shells would substantially reduce the amount of time I'd have to spend with him in the kitchen. But Sonny was determined to make a spinach and brie soufflé that he said his mother had made once. He didn't care that it was complicated, or that he'd never made it before, himself. "It's to die for," he kept saying. After he'd said it ten times, I thought, I wouldn't mind seeing you die for it. I finally said I would make green salad and garlic bread, and he was on his own with the soufflé.

Nature's Fresh Northwest was crowded. My mind was flooded with thoughts of Kyle: Kyle kissing me with his wide, warm mouth; Kyle telling me he wanted children with me; Kyle reaching for my hand by the Willamette River last week. I wanted him inside me. Sonny kept up a running patter.

"Oh, Revelle, there are three, no four kinds of brie, which is best? Normal spinach or organic spinach? Four bunches or five bunches?" I gritted my teeth in fury. Nothing with Sonny could ever be simple, and it was impossible to hurry him along. "Which of these egg farmers treat their chickens the best? There're so many choices: cage free, free range, grain fed, vegetarian fed . . . why aren't you paying attention, Revelle? Would you go find some white pepper? No, no, black pepper won't work in this recipe." I fought the desire to run out of the store and not stop until I was miles away.

The checkout line was painfully long, made lengthier by Sonny's energetic flirting with the cashier. She was a well-endowed child of about 17 who kept her long-lashed fawn eyes lowered like Bambi's, as bashful as if she'd never received attention from a man before. I sensed Sonny wanted me to feel jealous. I didn't. I wanted to tell Bambi I would take over her cash register if she would just sashay on over to Fideles House and make the goddamned soufflé with Sonny.

Back at the house, things were quiet, hushed, as if dinner and worship were in the air waiting to be born. I started making garlic bread with the garlic that Rachel had grown in the garden, first turning on the radio to avoid conversation. Sonny promptly switched it from the National Public Radio station to the cassette tape function, popping in a tape he chose from the tidy shelves. It was Johnny Cash singing "Ring Of Fire."

"Man, that guy can write a song," Sonny remarked as he cracked eggs into a large orange bowl.

"His wife wrote that song," I said as I sliced tomatoes on a cutting board with one of the knives that Paul had sharpened. A sharp knife made a big difference.

"She did not," Sonny replied automatically, as if writers of good songs were uniformly male.

"June Carter Cash wrote 'Ring of Fire' in 1963," I told Sonny. I was using my slow, patient voice that Paul had once said was designed for village idiots. "It was one of the biggest hits of Johnny Cash's career." I knew this because Marisol had written a paper in college on women's under-publicized contributions to popular culture. I found it irrelevant to add that June had co-written it with a man, Merle somebody or other. June had probably done most of the work.

"She wrote it when Johnny Cash was a drug addict and a jerk, and he kept burning her again and again. Then he cleaned up his act, so she married him. Then she trusted him enough to have a child." I glared at Sonny, who watched me closely, somewhat warily. I realized the knife in my hand and expression on my face might have something to do with that. The phone rang and I dropped the knife and quickly moved around the island to answer it, wiping my hands on a flour-sack towel.

"Fideles House, this is Revelle."

"Revelle?" Kyle's voice met my ear, as welcome as a kiss.

"Hi!" I said, my heart starting to pound and my face to burn. Sonny was five feet away.

"Can you talk?"

"Actually, I can't," I said. "I'm making dinner for the community right now, and we're running really late. Let me call you after worship is over, OK?"

"That won't work. We're having a big family dinner. These things go on a long time." Kyle's voice was glum. "My uncle has come in from New York."

"You mean the one who—?"

"Yeah."

"Oh, God!" I smacked my forehead. I wanted to say, "You have to go to dinners like that, with him there?"

"It'll be OK. I'll be OK," Kyle was assuring me. "It was such a long time ago, it's like we were both different people."

"Hm," I said, concerned, not convinced. I had never thought that somebody other than me had been raped at age seven.

"I'll call you tomorrow morning," he promised. I loved knowing that that call would in fact happen.

"Good!" I smiled. "Take care. Bye for now." I moved back to the cutting board without meeting Sonny's eyes and resumed slicing tomatoes. "That was Dorothy. She's making a lot of outreach calls lately."

"She calls you here?"

"I spend a lot of time here." I met his blue eyes now with anger and defiance. "What do you know about people who work twelve-step programs?"

"All I know is I want you to move back in with me," Sonny replied, his tanned face suddenly vulnerable. "I need you."

I refrained from screaming at him that he was late on needing me, as he was late with everything else in his life. It seemed to me that it had always been a love-hate relationship I had had with Sonny, and that I had used up all the light, frothy, good-tasting love in the first two years, and was now left with a long-ignored, huge mound of the bitter-tasting hatred.

I turned my back on him and sliced a cucumber, loving its fresh scent, wishing it to cool my blistered mind, my blistering temper.

Sonny struggled on with his spinach soufflé for 24 people with much drama and clattering through cupboards, eventually calling his mother for advice on whether a single, enormous casserole dish was likely to work. The conversation did not go well, from the part I heard of it.

"But I'm supposed to be living up here," he muttered at one point. "I'll lose her otherwise." And a moment later, "Well, I care."

We served dinner half an hour late, the community hastily emptying the bowls of salad and plates of garlic bread. Few touched the soufflé, which sat limp and unrisen in its single, over-sized casserole dish like a downtrodden, pre-Easter Christ.

I didn't hear a word of Rachel's sermon that evening. After the closing benediction, Marisol, Paul and Ruben helped me clean up the devastated kitchen while Sonny talked showily, animatedly with Rachel in the dining room. "Now that I've moved up here, I want to become an official member of Fideles," I heard him say. *No way*, I thought fiercely. *I'm getting custody of the church.*

When we were done I quickly asked Paul to take a walk with me, while Sonny still had Rachel's attention and wouldn't realize I was leaving. Paul looked a little surprised but readily agreed. We strolled down the still-light street in our sandals, the huge oak and maple trees making an extravagant green canopy above us, their roots making ripples, cracks and hills in the sidewalks that we stepped over. I told him I was leaving Sonny, and staying with a girlfriend while I figured out where to live next.

"Finally," Paul said feelingly. "Thank you, Jesus!" He raised his arms to the heavens like a Dust Bowl preacher who had finally conjured rain for the brittle crops.

"I'm glad you're happy, but I feel bloodied," I said. A three-legged terrier bounced over to us, wagging its tail, and I bent to pet it. "It's like I'm wounded," I said.

"Well, you are. Being with Sonny would wound anybody," Paul said. It felt like support.

"I've wounded him, too, though. It's cutting both ways." I didn't want to think about what Sonny's reaction would be when I told him I wasn't coming back.

"Yeah," Paul acknowledged. "Well. A wound is a doorway. We exit our old life through the wound."

I thought about that as we walked, trying it on for size. "So, I can exit my old life through my wound. Good. Yes! Did you make that up?"

"Nah. Robert Bly."

"Have you exited your old life through the wound Lena left?"

Paul didn't answer right away. I looked down at my worn-out sandals, feeling bad that it was the first time I'd asked him about himself in weeks. He stopped at a retaining wall that was straining to hold back a riotously overgrown garden, plants and flowers tumbling down in a colorful, tangled cascade. He picked two orange nasturtium blossoms, put one in his mouth, and gave the other to me. "I'm working on it," he said, then chewed.

I put my nasturtium blossom into my mouth. It was spicy, startling me, almost scaring me with its intensity. Then, right there on my tongue, it changed flavor. It became sweet, like clover honey.

Chapter 24
Shooting Star

"Sonny? Are you home?"

His truck was in the driveway, but shouldn't have been. I'd expected him to be at work. It was mid-afternoon, the Friday before Labor Day. I stood in the living room, sweating. I was wearing jeans and the camisole with "Cowgirl" scripted across it. It was too hot for jeans, but I had so little up at Erin's. I needed the rest of my clothes, which was why I had come here with black garbage bags. I wanted to quickly stuff them and be gone.

"I'm in the bathtub. Door's open," Sonny called. I stood still in the living room, my stomach knotting with the old anxiety I was trying to leave behind. Paul and I had talked about the best way to tell Sonny I wasn't just taking a break but was leaving the marriage.

"I think you should do it on the phone," Paul had said.

"That's cold. It's more respectful in person," I'd objected.

"He's not a respectful kind of guy. He's a wild card, and he's not going to like what you're telling him. If you're going to break up with him in person, I think I should be there," Paul had said.

"He's never hit me," I pointed out.

"Neither has any guy ever hit his wife, until the first time he hits his wife."

I considered. Paul had always been more street-smart than I was.

"OK, I'll go and get my things from the house on Friday while he's at work. Then I'll tell him on the phone that it's over."

"That's better," Paul had said, satisfied. Now, I wished he were here. I wished he were here. My mind gabbled the line from the Pink Floyd song over and over: Paul, I wish you were here.

"Why aren't you at work?" I called to Sonny as I went to the bedroom. I started quickly emptying my dresser drawers into a black garbage bag, stepping around the Coors beer cans and an empty vodka bottle on the floor. I should be gone within minutes.

"They laid me off," Sonny finally called from the bathroom. I heard splashing sounds and squishy footsteps, and then he was in the bedroom with me, naked and dripping. He had a California tan overlaid with a construction worker's tan: his face, neck and arms from mid-biceps down were reddish brown, and the rest of him medium tan except for everything his swim trunks usually covered. That skin was pale as a baby's. With the full-length mirror behind him doubling all the color contrasts, he looked goofy, like a cartoon version of a multicultural man. I felt inappropriate laughter bubbling up in me, which I quelled. Stress had always made me laugh and cry easily.

"They had too many people once the big job ended, plus I showed up late a couple of times," Sonny said. "With you gone, it's hard to feel like anything matters. Are you coming back?"

I dropped my eyes. "No. I'm leaving. I'm moving in with Marisol." I could see the indignity of having your wife break up with you when you were stark naked and dripping onto the floor. But there was no way I could wait around for him to dry off and get dressed in his leisurely, distractible way.

"You're seeing someone else. Aren't you?" His voice radiated heat.

"That's not the reason I'm leaving," I said. It was true that Kyle coincided in time with my marriage ending. But it was the way Sonny was, plus my original mistake in marrying him, that were the ultimate causes. My overpriced, debt-inducing education had at least taught me the difference between proximate cause and ultimate cause.

"Women always say that when they leave their husband for someone else. What's his name?" he demanded.

"It's nobody you know." Now I was getting mad, too. The marriage had been on his terms for the year of its lifespan, and now he was still assuming that all the choices were his, and none of them mine. The conversation needed to end. I moved toward the bedroom door, dragging my black garbage bag of clothes like an inept thief.

"Is it one of your dance students? Or is it that guy from church, Paul?" Sonny moved toward the door, blocking my way out.

"God no, not Paul!" I said, stamping my foot. Then I felt like a shithead, as if I'd castrated my friend. It upset me that Sonny had smeared dirt into the part of my life that was the cleanest.

"You can't throw our marriage away. You can't throw us away," Sonny said. He'd switched to his nice-guy voice, his lover persona. "I'm here now." He made a gesture drawing attention to his presence in the room, in the house. I hated that I was supposed to be impressed he was finally living in the same city as me, a year after we'd taken our vows. He reached for me, held me to his wet skin. I squirmed away. "Revelle, I feel more passion for you than I've ever felt for anyone in my life."

"Well, your passion didn't do me any good!" I heard myself roar. Sonny's desire was like Mike's desire had been: pleasurable for them, but useless to me in the end. "I never told you to feel passion for me! You're a child in a man's body. I can't have a child with another child!"

"But you knew exactly what I was like when you married me!" Sonny cried.

"You're right. I knew exactly what you were like!" I yelled back. "That didn't mean it ever worked for me!"

"But you *married* me!" he bellowed. His reddish brown face was going darker red. "You weren't being honest down in California!"

"You're right!" I screamed back, my throat opening full throttle. "I wasn't being honest in California! I was being *desperate*!"

Sonny's face exploded with pain, and my body convulsed with its own misery and fury, making me bend in two. I heard a crashing noise, and looked up to see that his fist had gone into the full-length mirror, shattering it. Shards glittered from the floor like mosaic pieces waiting to be put together, and jagged splinters clung to the mirror frame like oversized thorns. Sonny's face told me his rage had only started.

I fled from the house, leaving the bag of clothes behind because it would only slow me down and make me into easier prey. I could hear Sonny yelling from inside the house, but the truck was already carrying me away like a merciful ambulance. I imagined Sonny had been shouting, "Calamity Revelle," his moniker for me in our Magic Kingdom days. Calamity Revelle thudded dully in my mind, and I wished for a stiff shot of tequila, because I was a cowgirl, and tequila was what cowgirls drank.

The truck drove me onto the Fremont bridge and up and over the Willamette River, then guided me to Mount Tabor Park. I parked and wandered the forest trails in the muggy heat with no sense of direction at all, holding the maddeningly thick blanket that was my hair up off my neck with first one hand and then, when that arm tired, the other. All my ponytail holders had gotten left at the house. My hands themselves itched and hurt from eczema, and the expensive ointment that could soothe this was also still at the house. I wanted to cry from pain and frustration. Sonny's rage blocked me from the house, and buying new things to replace the old would just send me farther down the tunnel of debt that I had been drilling for months with *Dancing Fool*. In the past month I'd actually taken cash advances from my credit card with the lowest interest rate to make the minimum payments on each of my cards. That itself was a crazy cannibalism, the kind of thing Sonny might do, not me. You grew to be like the people closest to you. I wanted to be like Kyle, not Sonny. The random thought came to me that the deepest thing Kyle and I had in common was being half-breeds with fucked-up pasts. It was the reason his face had hit me like a thunderbolt the first time I'd seen it. We were both charming overachievers, working to pass in the mainstream as people who just happened to have great tans.

I trudged the trails in my overheated fugue state until the shadows of the Douglas fir trees were growing tall and thin like anorexic models. I managed to find the truck, and this time it took me down Hawthorne, to a parking spot that miraculously appeared two doors down from the Oasis. I found Kyle in his tiny theater office, dark head and bone-wide shoulders spread out over a spreadsheet, eating Tic Tacs.

"Hi!" he said, pulling himself up, face lighting into a smile. "It's great to see you. Want some Tic Tacs?"

"Sure," I said, letting him pour a few into my hand and tossing them back like Calamity's shot of tequila. "How's the new show coming along?"

"Better than I thought it would, but now it's the show after that that I'm worried about. The lead actor is talented, but flaky as hell. I have to ride him like a rented mule, and I still think the whole thing might fall apart." I nodded. That was easy to relate to.

"How are you doing?" Kyle asked me in a softer tone.

"Kind of a hard day. I just told Sonny I was leaving for good." I took his hand and tapped another Tic-Tac into my own hand, to have an excuse to touch him.

"You did?" I nodded. I wished I could change out of my sweaty Cowgirl camisole.

"Are you OK? Do you have a place to live?" He had felt bad in the past week that he had nothing to offer me in that way, since he lived with his sister.

"Marisol just invited me to move in with her family, even though her cousins are still there, too. Carmenita's sharing her room with me. She's excited; she thinks we're having nightly slumber parties. My other roommate is Isadora Duncan. A hamster," I explained. Maybe a little more detail than he'd needed.

"Listen, if you can hang around another hour, I can finish this spreadsheet and we can get out of here, go someplace together," he said. His large hazel eyes held mine.

"Sure. Just come get me down at the studio." I felt breathless but focused, now that I had time with Kyle to look forward to. At *Dancing Fool* I went through mail, returned phone calls, cleaned the fingerprinted wall-mirrors and gritty floor. I took a sponge bath in the bathroom and changed into a clean-looking white t-shirt that some dancer or yoga student had left behind.

Then Kyle and I were out in the late, long-shadowed sunlight, him opening the door of his huge old Chrysler and me sitting on the cracked green upholstery, hot even through my jeans. But now I welcomed the heat, loved being in my body, being with him. He leaned over from the driver's seat, took my face in his hands and kissed me. "How about the Gorge?" he murmured. I felt the words more than heard them, like Helen Keller. He wanted to take us east on 84, out the spectacularly cliffed corridor of the mighty Columbia, the river that forms the border between Oregon and Washington.

"Yes," I formed back with my lips, breathing into his mouth. "I love the Gorge."

ॐ

At the funky little restaurant on Oak Street in Hood River, he ordered a bloody Mary and I got a tequila sunrise.

"There was a movie in the 80's called Tequila Sunrise," Kyle remarked. I'd elected to sit next to him in the booth rather than across from him. I loved the warmth of his side against mine.

"I remember it. Mel Gibson, Michelle Pfeiffer." I felt as happy now as I'd felt tense and anxious all afternoon.

"And Kurt Russell. A messed-up love triangle. Like us."

"Well, they had guns, drugs and kids all mixed together," I pointed out. "Bad combination. We don't have any of those in our triangle."

"There's a difference," he conceded. I finished my tequila sunrise quickly. When I reached for the cherry at the bottom of the glass, Kyle said, "Those things are carcinogenic."

"So I live dangerously." I chewed with enjoyment, looking him in the eye.

"Evidently." He put his arm around me. "How did Sonny take the news?"

"Not well." We ordered new drinks.

"What's this?" He held the devastated palm of my left hand up between us. The skin could have been something a lizard would have left behind. The wedding ring was gone, tucked into my purse.

"Eczema. The doctor said it's a stress reaction. It's flared up the past year whenever Sonny has been around." Kyle nodded thoughtfully, head bent over our hands in a suggestion of a conjoint prayer.

"So you're on probation in this relationship," I said in my best sweet-but-tough-woman voice. "If I'm with you and the skin on my hands starts to crack and break again—"

I jerked my thumb over my shoulder. "I'm outta here," Kyle grinned.

"Outta here," I smiled, kissing his cheek, then his temple.

"I can do this," he said. "Republicans are can-do people."

"You're a Republican?" The tequila was hitting my empty stomach hard, and I thought I'd misheard him.

"You didn't know that?"

"No. I'm a die-hard Democrat. Now I know for sure I'm in a cross-cultural relationship."

"Hey, let's dance." He led me by the hand and I followed the trail of his confidence to where two other couples were already joined on the floor in the low light. The band was just a guitar and bass player, but they sounded good. Soulful. Kyle put his arms around me and I relaxed into him. I wanted everything to go away except him. The duo sang in harmony about how wild horses couldn't drag them away, and the slide guitar wandered around like a cowboy searching a desert for water. Kyle and I were each other's water. We hadn't held each other since the night on the Willamette River. My face was pressed to his smooth cheek, his Indian cheek that he rarely needed to shave. The nerve endings in my body felt as if every synapse they had ever been groping and searching for in my life had now been delivered to them, delicately locked into place by the taut, tenuous, landing of Kyle's body against mine.

"We need to get out of town together, he murmured. "We need a lost weekend, where nothing else exists except each other. I hate that neither of us has a place of our own where we can be together tonight." I didn't answer right away, because I felt grateful at this point that I had a place to live, at all, even not my own. The wild horses song ended, and the duo started a faster song. I started moving to it, hungry to dance, but Kyle led us back to our booth.

"We could go camping together," I suggested. "There's a great place on the beach where you bring your things down in wheelbarrows—"

"No thanks on camping. Sorry, but I don't find it romantic to slap at mosquitoes and struggle to make a fire. I'm not that kind of Indian."

I sighed. No camping was more of a setback than his being a Republican. We sipped our drinks. Then I remembered a casual conversation during the dinner of the fallen soufflé. "OK. Here's something. My friends Luke and Kat are leaving for B.C. tomorrow for a pottery show. They said I was welcome to stay at their place in Hebo. It's a little town near the coast."

"Really? I'm not working on Labor Day. Let's go then; it's just a couple of days away."

"I'll call them and let them know." I drained the last of my second tequila sunrise and suddenly sagged into him, the day-long flood of adrenaline drained from my body.

"What's wrong?" Kyle said. He was studying the menu. He probably hadn't eaten all day, either. He got lost in his work, the way I'd used to get lost in mine, before I got lost in this triangle of him, me and Sonny.

"All this lostness," I said. I felt deeply sad.

"Listen," Kyle said, shifting uncomfortably. "I need to say something. I've got a lot of stress in my life. The theater is barely staying afloat. Jewel is close to my family, and since she's mad at me for breaking up with her, my family is mad at me, too. I don't need all that bullshit. What I *do* need is for my relationship with you to be an escape from my stress. I love you, but I don't want to deal with sad faces or hear about problems. I'm not up for that."

"Ah," I said simply, lightly. I straightened my spine and neck like a dancer going on stage. We ordered food and ate. That helped both of us. I kept my face composed, attentive, not sad. We danced on the slow songs. I fed on the fact he loved me. The mournful, wandering slide guitar expressed my feelings so I didn't have to, the way music and art will often say the things we're not allowed to say, ourselves.

Later, driving back down the Gorge, Kyle said, "What's the best thing about walking a mile in someone else's moccasins?" His hand was on my blue-jeaned thigh. I looked to our left at Multnomah Falls, silvery strands coming down from the cliff like the necklace of God.

"I don't know. What?" I asked brightly. No stress over here, no sir, I thought.

"You get a new pair of moccasins, and you get to walk the hell away from the person who gave them to you."

"Funny," I said. "Cynical, but funny."

His hand moved on my leg. "I don't want to wait until Labor Day to make love to you," he said.

"I agree! We've got the river," I said, gesturing grandly toward it. I was a little drunk, but not very. He shook his head. "I'm serious," I said with much animation. "If you won't go camping with me, you have to show some flexibility." A woman often had to negotiate with a man.

"I can be flexible, but we're not making love in the river."

"On the river*bank*!" I smacked the bench-seat's cracked upholstery, I was so smitten with the idea. "Besides, this is the month of falling stars." I'd always wanted to call my eventual daughter Estrella, the Spanish word for star.

Twenty minutes later, I had Kyle pressed deep inside me and my spine pressed into the earth, on top of an old blanket we'd found in his trunk. The Columbia River was a dozen yards away. He was using a condom but I wouldn't have cared if he wasn't, I was so exhausted that night from overwork and worrying about doing the right thing and being responsible and self-controlled. I buried my mouth in the curve of his neck and looked up to see a shooting star blazing white against the dark sky before it was snuffed out by the earth's atmosphere. *My marriage is the shooting star,* I thought.

Kyle's lovemaking was slow and sinuous, so that my breath came in hitches. When I moved my mouth to the other side of his neck and opened my eyes again, I was startled to see the moon over his right shoulder, pale gold, full and whole and round, as opposite from snuffed out as a body could be. *I am the moon,* I thought. I breathed deeply, moved my hands along the flat, hard muscles of his back and curled my pelvis up to draw him closer in.

Chapter 25
Dodged Bullet

"I knew that something like this was going to happen," Kyle said. It was late afternoon of Labor Day, and he was referring to the fire that Sonny had set. Kyle's hands were gripping the steering wheel of his car hard, at exactly two o'clock and ten o'clock, and he was grim-faced, like a miserable driving student.

"Do you want me to be there with you?" he had asked me that morning when I'd told him what had happened and that the police officer was coming to take a report.

"Thanks for offering," I said, and thought a moment. Thinking was hard but doable, like when I'd lost my job and my dad had gotten cancer at the same time. "You know, I've got Marisol and Ruben here to help me with talk with the police," I said. "But I still want to get out into the country with you. Maybe you could buy the groceries and just pick me up around 3:00."

Driving west now on Highway 6 late in the day meant the sun was in our eyes. I had shed the cowgirl camisole, and was wearing an embroidered peasant blouse of Marisol's that I'd once said was cute. She'd insisted today on giving it to me since most of my clothes were destroyed.

"I knew that something like this was going to happen, too," I finally replied to Kyle. "That didn't stop either of us." I watched the Wilson River on my right as we traveled west through the Tillamook Forest. Like the Columbia, the Wilson flowed to the ocean. Here at summer's end, it was the lowest and driest I'd ever seen it. *I am the Wilson River*, I thought.

"Right," he said. A few more miles of forest. Pregnant silence. Then, "Are you sorry now that you ever laid eyes on me?"

I swung my head to look at him. "Not a bit. Oh no, Kyle." His face relaxed a little. "Might have been nice to have met you a little earlier, maybe," I smiled. "Like before I ever met Sonny."

Kyle nodded. More miles, the silence rich now instead of edgy.

"You caught the bullet I dodged," Kyle said.

I thought about that awhile. The fire and now the drive west seemed to have slowed time down for me. Instead of dreading some explosive event in the near future, as I'd been doing, the explosion had happened, kicking me backward into the present moment. It was a warp effect that I found helpful. "You mean that Sonny would have gone after you if he'd known who you were?" I asked him. I'd never let Sonny know anything about Kyle.

Kyle nodded. "Did I ever tell you about when I was a junior in high school and I got together with a cheerleader? She'd been going with this football player, and she told me she'd broken up with him. Actually, she told me that he had broken up with her, which I thought meant things would be OK if I was with her. But it didn't work that way. Word got out about me and her, and the football player came after me in the parking lot after school. Sent me to the hospital. Stitches in my scalp."

"Oh my God," I said. "That's awful."

"I didn't deserve that bullet," he went on. "But I probably deserved this one. I knew that you were married to him and that he still wanted you. I knew that seeing you was a risk for me. But I didn't think much about putting you at risk. You caught Sonny's bullet. I hadn't meant to dodge it. But I did. I'm sorry about that."

"Thanks," I said after a minute, at a loss for anything else to say. The self-help books didn't tell you how to navigate situations driven by fires and lovers. We turned onto the gravel road after the bridge and followed the map. At the Kavanaughs' house we unpacked the car, putting groceries in the kitchen and our overnight bags in the bedroom. It was early evening by now, and I realized I had been with other people nonstop since Sonny had knocked on the door that morning. I badly needed time by myself in a wildish place. Hopefully I'd hear a wiser voice than my own guide me on whether to have Sonny arrested.

"I'm going to take a run," I told Kyle, in as cheerful a tone as possible.

"Sure," he replied. "I'll make some business calls. I brought my calling card with me." The type of thing Sonny wouldn't have thought to do. The type of situation where he'd have rung up a $50 long distance bill, and forgotten to mention it to the people whose phone it was. But I could take Kyle anywhere.

Starting down the gravel road into the low-slung sunbeams, I felt the old relief. The earth was so stable. The lovely pressure of gravity went into the soles of my feet, up my calves and thighs, on into my pelvis. The earth never betrayed me. I breathed from my belly and pranced a little, flexing my ankles so they wouldn't get mini-sprains from the sharp little gravelly angles of the road. Then I settled into a good, medium pace, telling myself that every step moved me farther away from the fire.

A mile or so down the road I found three horses grazing in a pasture: a leggy bay, a rawboned chestnut, and a dappled gray that I could see was a pregnant mare. They raised their heads and looked at me with interest, chewing and pricking their ears toward me. I felt invited to visit, so I went to the fence and said hello.

Surprisingly, they all walked toward me, as if I had food for them, or they knew me. They stopped at the fence and looked at me alertly. I looked back at them, engaged, and bounced on my toes, feeling a bit excited. The bay tossed his handsome head up and down, as if sharing the feeling. The chestnut pawed the ground. I trotted alongside the fence a few yards, looking over my shoulder to keep eye contact, inviting them to move with me. They came right along. I was delighted. Fellow dancers!

"Hey, guys," I said. "Is there any way you could pay me for this? I wouldn't normally ask, but there's been kind of a financial setback."

The gray tossed her head gracefully. "No problem," I imagined her saying. "We've got you covered."

That did it. I capered and pranced fifty yards in one direction, then back again. They mirrored me on the other side of the fence, trotting and turning on cue. I felt their energy like an infusion into my thigh muscles, burning warm and bright. I ran faster and they moved from trotting to cantering, a beautiful rocking gait, and then when I leaped up and down in an outburst of excitement, they responded by taking off at a gallop around their pasture, the bay leading and the others following, their manes flying and tails held high as they stretched out their legs. I executed some pirouettes to celebrate our cross-species communion. The horses had vaulted me briefly back into joy.

Back in our borrowed house, I found Kyle had started dinner. He poured us glasses of Chardonnay, half-chilled because he'd stuck it in the freezer during my run. "What are we drinking to?" I asked.

He considered a minute, his glass poised. "The end of summer and the end of a bad marriage."

I smiled, inclined my head, and looped my arm through his so our bodies were joined in space as we drank.

"That was a dance move," he said. "Two of them. Starting with the head bow."

"Good memory. Good student," I smiled, and turned my head to kiss him. His lips were full and pillowy, and I rested on them a moment with a sense of solace. But he pulled away.

"Don't get me started," he said. "Not 'til later." I felt a stab of alarm in my stomach. I didn't feel sexual at all. Having my possessions destroyed was the opposite of an aphrodisiac. But he was obviously counting on making love, and I didn't have the strength for conflict of any kind, not after the fire.

Kyle had brought salmon, crusty bread, corn on the cob, and lettuce and tomatoes for salad. We made dinner together as we sipped the wine, and then ate outdoors on the deck. The sun had set, and the air was cooling. We talked about simple things, the people he had called while I was running, the days getting shorter as we approached the autumn equinox, the Indian he had bought the salmon from under the Bridge of the Gods on the Columbia River. Small talk was another small solace.

"This big old Indian stood up there in the bed of his truck and showed me where this fish was bruised from a seal bite," Kyle was telling me. "You could see the teeth marks. That's why he gave me the whole fish for five dollars." Kyle loved discounts and bargains.

"Aaahhhh," I poured my voice out like honey and leaned toward him confidentially. "I was wondering why I was feeling the early symptoms of rabies."

His long-lashed eyes opened wide in alarm. "Are you kidding?"

I held his gaze soberly for a few beats. Then, a sweet smile. "Yes."

"You had me. Let's wash the dishes and use the hot-tub," Kyle said, and so we did. I wore my two-piece bathing suit. Kyle took my cue and wore his boxers. I welcomed the heat of the water, and did slow, dreamy twirls in the center of the tub until Kyle pulled me into his arms and held me to him, his head next to mine over my right shoulder.

"I'm really glad we're here together," he said.

"Me too."

"If someone had asked me after that first time I met you whether I would ever get to be with you here like this, I'd have said it was impossible."

"You mean because I was married?" I heard myself speak of marriage in the past tense for the first time, and realized the fire had etched a sharp line in my life, creating a past that I could distance myself from. My present and my future would be distinctly *after* the fire. Even tonight was after the fire, and that thought buoyed me more than the water in the hot tub.

"The ring I saw on your finger was only part of it. You had all this presence and grace," Kyle said. "It was as if you'd written the book on how to be joyful inside your body, and you were friendly enough to show the rest of us how we could be joyful inside our own bodies."

"Wow. You really got that from me?"

"I did. Of course, you're not that happy now."

I turned my head and pulled away a little to make eye contact. "Can you carry the happiness for both of us for awhile, do you think?" My tone was light, but I really didn't know at this point how we would make it otherwise. Just a few nights earlier in Hood River he'd said he wanted our relationship to be his escape from problems. I was hoping he'd been having a bad day.

He started kissing my neck, above the water line. "I can try." He spoke the words between kisses, one word per kiss, his hands moving on my breasts. "But you can help trigger it. My happiness, I mean."

Alarm stabbed my stomach again. I remembered the summer I'd been a counselor at a church camp, and the director had directed all of us to speak up quickly with a certain word if someone said something that hurt us.

"Ouch," I said softly.

"Hm?" he said against my neck.

"Kyle, I'm crazy about you," I said. "But this isn't the right night for me to make love. I feel too fragile." It took everything I had to get the words out. I sat in his arms, frozen still in the steaming water.

"You're safe. Sonny's going to go to jail. I'm here to protect you."

But you dodged his bullet. I took it instead, I thought angrily, even knowing it wasn't fair, that nobody could protect you from everything. And I'd created the whole situation by choosing to marry Sonny in the first place. I was silent, all out of spoken words like a sack emptied of sugar.

After awhile we got out of the hot tub, dried off and climbed up into Luke and Kim's four-poster bed. I wore my long dark-blue nightgown with the ribbony straps that crossed low on my back, and Kyle wore another pair of boxers. Almost immediately we reached for each other in the dark, urgent and intense, as if we'd been separated, wrapping our arms tightly around each other. It was the first time we'd gotten to stretch out in a bed together. I wanted to be held and he wanted to kiss, so we did both. He was hard against my thigh, breathing hard, lifting my hips, pulling my long nightgown up around my waist. I wanted him to back off, but my volition was gone. All my strength had been used up by the awful day.

"I love you, Revelle," he said. "I need to be close to you." Then he slipped inside me and suddenly I was alive again instead of dead, moving with him, connected to him and to a force larger than myself. I craved that connection. He wasn't using a condom, but when he came I didn't flinch. My life felt so out of control that I couldn't imagine controlling anything at all. Getting pregnant would make just as much sense as the fire made. A child would give me focus and structure.

"I'm sorry," Kyle said, our limbs still entangled. "I just want you so goddamned much."

"It's OK," I told him. I didn't know which thing he was sorry for, but I needed badly for things to be OK between us. We curled up to sleep together for the first time, finding ways to keep touching while also getting comfortable.

The fire gave me the queer, perverse benefit of confirming my decision to leave Sonny. Kyle would never have torched my truck and possessions. I was drifting off to sleep when an image of Kyle floated in my mind. I was on one side of him with Sonny in the middle-distance, his head turned sharply toward us. I was absorbed in Kyle's beautiful, high-cheek-boned face. Sonny lifted a gun and fired. Kyle, who had been watching Sonny, dived face-first to the ground, and I took the bullet in my heart, soundless and wordless. I fell, crumpling down onto Kyle, while Sonny stood, calm and proud, the sun at his back.

Chapter 26
Seeing Things Whole

We woke early the next morning and I made coffee, then toast from the bread left over from dinner. Kyle had brought baguette bread, the fresh, crusty kind that helped you imagine you might be somewhere romantic like France, but I couldn't finish even a slice of it. My eating had diminished when I'd thrown myself into developing the show, and then when Sonny had moved up, food had started feeling foreign, hard to deal with, and my clothes were now draping from me in little folds. The other day Marisol had quietly asked me if I might be developing anorexia.

"Well, anorexics think they're fat, and are trying to lose weight. But I know I'm thin, and I'm not," I'd replied. "I'll try to eat more." That hadn't eased her worried expression.

"That flaky lead actor has disappeared," Kyle announced. He'd been on the phone again. "I think he snorts too much coke. The show is on the verge of falling apart."

I regarded him over my coffee. So was I. "Do you need to go back to town?"

"I really do. I'm sorry. Do you want to come with me, or stay here? I could probably make it back out tonight."

"It depends." I called Mary at her cousin's house, since she'd told me yesterday to call her if I needed help. Miraculously, she picked up on the first ring. I almost wept with relief when she said she would come out and join me that afternoon.

I kissed Kyle good-bye without saying much, and watched his big boat of a Chrysler jounce down the gravel road. He needed new shock absorbers, but couldn't afford them. Our shared history was of me being the idea person, the creative force, and him embracing the ideas, supporting and honing them, doing problem-solving and putting it all out into the world to let it shine. The change was that now he was doing all that for other people, not me.

The phone rang, startling me. It was Pastor Rachel. She asked me how I was doing, and then told me Sonny had called her. Twice in the last 24 hours, in fact. "I'm not hearing any remorse from him," she said. "At one point he was wondering if it was all a bad dream he'd had."

"Oh," I said, halting my pacing. "I wish that it was."

"I did something I almost never do," Rachel went on. "I told him he can't come to Fideles House at this point. He can't just pretend nothing has happened."

"Thank you," I said.

"I feel a little foolish now that I had thought marriage counseling was going to make a difference," she said. "This kind of craziness is more . . . off the scale."

"I'm sorry I brought craziness into our community," I said.

"Revelle, his behavior isn't your fault."

My own behavior hadn't been so great, either, but rather than saying that, I thanked her for calling and wrapped up the conversation. It was so humiliating for your husband to set fire to your possessions. It was like a headline in the local newspaper stating you were garbage, needing to be disposed of rapidly. At some points that morning I felt like garbage. Normal women didn't have things like this happen to them, so I'd clearly brought at least part of the fire onto myself.

My mind was as jittery and jumpy that day as a gazelle with lions in the vicinity. I prayed periodically, asking for God's love and comfort, but I couldn't feel those things, the way I couldn't feel desire for food, or the taste of it in my mouth. I checked the clock compulsively, wishing time would hurry up so Mary would arrive. I went running but was disappointed to not see the horses this time. The early afternoon found me at the double kitchen sink with most of the clothes I now owned, washing the small pile by hand like a pioneer woman. I swirled my socks and running shorts around in the sudsy water, where the soap made them slippery, then in the clear water, where the clothes regained their friction. My mom's words had been friction on my nerves when I'd called her. After she'd gotten over her shock, she'd said matter of factly, "This wouldn't have happened if you hadn't gotten involved with Kyle." So, I'm the village's biggest idiot, I thought. And, she wanted me to have Sonny arrested. When I was noncommittal she said, "What might he do to you next if he knows you won't do anything about it?" Officer Chilstrom had said the same thing yesterday.

I moved around in my hip-yoke skirt and dusty rose camisole, rolling my wet clothes into towels to sop up the moisture, then laying both clothes and towels outside on the rails of the deck to dry in the sun. When Mom had asked if I needed money, I'd thanked her for offering and said, let's wait and see. Walking back inside, I smacked my hand furiously on the side of the house. A set of sparrows in the tree on my right spurted away, cheeping in alarm. I was 34 years old, educated and able-bodied, but would have been practically destitute if I didn't have great friends. I had a divorce in my near future, which would cost money. And Kyle would probably interpret any delay on the divorce as lack of commitment to him. He liked being in a relationship and would want no sign he might be alone. My life was a pressure cooker.

Paul called, surprising me with the news that the truck was still drivable. The fire had stayed confined to the truck's bed. He and Ruben were offering to go to the dump with me. "We're willing to just do it for you, but not everything in the truck is burned," he said in his slow, kind way. "It might be better for you to make the decisions on what to keep and what to throw away." We made a plan to go to the dump together when I was back in town.

"I have fantasies of beating Sonny up," he said flatly. I breathed for a minute, absorbing the thought. Grandpa Joe's spirit seemed to have entered the room. *Forgiveness was for those too weak to take revenge.*

"But Marisol says this is your own battle to fight," he added.

"She means I need to take care of myself. She's right." I dropped to the faded Oriental rug in the living room, legs spread wide, and bent my forehead to my left knee. After a minute I said, "Is it hard to be my friend, Paul?"

"You have no idea." His voice was heavy, as if exhausted. Tears sprang to my eyes.

"I love you," I whispered.

"I know," he said unhappily.

Mary arrived as the shadows of the trees were starting to lengthen, eager-faced and a bit disheveled, carrying a bag of groceries and her huge, colorful Guatemalan purse. She hugged me close, which felt wonderful, like falling into the arms of the original earth mother. "I'm making my famous chicken salad for supper," she said as she set grapes, crackers, mayonnaise, almonds, a lemon and two chicken breasts onto the kitchen counter. Being from Kansas, the last meal of the day was supper to Mary. She was wearing the same mud-colored dress as the day I'd first met her, which was, two years and three months ago, almost to the day. My mind was latching onto little facts like that, as if tracking them would prove I was smart as a whip and somehow in control of my life.

We sat on the sofa and I caught her up on news and phone calls. Her brown eyes held mine with complete concentration. She nodded at different points, asking clarifying questions now and then.

"What am I not seeing?" I finally asked her. Everything looked awful to me, and I needed a different set of eyes.

"Well, most people in your shoes would have some post-traumatic stress disorder going forward from something like this. You know, PTSD." Mary had been a chaplain in a hospital before working at the Claremont colleges.

"PTSD? Like Vietnam vets have?"

She nodded. "You'll have trouble concentrating. You won't perform anything as well as you did before the fire."

Except sex, I thought. Or, maybe that, too.

I forced myself into business-mind. "So if I was having trouble earning a living before, it'll be even harder now?" Another nod. If Mary had come out here to the countryside to lend encouragement, we were moving in the wrong direction. I dropped my head into my hands.

"OK. Maybe we should just deal with today," she said gently. I nodded without raising my head.

"So you're living now with Marisol and Ruben. That's good."

"It is good." I lifted my face and held her gaze again.

"And the police took the report. So the next step would be to have Sonny arrested. Is that right?" I broke eye contact and stiffened. The warm room got warmer in the silence. My armpits were wet with sweat.

"Help me understand why you'd hesitate to have Sonny arrested," Mary finally said, shifting her body to get more comfortable.

"It seems so vengeful." My stomach was in knots. I remembered the time I'd almost brained Sonny with the bottle of wine, and the time earlier in my life when my revenge had been ruthless.

"No. It's just holding your own. Just taking care of yourself. What's the real problem?"

"I'm afraid he'd get raped by other prisoners. It happens all the time. I've read about it." My voice was strained, high-pitched. I struggled to modulate it, bring it back down to how it was supposed to sound. "I can't set him up for that. Nobody deserves it, no matter what they've done."

"Why do you assume Sonny would get raped?"

"He's so good-looking," I said miserably. "Good-looking people are targets." On that I was positive.

"But he's also tall and strong. He's been in fights before," Mary pointed out. "I don't picture him being in danger. He'll go to a local jail. Those aren't nearly as violent as prisons." But I still felt a rising panic at the idea of having Sonny arrested. Mary had no idea of how aggressive, how dangerous I'd been in the past. Nobody did. That was what made me feel crazy.

I moved restlessly. "I need to take a break," I said.

"OK," she said. "How about some iced tea?" I nodded gratefully. While she boiled water and sliced the lemon I went outside and rearranged clothes and towels on the deck, turning them, getting the moist parts out into the sun for the last hours of daylight. Then I stretched to the sky, trying to relax. The shadow I threw onto the house was taller than Sonny's body.

"Thanks." I gulped the cold tea and sat down this time on the living room floor, my back up against the sofa, legs stretched straight out. Mary settled herself down next to me, with a bit more effort.

"There's something I've never told you about," I began. Mary reached over and held my hand. I loved her touch, but it made something shudder in me that was already cracked, like a dam on the Columbia River that had been stressed by an enormous snowpack melting into it and was in danger of being breached.

"Remember the man who raped me when I was little?" Mary nodded immediately, almost as if she'd expected me to bring him up.

"I didn't tell you the whole story." I started to tremble, the dam breaking. Mary stroked my bare arm with her free hand and waited.

"When I was 16 I maimed him. I tripped him so he fell down the bleachers at a basketball game. Nobody ever knew it was me." I gasped, the river crashing over the dam. I was in whitewater now, careening toward the ocean. "They took him to the hospital. I might have made him into a quadriplegic. I might have killed him. I don't know." The truth was now dislodged from my body and in the living room with us, a hideous, exposed incubus.

Mary pulled me firmly against the side of her solid body. I bent my knees up and moved farther into her, out of the water onto the river beach, rocking against her.

"And this is the first time you've told anyone, right?" she said. If she felt any shock that I had maimed a man, there was no evidence of it.

I nodded, several times so that it was distinguishable from my trembling. I had goose bumps on my arms, as cold now as I'd been hot earlier. It was only Mary's body holding mine that was keeping me on the river beach, in the here and now.

"God wants to forgive you for hurting him." Her words hung in the air like a remarkable object, like a chalice made of diamonds that had been invisible and was suddenly unveiled, catching and throwing prisms of late summer sunlight across the living room.

I captured one of the prisms of light into a thought. "The *rapist* should be asking for God's forgiveness!"

"Of course he should. But you only have control over your own relationship with God."

"I'm not forgiving that man for raping me when I was seven!" I went on rebelliously.

"That's not on the table," Mary said. She was unflappable. If I'd been a Nazi war criminal who'd made lampshades out of children's skin she wouldn't have blinked or otherwise been intimidated. "You said you feel guilty for attacking him. We're talking about you asking God's forgiveness for that."

"It's complicated," I said, looking fretfully around the room, the chalice no longer in sight. I'd known it wouldn't stick around.

"Don't get bogged down in the details," Mary said mildly. "God doesn't."

"It's all so big," I said, but feebly, knowing where Mary was taking me, where we were going.

"There is absolutely nothing that God cannot forgive, is not waiting to forgive," she said, so quietly that the songbirds' notes outdoors were audible through it, lacing into the room like the lavender ribbons woven into the edges of Kat's kitchen curtains.

"Nothing," she whispered, like the reverse image of an exclamation point.

I stacked our four hands in a tower on my bare left knee. We bowed our heads.

"Spirit," I began, drawing a deep, shuddering breath. Then I slipped from the river-beach back into the water, away from Mary, and was crying, wrenching sobs from my gut, the roiling whitewater of my guilt pouring out as tears.

"I ruined his life," I choked out.

"We don't know that. For all we know, being injured might have brought him to Jesus and asking for forgiveness, himself," Mary replied. She was crisp and fast-paced now, the lifeguard swimming along in the rapids beside me. "We can't know how God's will plays itself out. But we do know God wants to forgive you. And you're sick from needing it." My nose was streaming even more heavily than my eyes, and Mary removed her right hand from our prayer-tower, dug a red bandana out of her Guatemalan purse and handed it to me. I reclaimed my own hands to blow my nose into the soft old cotton and wiped my eyes, breathing short, hard and fast.

"Put your head between your knees, Revelle." Mary was worried I'd hyperventilate and pass out. "Breathe slowly." I obeyed, bending my forehead down onto the Oriental rug like a pilgrim seeking Mecca. It worked. I slowly sat up.

"OK," Mary said. "I'm going to get us started, and then it'll be your turn." I nodded, stomach churning like when I'd stood on the high diving board for the first time at age nine. We restacked our hands on my knee. The solid old sofa supported our backs.

"Mother-father God, we step into your circle of grace and power," Mary said. Her tone was low and confidential, as if consulting with a lover. "We know your vision of Revelle is shining and whole. We know you want to protect Revelle from further danger. There's a barrier to that protection. Please hear Revelle's prayer."

We sat in silence, eyes closed. I smelled the lemon from our iced tea. A horse neighed in the distance, possibly my friend the pregnant mare, starting high and then huskily sliding on down to low, rumbling notes. I remembered how still the pastures had been at dusk the night before, and tried to quiet my mind to be like them. I felt the softest of vibrations in the room. The Holy Spirit had entered.

"Spirit," I began. And something shifted in me then, away from cowering as a victim and being Sonny's prey, and stepped into the shadow, the predator part of my own nature. "You know exactly what I did when I was sixteen. You know my crazy mixed-up heart, how glad I was in that moment to have gotten revenge. And then how ashamed I've been all these years. How alone I've felt with the secret." The predator in me blinked.

"Spirit, I need your forgiveness for hurting him," I whispered. "Please forgive me." Mary's and my hands were sweating into each other, making my knee slick underneath them. We breathed in and out, smelling each other's tea breath. The predator in me had turned and was slowly walking away. The tip of its tail twitched slightly.

The atmosphere in the room changed as sharply as if our bodies were conducting lightning from the sky down into the ground. We leaned into the charge in the air, Mary at my side, my tailbone supported by the floor, which was supported by the earth.

My hand was guided to move to the table on my right that held my tan canvas purse. Slowly, gentle-handed as Jesus, I took the two cards out of it, then lifted Luke and Cat's big, chunky beige phone onto my lap. My forefinger circumscribed one numeral after another on the old rotary dial, first from the calling card Kyle had given me, then from Officer Chilstrom's card. I could feel Grandpa Joe's essence in the room, not the violent part, but the part that had wanted to keep me safe from harm. His spirit and Officer Chilstrom's spirit stood in the room over by the picture window, nodding, pleased that this woman was neither stalking prey nor fleeing from a predator now, but just standing her ground. Him, her, him dancin'.

Like any good, old-fashioned thing, the phone worked at a slow pace. My right forefinger traced arc after arc, creating a buzzing sound with each number like the bees in the bee-bushes at my elementary school, except that the bees would not hurt me now. The arcs created a set of spirals in the rebirthed atmosphere, a ring of protection I had not thought I merited.

"Thank you," I whispered before I started talking.

Reader's Guide for discussion groups

1. The story is launched into motion by multiple reversals. Have you ever had two or more reversals happen at the same time in your life, i.e. job loss, relationship loss, serious illness in the family, imminent loss of home? How did the reversals impact your quality of life, and your ability to make good choices?

2. The novel suggests in the opening chapter that beauty is actually a liability, making a person into a target. Had you ever seen beauty that way before? Does that notion seem to have any accuracy to you?

3. What reaction did you have to Revelle being assaulted as a child? How did you feel about her counter-assault as a teenager? How would you feel if she had refrained from ambushing the rapist, and the pedophile had presumably gone on to assault many more children before dying a natural death?

4. Have you known anyone as unpredictable or erratic as Sonny? If so, how did that person impact your life, or how did you shield yourself from troubling impacts that could have happened?

5. Discuss the concept of luck, i.e. how some people tend to be lucky, and others not so lucky. How many of Revelle's problems would you characterize as driven by bad luck, and how many driven by poor choices on her part?

6. This story has several characters with mixed ethnic backgrounds (Revelle is half Palestinian, Marisol is half Mexican, Kyle is half Apache Indian). Whether in the novel or in real life, do you think people of mixed ethnicity are better off ignoring their non-white heritage and blending into the mainstream as much as possible, or actively engaging with their heritage?

7. The novel has a recurring motif of the natural world in general, and horses in particular. What roles do the natural world and horses seem to play in Revelle's life?

8. Many characters in literature and real life benefit from twelve-step groups, including Paul in this story. Revelle, though, has a troubled relationship with AlAnon. Why do you think that is?

9. Of all the characters in Revelle, which did you connect with the most on an emotional level? How do you explain that connection?

10. The novel suggests at the beginning, after arson has been committed, that predator and prey (i.e. victims and victimizers) are not always what they seem, and may periodically trade identities. Does that notion 'pay off' for you, or do you feel that victims and victimizers are two fundamentally separate groups of people?

11. Revelle collects advice from people throughout the story, some of which she takes and some of which she doesn't. At what point would you most like to have given her advice, and what would you like to tell her?

CPSIA information can be obtained at www.ICGtesting.com
Printed in the USA
BVOW081731200113

311100BV00001B/6/P